D0804660

The Power Unchained . . . .

The nomads had broken through the stockade, and as Marika sat helplessly in the momentary haven of the watchtower, she saw the huntresses of her pack slain one by one. In horror, she glimpsed her litter mate Kublin race out from under a platform, his side open in a bloody wound. Two slavering nomads pursued him.

Black emotion boiled inside Marika, hot and furious. Something took control. She saw Kublin's pursuers through a dark fog, moving in slowed motion. It was as though she could see through them, see them without their skins. And she could see drifting ghosts, like the ghosts of all her foredams, hovering over the action. She willed a lethal curse upon the hearts of Kublin's pursuers.

They pitched forward, shrieking, losing their weapons, clawing their breasts.

Marika gasped. What? Had she done that? Could she *kill* with the touch?

Also by Glen Cook

Passage at Arms

Published by
POPULAR LIBRARY

ATTENTION: SCHOOLS AND CORPORATIONS

POPULAR LIBRARY books are available at quantity discounts with bulk purchase for educational, business, or sales promotional use. For information, please write to SPECIAL SALES DEPARTMENT, POPULAR LIBRARY, 75 ROCKEFELLER PLAZA, NEW YORK, N Y 10019

**ARE THERE POPULAR LIBRARY BOOKS
YOU WANT BUT CANNOT FIND IN YOUR LOCAL STORES?**

You can get any POPULAR LIBRARY title in print. Simply send title and retail price, plus 50¢ per order and 50¢ per copy to cover mailing and handling costs for each book desired. New York State and California residents add applicable sales tax. Enclose check or money order only, no cash please, to POPULAR LIBRARY, P.O. BOX 690, NEW YORK, N Y 10019

DARKWAR TRILOGY·1
DOOMSTALKER
BY GLEN COOK

POPULAR LIBRARY

An Imprint of Warner Books, Inc.

A Warner Communications Company

POPULAR LIBRARY EDITION

Copyright © 1985 by Glen Cook
All rights reserved.

Popular Library books are published by
Warner Books, Inc.
75 Rockefeller Plaza
New York, N.Y. 10019

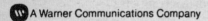 A Warner Communications Company

Printed in the United States of America

First Printing: August, 1985

10 9 8 7 6 5 4 3 2 1

For the wonderful ground crew folk of StarBase Tulsa.
You help me walk the stars.

BOOK ONE:
THE PACKSTEAD

Chapter One

I

It was the worst winter in memory. Even the Wise conceded that early on. The snows came out of the Zhotak early, and by Manestar Morning they stood several paws deep. They came on bitter winds that found every crack and chink in the Degnan loghouses till in frustration the older females ordered the males out to cover the curved roofs with blocks of sod. The males strove valiantly, but the ice-teethed wind had devoured the warmth of the ground. The earth would not yield to their tools. They tried packing the roofs with snow, but the ceaseless wind carried that away. The ranks of firewood dwindled at an alarming rate.

It was customary for the young of the pack to roam the nearby hills in seach of deadwood when they had no other chores, but this bitter winter the Wise whispered into the ears of the huntresses, and the huntresses ordered the pups to remain within sight of the packstead palisade. The pups sensed the change and were uneasy.

Nobody said the word "grauken." The old, terrible stories were put aside. Nobody wanted to frighten the little ones.

But the adults all knew weather like this conjured the beast lying so near the surface of the meth.

Game would be scarce on the Zhotak. The nomad packs of the northland would exhaust their stored food early. They would come south before long. Some did even during the milder winters, stealing where they could, fighting if they had to to seize the fruits of the labors of their sedentary cousins.

And in the terrible winters—as this promised to become—they even carried off young pups. Among meth, in the heart of the great winter, hunger knew no restraint.

In the fireside tales the grauken was a slavering beast of shadowed forests and rocky hills that lay in wait for careless pups. In life, the grauken was the hunger that betrayed civilization and reason. The Degnan Wise whispered to the huntresses. They wanted the young to develop the habit of staying close and alert long before the grauken came snarling up from its dark place of hiding.

Thus, another burden fell upon the harried males. They ventured out in armed parties, seeking firewood and long, straight logs suitable for construction. To their customary exhausting duties were added the extension and strengthening of the spiral stockade of needle-pointed logs and the bringing of snow into the loghouses to melt. The water produced, they returned to the cold, where they poured it into forms and froze it into blocks. With these ice cakes they sheathed the exteriors of the loghouses, bit by bit.

This winter's wind was like none the pack had ever known. Even the Chronicle did not recall its like. Never did it cease its bicker and howl. It became so cold the snow no longer fell. Who dared take a metal tool into a bare paw risked losing skin. Incautious pups suffered frostbitten muzzles. Fear glimmered in the eyes of the Wise as they bent their toothless heads together by the fires and muttered of signs and evil portents. The sagan, the wisest of the Wise, burned incense and made sacrifice daily. All the time she was awake her shaky, pain-deformed old paws wove powerful fetishes and banes to mount over the entrances to the loghouses. She commanded ceremonies of propitiation.

And the wind continued to blow. And the winter grew more cold. And the shadow of fear trickled into the bravest of hearts.

Huntresses found unfamiliar meth tracks just a few hours away from the packstead, up near the boundary with the Laspe hunting grounds. They might have been made by Laspe huntresses ranging out of their territory, seeking what small game did not hibernate. But the snow held no scent. Fears of the worst became haunting. Could it be that savages from the north were scouting the upper Ponath already?

Remnants of an old fire were found at Machen Cave, not far north of the packstead. Even in winter only the brave, the desperate, or the foolish nighted over in Machen Cave. The Laspe, or any other of the neighbors, would have traveled on by night rather than have sheltered there. So the Wise whispered and the huntresses murmured to one another. Those who knew the upper Ponath knew that darkness dwelt within Machen Cave.

II

Marika, Skiljan's pup, reached her tenth birthday during the worst of winters, when the fear lurked in the corners of her dam's loghouse like shadows out of the old stories the old females no longer told. She and the surviving pups of her litter, Kublin and Zamberlin, tried to celebrate the event in traditional pup fashion, but there was no breaking the gloom of their elders.

Skits drawn from folklore were customary. But Marika and Kublin had created their own tale of adventure, and over the protests of conservative Zamberlin, had rehearsed it for weeks. Marika and Kublin believed they would aston-ish their elders, Zamberlin that they would offend the hide-bound Wise. In the event, only their dam proved insufficiently distracted to follow their story. All their expectations were disappointed. They tried flute and drums. Marika had a talent for the flute, and Zamberlin enthusiasm on the skins. Kublin tried to sing.

One of the old females snarled at the racket. They failed to stop sufficiently soon. Skiljan had to interpose herself between the old female and the pups.

The pups tried juggling, for which Marika had an exceptional talent. In summertime the old females always watched and cooed in amazement. She seemed able to command the balls in the air. But now even their dam showed no interest.

Desolate, the pups slinked into a corner and huddled for warmth. The chill was as much of the heart as of the flesh.

In any other season their elders would have snapped at them, telling them they were too old for such foolishness. In this dread season the old ignored the young, and the young stayed out of the path of the old, for tempers were short and civilization's edge lay very near the surface. A meth who slipped over could kill. They were a race with only the most tenuous grasp on civilized behavior.

Marika huddled with her littermates, feeling the rapid patter of their hearts. She stared through the smoky gloom at her elders. Kublin whimpered softly. He was very frightened. He was not strong. He was old enough to know that in the hard winters weakling males sometimes had to go.

In name the loghouse was Skiljan's Loghouse—for Marika's dam—though she shared it with a dozen sisters, their males, several older females, and all their pups. Skiljan commanded by right of skill and strength, as her dam had before her. She was the best huntress of the pack. She ranked second in physical endurance and strength, and first in will. She was among the smartest Degnan females. These being the qualities by which wilderness meth survived, she was honored by all who shared her loghouse. Even the old females deferred when she commanded, though it was seldom she ignored their advice. The Wise had more experience and could see behind veils youth drew across the eyes. In the councils of the packstead she spoke second only to Gerrien.

There were six similar loghouses in the Degnan packstead. None new had been erected within living memory. Each was a half cylinder lying on its side, ninety feet long and a dozen high, twenty-five wide. The south end, where the entrance was, was flat, facing away from winter's winds. The north end was a tapering cone covering a root cellar, providing storage, breaking the teeth of the wind. A loft hung six feet above the ground floor, half a foot above the average height of an adult meth female. The young slept up there in the warmth, and much that had to be stored was tucked away in the loft's dark crannies and recesses. The loft was a time vault, more interesting than the Chronicle in what it told of the Degnan past. Marika and Kublin passed many a loving hour probing the shadows, disturbing vermin, sometimes bringing to light treasures lost or forgotten for generations.

The loghouse floor was earth hammered hard by generations of feet. It was covered with skins where the adults slept in clumps, males to the north, old females between the two central firepits, females of breeding age to the south, nearest the door. The sides of the loghouse were piled with firewood and tools, weapons, possessions, and such food stores as were not kept in the unheated point of the structure. All this formed an additional barrier against the cold.

A jungle of foods, skins, whatnots hung from the joists supporting the loft, making any passage through the loghouse tortuous and interesting.

And the smells! Over all was the rich smell of smoke, for smoke found little escape in winter, when warmth was precious. Then there was the smell of unwashed bodies, and of the hanging sausages, fruits, vegetables. In summer the Degnan pack spent little time indoors, fleeing the thick, rank interior for sleep under the stars. In summer adult meth spoke longingly of the freedom enjoyed by the nomadic meth of the Zhotak, who were not tied to such pungent spirit traps. (The nomads believed built houses held one's spirit prisoner. They sheltered in caves or pitched temporary hide tents.) But when the ice wind began to moan out of the Zhotak, old folks lost that longing. Settled meth, who raised a few scrawny vegetables and grains and who gleaned the forests for game and fruits that could be dried and preserved, survived the winters far more handily than their footloose cousins.

"Marika!" old Zertan snapped. "Come here, pup."

Marika shivered as she disentangled herself from her littermates. Her dam's dam was called Carque by all the pups of the packstead—a carque being a rapacious flyer of exceedingly foul temper. Zertan had bad teeth. They pained her constantly, but she would not have them pulled and refused to drink goyin tea. She was a little senile and a lot crazy and was afraid that enemies long dead would steal up on her if she risked the drowsiness caused by the analgesic tea.

Her contemporaries called her Rhelat—behind her back. The rhelat was a carrion eater. It had been known to kill things and wait for them to ripen. Zertan's rotten teeth gave her particularly foul breath.

Marika presented herself, head lowered dutifully.

"Pup, run to Gerrien's loghouse. Fetch me those needles Borget promised me."

"Yes, Granddam." Marika turned, caught her dam's eye. What should she do? Borget was dead a month. Anyway, she had been too feeble to make needles for longer than Marika could remember.

Granddam was losing her grip on time again. Soon she would forget who everyone was and begin seeing and talking to meth dead for a generation.

Skiljan nodded toward the doorway. A pretense would be made. "I have something you can take to Gerrien, since you are going." So the trip would not be a waste.

Marika shrugged into her heavy skin coat and the boots with otec fur inside, waited near the doorway. Zertan watched as if some cunning part of her knew the quest was fabulous, but insisted Marika punish herself in the cold anyway. Because she was young? Or was Zertan grasping for a whiff of the power that had been hers when the loghouse had carried her name?

Skiljan brought a sack of stone arrowheads, the sort used for everyday hunting. The females of her loghouse were skilled flakers. In each loghouse, meth occupied themselves with crafts through the long winters. "Tell Gerrien we need these set to shafts."

"Yes, Dam." Marika slipped through heavy hangings that kept the cold from roaring in when the doorway was open. She stood for a moment with paw upon the latch before pushing into the cold. Zertan. Maybe they ought to rid themselves of crazy old females instead of pups, she thought. Kublin was far more useful than was Granddam. Granddam no longer contributed anything but complaint.

She drew a last deep, smoky breath, then stepped into the gale. Her eyes watered instantly. Head down, she trudged across the central square. If she hurried she could make it before she started shivering.

The Degnan loghouses stood in two ranks of three, one north, one south, with fifty feet of open space between ranks. Skiljan's loghouse was the middle one in the northern rank, flanked by those of Dorlaque and Logusz. Gerrien's was the end loghouse on Marika's left as she faced south. Meth named Foehse and Kuzmic ruled the center and right loghouses, respectively. Seldom did any but Gerrien have much impact on Marika's life. Gerrien and Skiljan had been both friends and competitors since they were pups.

The packstead stockade, and the lean-tos clutching its skirts, clung close to the outer loghouses and spiraled around the packstead twice. Any raider would have to come in through a yard-wide channel, all the way around, to reach her goal. Unlike some neighboring packs, the Degnan made no effort to enclose their gardens and fields. Threats came during winter anyway. Decision had been made in the days-of-building to trade the risk of siege in growing time for the advantage of having to defend a shorter palisade.

The square between loghouse ranks seemed so barren, so *naked* this time of year. In summer it was always loosely controlled chaos, with game being salted, hides being tanned, pups running wild.

Six loghouses. The Degnan packstead was the biggest in this part of the upper Ponath, and the richest. Their neighbors envied them. But Marika, whose head was filled with dreams, did not feel wealthy. She was miserable most of the time, feeling deprived by birth.

In the south there were places called cities, tradermales said. Places where they made the precious iron tools the Wise accepted in exchange for otec furs. Places where many packs lived together in houses built not of logs but of stone. Places where winter's breath was ever so much lighter, and the stone houses turned the cold with ease. Places that, just by being elsewhere, by definition would be better than here.

Many an hour had she and Kublin passed dreaming aloud of what it would be like to live *there*.

Tradermales also told of a stone place called a packfast, which stood just three days down the nearby river, where that joined another to become the Hainlin, a river celebrated in the Chronicle as the guide which the Degnan had followed into the upper Ponath in ancient times. Tradermales said a real road started below the packfast, and wound through mountains and plains southward to great cities whose names Marika could never recall.

Marika's dam had been to that stone packfast several times. Each year the great ones who dwelt there summoned the leading females of the upper Ponath. Skiljan would be gone for ten days. It was said there were ceremonies and payments of tribute, but about none of that would Skiljan speak, except to mutter under her breath, "Silth bitches," and say, "In time, Marika. In due time. It is not a thing to be rushed." Skiljan was not one to frighten, yet she seemed afraid to have her pups visit.

Other pups, younger than Marika, had gone last summer,

returning with tales of wonder, thrilled to have something about which to brag. But Skiljan would not yield. Already she and Marika had clashed about the summer to come.

Marika realized she had stopped moving, was standing in the wind and shivering. Dreamer, the huntresses and Wise called her mockingly—and sometimes, when they thought she was not attentive, with little side glances larded with uncertainty or fright—and they were right. It was a good thing pups were not permitted into the forest now. Her dreaming had become uncontrolled. She would find some early frostflower or pretty creekside pebble and the grauken would get her while she contemplated its beauty.

She entered Gerrien's loghouse. Its interior was very like Skiljan's. The odors were a touch different. Gerrien housed more males, and the wintertime crafts of her loghouse all involved woodworking. Logusz's loghouse always smelled worst. Her meth were mainly tanners and leather workers.

Marika stood before the windskins, waiting to be recognized. It was but a moment before Gerrien sent a pup to investigate. This was a loghouse more relaxed than that ruled by Skiljan. There was more merriment here, always, and more happiness. Gerriaen was not intimidated by the hard life of the upper Ponath. She took what came and refused to battle the future before it arrived. Marika sometimes wished she had been whelped by cheerful Gerrien instead of brooding Skiljan.

"What?" demanded Solfrank, a male two years her elder, almost ready for the rites of adulthood, which would compel him to depart the packstead and wander the upper Ponath in search of a pack that would take him in. His chances were excellent. Degnan males took with them envied education and skills.

Marika did not like Solfrank. The dislike was mutual. It extended back years, to a time when the male had thought his age advantage more than overbalanced his sexual handicap. He had bullied; Marika had refused to yield; young teeth had been bared; the older pup had been forced to submit. Solfrank never would forgive her the humiliation.

The grudge was well-known. It was a stain he would bear with him in his search for a new pack.

"Dam sends me with two score and ten arrowheads ready for the shaft." Marika bared teeth slightly. A hint of mockery, a hint of I-dare-you. "Granddam wants the needles Borget promised."

Marika reflected that Kublin *liked* Solfrank. When he was not tagging after her, he trotted around after Gerrien's whelp—and brought back all the corrupt ideas Solfrank whispered in his ear. At least Zamberlin knew him for what he was and viewed him with due contempt.

Solfrank bared his teeth, pleasured by further evidence that those who dwelt in Skiljan's loghouse were mad. "I'll tell Dam."

In minutes Marika clutched a bundle of ready arrows. Gerrien herself brought a small piece of fine skin in which she had wrapped several bone needles. "These were Borget's. Tell Skiljan we will want them back."

Not the iron needles. The iron were too precious. But . . . Marika did not understand till she was outside again.

Gerrien did not expect Zertan to live much longer. These few needles, which had belonged to her sometime friend— and as often in council, enemy—might pleasure her in her failing days. Though she did not like her granddam, a tear formed in the corner of Marika's eye. It froze quickly and stung, and she brushed at it irritably with a heavily gloved paw.

She was just three steps from home when she heard the cry on the wind, faint and far and almost indiscernible. She had not heard such a cry before, but she knew it instantly. That was the cry of a meth in sudden pain.

Degnan huntresses were out, as they were every day when time were hard. Males were out seeking deadwood. There might be trouble. She hurried inside and did not wait to be recognized before she started babbling. "It came from the direction of Machen Cave," she concluded, shuddering. She was afraid of Machen Cave.

Skiljan exchanged looks with her lieutenants. "Up the ladder now, pup," she said. "Up the ladder."

"But Dam . . ." Marika wilted before a fierce look. She scurried up the ladder. The other pups greeted her with questions. She ignored them, huddled with Kublin. "It came from the direction of Machen Cave."

"That's miles away," Kublin reminded.

"I know." Maybe she had imagined the cry. Dreamed it. "But it came from that direction. That's all I said. I didn't claim it came from the cave."

Kublin shivered. He said nothing more. Neither did Marika.

They were very afraid of Machen Cave, those pups. They believed they had been given reason.

III

It had been high summer, a time when danger was all of one's own making. Pups were allowed free run of forest and hill, that they might come to know their pack's territory. Their work and play were all shaped to teach skills adults would need to survive to raise their own pups.

Marika almost always ran with her littermates, especially Kublin. Zamberlin seldom did anything not required of him.

Kublin, though, hadn't Marika's stamina, strength, or nerve. She sometimes became impatient with him. In her crueler moments she would hide and force him to find his own way. He did so whining, complaining, sullenly, and slow, but he always managed. He was capable enough at his own pace.

North and east of the packstead stood Stapen Rock, a bizarre basalt upthrust the early Wise designated as spiritually and ritually significant. At Stapen Rock the Wise communed with the spirits of the forest and made offerings meant to assure good hunting, rich mast crops, fat and juicy berries, and a plentitude of chote. Chote being a knee-high

plant edible in leaf, fruit, and fat, sweet, tuberous root. The
root would store indefinitely in a dark, cool, dry place.

Stapen Rock was the chief of five such natural shrines
recalling old Degnan animistic traditions. Others were dedi-
cated to the spirits of air and water, fire and the underworld.
The All itself, supercessor of the old way, was sanctified
within the loghouses themselves.

Machen Cave, gateway to the world below, centered the
shadowed side of life. Pohsit, sagan in Skiljan's loghouse,
and her like visited Machen Cave regularly, propitiating
shadows and the dead, refreshing spells which bound the
gateway against those.

The Degnan were not superstitious by the standards of
the Ponath, but in the case of shadows no offering was
spared to avert baleful influences. The spells sealing the
cave were always numerous and fresh.

Marika played a game with herself and Kublin, one that
stretched their courage. It required them to approach the
fane nearer than fear would permit. Timid, Kublin remained ever close to her when they ran the woods. If,
perforce, he went with her.

Marika had been playing that game for three summers.
In the summer before the great winter, though, it ceased
being pup play.

As always, Kublin was reluctant. At a respectful distance
he began, "Marika, I'm tired. Can we go home now?"

"It's just the middle of the afternoon, Kublin. Are you an
infant that needs a nap?" Then distraction. "Oh. Look."

She had spotted a patch of chote, thick among old leaves
on a ravine bank facing northward. Chote grew best where
it received little direct sunlight. It was an ephemeral plant,
springing up, flowering, fruiting, and wilting all within
thirty days. A patch this lush could not have gone unnoticed.
In fact, it would have been there for years. But she would
report it. Pups were expected to report discoveries. If nothing else, such reports revealed how well they knew their
territory.

She forgot the cave. She searched for those plants with

two double-paw-sized leaves instead of one. The female chote fruited on a short stem growing from the crotch where the leaf stems joined. "Here's one. Not ripe. This one's not ripe either."

Kublin found the first ripe fruit, a one-by-one-and-a-half-inch ovoid a pale greenish yellow beginning to show spots of brown. "Here." He held it up.

Marika found another a moment later. She bit a hole, sucked tangy, acid juice, then split the shell of the fruit. She removed the seeds, which she buried immediately. There was little meat to chote fruit, and that with an unpalatable bitterness near the skin. She scraped the better part carefully with a small stone knife. The long meth jaw and carnivore teeth made getting the meat with the mouth impossible.

Kublin seemed determined to devour every fruit in the patch. Marika concluded he was stalling. "Come on."

She wished Zamberlin had come. Kublin was less balky then. But Zamberlin was running with friends this year, and those friends had no use for Kublin, who could not maintain their pace.

They were growing apart. Marika did not like that, though she knew there was no avoiding it. In a few years they would assume adult roles. Then Zambi and Kub would be gone entirely. . . .

Poor Kublin. And a mind was of no value in a male.

Across a trickle of a creek, up a slope, across a small meadow, down the wooded slope bordering a larger creek, and downstream a third of a mile. There the creek skirted the hip of a substantial hill, the first of those that rose to become the Zhotak. Marika settled on her haunches a hundred feet from the stream and thirty above its level. She stared at the shadow among brush and rocks opposite that marked the mouth of the cave. Kublin settled beside her, breathing rapidly though she had not set a hard pace.

There were times when even she was impatient with his lack of stamina.

Sunlight slanted down through the leaves, illuminating

blossoms of white, yellow, and pale red. Winged things flitted from branch to branch through the dapple of sunlight and shadow, seeming to flicker in and out of existence. Some light fell near the cave mouth, but did nothing to illuminate its interior.

Marika never had approached closer than the near bank of the creek. From there, or where she squatted now, she could discern nothing but the glob of darkness. Even the propitiary altar was invisible.

It was said that meth of the south mocked their more primitive cousins for appeasing spirits that would ignore them in any case. Even among the Degnan there were those who took only the All seriously. But even they attended ceremonies. Just in case. Ponath meth seldom took chances.

Marika had heard that the nomad packs of the Zhotak practiced animistic rites which postulated dark and light spirits, gods and devils, in everything. Even rocks.

Kublin had his breath. Marika rose. Sliding, she descended to the creek. Kublin followed tautly. He was frightened, but he did not protest, not even when she leapt the stream. He followed. For once he seemed determined to outgut her.

Something stirred within Marika as she stared upslope. From where she stood the sole evidence of the cave's presence was a trickle of mossy water on slick stone, coming from above. In some seasons a stream poured out of the cave.

She searched within herself, trying to identify that feeling. She could not. It was almost as if she had eaten something that left her slightly irritable, as though there was a buzzing in her nerves. She did not connect it with the cavern. Never before had she felt anything but fear when nearby. She glanced at Kublin. He now seemed more restless than frightened. "Well?"

Kublin bared his teeth. The expression was meant to be challenging. "Want me to go first?"

Marika took a couple of steps, looked upslope again. Nothing to see. Brush still masked the cave.

Three more steps.

"Marika."

She glanced back. Kublin looked disturbed, but not in the usual way. "What?"

"There's something in there."

Marika waited for an explanation. She did not mock. Sometimes he could tell things that he could not see. As could she. . . . He quivered. She looked inside for what she felt. But she could not find it.

She did feel a presence. It had nothing to do with the cave. "Sit down," she said softly.

"Why?"

"Because I want to get lower, so I can look through the brush. Somebody is watching. I don't want them to know we know they're there."

He did as she asked. He trusted her. She watched over him.

"It's Pohsit," Marika said, now recalling a repeated unconscious sense of being observed. The feeling had left her more wary than she realized. "She's following us again."

Kublin's immediate response was that of any pup. "We can outrun her. She's so old."

"Then she'd know we'd seen her." Marika sat there awhile, trying to reason out why the sagan followed them. It had to be cruel work for one as old as she. Nothing rational came to mind. "Let's just pretend she isn't there. Come on."

They had taken four steps when Kublin snagged her paw. "There *is* something in there, Marika."

Again Marika tried to feel it. This sense she had, which had betrayed Pohsit to her, was not reliable. Or perhaps it depended too much upon expectation. She expected a large animal, a direct physical danger. She sensed nothing of the sort. "I don't feel anything."

Kublin made a soft sound of exasperation. Usually it was the other way around, Marika trying to explain something sensed while he remained blind to it.

Why did Pohsit follow them around? She did not even

like them. She was always saying bad things to Dam. Once again Marika tried to see the old meth with that unreliable sense for which she had no name.

Alien thoughts flooded her mind. She gasped, reeled, closed them out. "Kublin!"

Her littermate was staring toward the mouth of the cave, jaw restless. "What?"

"I just . . ." She was not sure what she had done. She had no referents. Nothing like it had happened before. "I think I just heard Pohsit thinking."

"You what?"

"I heard what she was thinking. About us—about me. She's scared of me. She thinks I'm a witch of some kind."

"What are you talking about?"

"I was thinking about Pohsit. Wondering why she's always following us. I reached out like I can sometimes, and all of a sudden I heard her thinking. I was inside her head, Kublin. Or she was inside mine. I'm scared."

Kublin did not seem afraid, which amazed Marika. He asked, "What was she thinking?"

"I told you. She's sure I'm some kind of witch. A devil or something. She was thinking about having tried to get the Wise to . . . to . . ." That entered her conscious mind for the first time.

Pohsit was so frightened that she wanted Marika slain or expelled from the packstead. "Kublin, she wants to kill me. She's looking for evidence that will convince Dam and the Wise." Especially the Wise. They could overrule Skiljan if they were sufficiently determined.

Kublin was an odd one. Faced with a concrete problem, a solid danger, he could clear his mind of fright and turn his intellect upon the problem. Only when the peril was nebulous did he collapse. But Marika would not accept his solution to what already began to seem an unlikely peril.

Kublin said, "We'll get her up on Stapen Rock and push her off."

Just like that, he proposed murder. A serious proposal. Kublin did not joke.

Kublin—and Zamberlin—shared Marika's risk. And needed do nothing but be her littermates to be indicted with her if Pohsit found some fanciful charge she could peddle around the packstead. They shared the guilty blood. And they were male, of no especial value.

In his ultimate powerlessness, Kublin was ready to over-react to the danger.

For a moment Marika was just a little frightened of him. He meant it, and it meant no more to him than the squash-ing of an irritating insect, though Pohsit had been part of their lives all their lives. As sagan she had taught them their rituals. She was closer, in some ways, than their dam.

"Forget it," Marika said. By now she was almost con-vinced that she had imagined the contact. "We came to see the cave."

They were closer than ever they had dared, and for the first time Kublin had the lead. Marika pushed past him, asserting her primacy. She wondered what Pohsit thought now. Pups were warned repeatedly about Machen Cave. She moved a few more steps uphill.

Now she saw the cave mouth, black as the void between the stars when the moons were all down. Two steps more and she dropped to her haunches, sniffed the cold air that drifted out of the darkness. It had both an earthy and slightly carrion tang. Kublin squatted beside her. She said, "I don't see any altar. It just looks like a cave."

There was little evidence anyone ever came there.

Kublin mused, "There *is* something in there, Marika. Not like any animal." He closed his eyes and concentrated.

Marika closed hers, wondering about Pohsit.

Again that in-smash of anger, of near insane determina-tion to see Marika punished for a crime the pup could not comprehend. Fear followed the thoughts, which were so repugnant Marika's stomach turned. She reeled away and her sensing consciousness whipped past her, into the shadows within Machen Cave.

She screamed.

Kublin clapped a paw over her mouth. "Marika! Stop! What's the matter, Marika?"

She could not get the words out. There *was* something there. Something big and dark and hungry in a way she could not comprehend at all. Something not of flesh. Something that could only be called spirit or ghost.

Kublin seemed comfortable with it. No. He was frightened, but not out of control.

She recalled Pohsit across the creek, nursing inexplicable hatreds and hopes. She controlled herself. "Kublin, we have to get away from here. Before *that* notices us."

But Kublin paid not attention. He moved forward, his step dreamlike.

Had Pohsit not been watching, and malevolent, Marika might have panicked. But the concrete danger on the far bank kept her in firm control. She seized Kublin's arm, turned him. He did not struggle. But neither did he cooperate. Not till she led him to the creekside, where the glaze left his eyes. For a moment he was baffled as to where he was and what he was doing there.

Marika explained. She concluded, "We have to go away as though nothing happened." That was critical. Pohsit was looking for something exactly like what had happened.

Once Kublin regained his bearings, he managed well enough. They behaved like daring pups loose in the woods the rest of the day. But Marika did not stop worrying the edges of the hundred questions Machen Cave had raised.

What was that thing in there? What had it done to Kublin?

He, too, was thoughtful.

That was the real beginning. But till much later Marika believed it started in the heart of that terrible winter, when she caught the scream of the meth on the breast of the cold north wind.

Chapter Two

I

Having questioned Marika till she was sure her scream was not one of her daydreams, Skiljan circulated through the loghouses and organized a scouting party, two huntresses from each. After Marika again told what she had heard, they left the packstead. Marika climbed the watchtower and watched them pass through the narrows around the stockade, through the gate, then lope across the snowy fields, into the fangs of the wind.

She could not admit it, even to herself, but she was frightened. The day was failing. The sky had clouded up. More snow seemed in the offing. If the huntresses were gone long, they might get caught in the blizzard. After dark, in a snowfall, even the most skilled huntress could lose her way.

She did not stay in the tower long. A hint of what the weather held in store came as a few ice pellets smacked her face. She retreated to the loghouse.

She was frightened and worried. That scream preyed upon her.

Worry tainted the rank air inside, too. The males prowled

nervously in their territory. The old females bent to their work with iron determination. Even Zertan got a grip on herself and tended to her sewing. The younger females paced, snarling when they got in one another's way. The pups retreated to the loft and the physical and emotional safety it represented.

Marika shed coat and boots, hung the coat carefully, placed her boots just the right distance from the fire, then scampered up the ladder. Kublin helped her over the edge. She did not see Zamberlin. He was huddled with his friends somewhere.

She and Kublin retreated to a shadow away from the other pups. "What did you see?" he whispered. She had asked him to scale the tower with her, but he had not had the nerve. For all his weakness, Marika liked Kublin best of all the young in the loghouse.

He was a dreamer, too. Though male, he wanted much what she did. Often they sat together filling one another's heads with imaginary details of the great southern cities they would visit one day. Kublin had great plans. This summer coming, or next at the latest, he would run away from the packstead when the tradermales came.

Marika did not believe that. He was too cautious, too frightened of change. He might become tradermale someday, but only after he had been put out of the packstead.

"What did you see?" he asked again.

"Nothing. It's clouded up. Looks like there's an ice storm coming."

A whimper formed in Kublin's throat. Weather was one of countless terrors plaguing him for which there was neither rhyme nor reason. "The All must be mad to permit such chaos." He did not understand weather. It was not orderly, mechanical. He hated disorder.

Marika was quite content with disorder. In the controlled chaos of a loghouse, disorder was the standard.

"Remember the storm last winter? I thought it was pretty."

The packstead had been sheathed in ice. The trees had

become coated. The entire world for a few hours had been encrusted in crystal and jewels. It was a magical time, like something out of an old story, till the sun appeared and melted the jewels away.

"It was cold and you couldn't walk anywhere without slipping. Remember how Mahr fell and broke her arm?"

That was Kublin. Always practical.

He asked, "Can you find them with your mind-touch?"

"Shh!" She poked her head out of their hiding place. No other pups within hearing. "Not inside, Kublin. Please be careful. Pohsit."

His sigh told her he was not going to listen to another of her admonitions.

"No. I can't. I just have the feeling that they're moving north. Toward Stapen Rock. We knew that already."

Only Kublin knew about her ability. Abilities, really. Each few major moons since last summer, it seemed she discovered more. Other than the fact that Pohsit was watching, and hating, she had no idea why she should keep her talents hidden. But she was convinced it would do her no good to announce them. Driven by Pohsit, the old females often muttered about magic and sorcery and shadows, and not in terms of approbation, though they had their secrets and magics and mysteries themselves—the sagan most of all.

Carefully worded questions, asked of all her fellow pups, had left Marika sure only she—and Kublin a little—had these talents. That baffled her. Though unreliable and mysterious, they seemed perfectly natural and a part of her.

Considering mysteries, considering dreams and stories shared, Marika realized she and Kublin would not be together much longer. Their tenth birthdays had passed. Come spring Kublin and Zamberlin would begin spending most of their time at the male end of the loghouse. And she would spend most of hers with the young females, tagging along on the hunt, learning those things she must know when she came of age and moved from the loft to the south end of the loghouse.

Too soon, she thought. Three more summers. Maybe four, if dam kept forgetting their age. Then all her freedom would be gone. All the dreams would die.

There would be compensations. A wider field to range beyond the stockade. Chances to visit the stone packfast down the river. A slim maybe of a chance to go on down the road to one of the cities the tradermales told tales about.

Slim chance indeed. While she clung to them and made vows, in her most secret heart she knew her dreams were that only. Huntresses from the upper Ponath remained what they were born. It was sad.

There were times she actually wished she were male. Not often, for the lot of the male was hard and his life too often brief, if he survived infancy at all. But only males became traders, only males left their packsteads behind and wandered where they would, carrying news and wares, seeing the whole wide world.

It was said that the tradermales had their own packfasts where no females ever went, and their own special mysteries, and a language separate even from the different language used among themselves by the males she knew.

All very marvelous, and all beyond her reach. She would live and die in the Degnan packstead, like her dam, her granddam, and so many generations of Degnan females before them. If she remained quick and strong and smart, she might one day claim this loghouse for her own, and have her pick of males with whom to mate. But that was all.

She crouched in shadows with Kublin, fearing her deadly plain tomorrows, and both listened to inner voices, trying to track their dam's party. Marika sensed only that they were north and east of the packstead, moving slowly and cautiously.

Horvat, eldest of the loghouse males, called dinner time. The keeping of time was one of the mysteries reserved to his sex. Somewhere in a small, deep cellar beneath the north end of the house, reached by a ladder, was a device by which time was measured. So it was said. None but the males ever went down there, just as none but the huntresses descended into the cellar beneath the southern end of the loghouse. Marika never had been down, and would not be allowed till the older huntresses were confident she would reveal nothing of what she learned and saw. We are strange, secretive creatures, Marika reflected.

She peeped over the edge of the loft and saw that none of the adults were hastening to collect their meals. "Come on, Kublin. We can be first in line." They scrambled down, collected their utensils quickly.

Two score small bodies poured after them, having made the same discovery. The young seldom got to the cookpots early. Oftentimes they had to make do with leavings, squabbling among themselves, with the weakest getting nothing at all.

Marika filled her cup and bowl, ignoring the habitual disapproving scowls of the males serving. They had power over pups, and used it as much as they dared. She hurried to a shadow, gobbled as fast as she could. There were no meth manners. Meth gobbled fast, ate more if they could, because there was no guarantee there was going to be another meal anytime soon—even in the packsteads, where fate's fickleness had been brought somewhat under control.

Kublin joined Marika. He looked proud of himself. Clinging to her shadow, he had been fast enough to get in ahead of pups who usually shoved him aside. He had filled his cup and bowl near spilling deep. He gobbled like a starved animal. Which he often was, being too weak to seize the best.

"They're worried bad," Marika whispered, stating the obvious. Any meth who did not jump at a meal had a mind drifting a thousand miles away.

"Let's get some more before they wake up."

"All right."

Marika took a reasonable second portion. Kublin loaded up again. Horvat himself stepped over and chided them. Kublin just put his head down and doggedly went on with his plunder. They returned to the shadow. Marika ate more leisurely, but Kublin gobbled again, perhaps afraid Horvat or another pup would rob him.

Finished, Kublin groaned, rubbed his stomach, which actually protruded now. "That's better. I don't know if I can move. Do you feel anything yet?"

Marika shook her head. "Not now." She rose to take her utensils to the cleaning tub, where snow had been melted into wash water. The young cared for their own bowls and utensils, female or not. She took two steps. Maybe because Kublin had mentioned it and had opened her mind, she was in a sensitive state. Something hit her mind like a blow. She had felt nothing so terrible since that day she had read Pohsit. She ground her teeth on a shriek, not wanting to attract attention. She fell to her knees.

"What's the matter, Marika?"

"Be quiet!" If the adults noticed . . . If Pohsit . . . "I–I felt something bad. A touch. One of them . . . one of our huntresses is hurt. Bad hurt." Pain continued pouring through the touch, reddening her vision. She could not shut it out. The loghouse seemed to twist somehow, to flow, to become something surreal. Its so well known shapes became less substantial. For an instant she saw what looked like ghosts, a pair of them, bright but almost shapeless, drifting through the west wall as though that did not exist. They bobbed about, and for a second Marika thought them like curious pups. One began to drift her way as though aware of her awareness. Then the terrible touch ended with the suddenness of a dry stick breaking. The skewed vision departed with it. She saw no ghosts anymore, though for an instant she thought she sensed a feathery caress. She was not sure if it was upon her fur or her mind.

"They're in trouble out there, Kublin. Bad trouble."

"We'd better tell Pobuda."

"No. We can't. She wouldn't believe me. Or she would want to know how I knew. And then Pohsit . . ." She could not explain the exact nature of her fear. She was certain it was valid, that her secret talents could cause her a great deal of grief.

But Kublin did not demand an explanation. He knew her talents, and he was intimate with fear. Its presence was explanation enough for him.

"I'm scared, Kublin. Scared for Dam."

II

The scouting party returned long after nightfall. Nine of them. Two of those were injured. With them came two injured strangers and a wild, bony skeleton of a male in tattered, grubby furs. The male stumbled and staggered, and was dragged partway by the huntresses. His paws were bound behind him, but he did not cringe like the cowardly males Marika knew.

Because Skiljan had led the party, the Wise and adult females of all the loghouses crowded into her loghouse. Skiljan's males cleared room and retreated to their chilly northern territory. The more timid withdrew to the store-room or their cellar. But Horvat and the other old ones remained watching from behind the barricade of their firepit.

The pups fled to the loft, then fought for places where they could look down and eavesdrop. Marika was big enough, ill-tempered enough, and had reputation enough to carve out a choice spot for herself and Kublin. She could not draw her attention away from the male prisoner, who lay in the territory of the Wise, watched over by the sagan and the eldest.

Skiljan took her place near the huntress's fire. She scanned her audience while it settled down with far more than customary snarling and jostling. Marika supposed the adults knew everything already, the huntresses having scattered to their respective loghouses before coming to Skiljan's. She hoped for enlightenment anyway. Her dam was methodical about these things.

Skiljan waited patiently. Three Degnan huntresses had

not returned. Tempers were rough. She allowed the jostling
to settle of its own inertia. Then she said, "We found eight
nomads denned in a lean-to set on the leeward side of
Stapen Rock. On the way there we found tracks indicating
that they have been watching the packstead. They have not
been there long, though, or we would have noticed their
tracks while hunting. The cry heard and reported by my pup
Marika came when they ambushed four huntresses from the
Greve packstead."

That caused a stir which was awhile settling out. Marika
wondered what her dam would have to say about neighbors
poaching, but Skiljan let it go by, satisfied that the fact had
sunk in. She ignored a call from Dorlaque for a swift
demonstration of protest. Such an action could cause more
trouble than it was worth.

"Four Greve huntresses ambushed," Skiljan said. "They
slew two. We rescued the other two." The Greve in question
were trying to appear small. Dorlaque had not finished her
say, though no one but they were listening. Skiljan continued, "The nomads butchered one of the dead."

Growls and snarls. Ill-controlled anger. Disgust. A little
self-loathing, for the grauken never lurked far beneath the
surface of any meth. Someone threw something at the
prisoner. He accepted the blow without flinching.

"Our sisters from Greve packstead overheard some of
their talk while they were captives. The speech of the
Zhotak savages is hard to follow, as we all know, but they
believe the group at Stapen Rock was an advance party
charged with finding our weaknesses. They belong to an
alliance of nomad packs which has invaded the upper
Ponath. They number several hundred huntresses and are
arming their males." She indicated the prisoner. "This
group was all male, and very well armed."

Again an angry stir, and much snarling about stupid
savages fool enough to give males weapons. Marika sensed a
strong current of fear. Several hundred huntresses? It was
hard to imagine such numbers.

"What became of the other nomads?" she wanted to ask.

But she knew, really. Her dam was a cautious huntress. She would have scouted Stapen Rock well before doing anything. She would have made no move till she knew exactly what the situation was. Then she would have had her companions fill the shelter with arrows and javelins. That three Degnan huntresses had not returned said the nomads, male or no, had been alert and ready for trouble.

"I wonder if any nomads got away," she whispered. Then, "No. Dam would still be tracking them."

Kublin shook beside her. She could have shaken herself. This was bad, bad news. Too much blood. The nomads might appease their consciences with claims of blood feud now, and never mind that they were guilty of a dozen savage crimes. Meth from the Zhotak did not think like normal meth.

Near chaos reigned below. Each of the heads of loghouse had her own notion of what should be done now. Hotheads wanted to go out in the morning, in force, and hunt nomads before nomads came to the packstead. More cautious heads argued for buttoning up the stockade now, and forget the customary search for deadwood and small game. Some vacillated, swinging back and forth between extremes. Because Gerrien took no firm position, but simply listened, there was no swift decision.

Dorlaque shouted a proposal for arming the males within the stockade, a course never before taken except in utmost extremity. Males could not be trusted with weapons. They were emotionally unstable and prone to cowardice. They might flee from their own shadows and cost the packstead precious iron tools. Or in their panic they might turn upon the huntresses. Dorlaque was shouted down.

It went on till Marika grew sleepy. Beside her, Kublin kept drifting off. Many of the younger pups had gone to their pallets. Skiljan entered nothing into the debate but an occasional point of order, refereeing.

After all the arguments had gone around repeatedly, unto exhaustion, Gerrien looked up from her paws. She surveyed the gathering. Silence fell as she rose. "We will question the prisoner." But that went without saying. Why else would Skiljan have brought him in? "And we will send a messenger to the silth packfast."

Marika came alert immediately. A low growl circulated among the Wise. Pohsit tried to rise, but her infirmities betrayed her. Marika heard her snarl, "Damned silth witches." Several voices repeated the words. Huntresses protested.

Marika did not understand.

Gerrien persisted. "Each year they take tribute. Some years they take our young. In return they are pledged to protect us. We have paid for a long time. We will call in their side of the debt."

Some began to snarl now. Many snapped their jaws unconsciously. There was a lot of emotion loose down there, and Marika could not begin to fathom it. They must be treading the edge of an adult mystery.

Skiljan shouted for silence. Such was her presence at that moment that she won it. She said, "Though I am loath to admit it, Gerrien is right. Against several hundred huntresses, with their males armed, no packstead is secure. Our stockade will not shield us, even if we arm our own males and older pups. This is no vengeance raid, no counting of coup, not even blood feud between packs. Old ways of handling attackers will not suffice. We cannot just seal the gate and wait them out. Hundreds are too many."

"Question the male first," Dorlaque demanded. "Let us not be made fools. Perhaps what the Greve huntresses heard was a lie by rogue males."

Several others joined her in arguing for that much restraint. Skiljan and Gerrien exchanged glances, Gerrien nodding slightly. Skiljan gave Dorlaque what she wanted. "We will send no messenger until we have questioned the captive."

Dorlaque carried on like she had won a major battle. Marika, though, watched Pohsit, who was plotting with her cronies among the Wise.

Skiljan said, "Two courses could be followed. We could

scatter messengers to all the packsteads of the upper Ponath and gather the packs in one holdfast, after the fashion of those days when our foredams were moving into the territory. Or we can bring in outside help to turn away outside danger. Any fool will realize we cannot gather the packs at this time of year. The Wise and the pups would perish during the journey. Whole packs might be lost if a blizzard came down during the time of travel. Not to mention that there is no place to rally. The old packfast at Morvain Rocks has been a ruin since my granddam's granddam's time. It would be impossible to rebuild it in this weather, with Zhotak huntresses nipping around our heels. The reconstruction is a task that would take years anyway, as it did in the long ago. So the only possible choice is to petition the silth."

Now Pohsit came forward, speaking for her faction among the Wise. She denounced the silth bitterly, and castigated Skiljan and Gerrien for even suggesting having unnecessary contact with them. Her opposition weakened Skiljan in the eyes of her neighbors.

But the sagan did not speak for a unanimous body of the Wise. Saettle, the teacher of Skiljan's loghouse, represented another faction arguing against Pohsit. She and the sagan squared off. They were no friends anyway. Marika was afraid fur would fly, and it might have had the prisoner not been there to remind everyone of a very real external threat. Fear of the nomads kept emotions from running wild.

Who were these silth creatures? The meth of the packfast down at the joining of rivers. But what was so terrible about them? Why did some of the Wise hate them so? Pohsit seemed as irrational about them as she was about Marika herself.

Was it because they feared the silth would displace them? There seemed an undercurrent of that.

Unexpectedly, old Zertan shrieked, "Trapped between grauken and the All! I warned you. I warned you all. Do not stint the rituals, I said. But you would not listen."

After the first instant of surprise, Granddam was talking

to air. Even her contemporaries ignored her. For a moment Marika pitied her. To this end an entire life. To become old and ignored in the loghouse one once ruled.

Marika firmed her emotions. Zertan had had her day. Her mind and strength were gone. It was best she stepped aside. Only, among the meth, one never stepped. One was pushed. All life long, one pushed and was pushed, and the strong survived.

And where did that leave the Kublins, brilliant but physically weak? Kublin, Marika knew, would not be alive now had he not been blessed with a mind that overshadowed those of the other pups. He was able to think his way around many of his weaknesses and talk his way out of much of the trouble that found him.

Below, the policy discussion raged on, but the real decisions had been made. The prisoner would be questioned, then a runner would be sent to the packfast. Everyone would remain inside the stockade till she returned. Food and firewood rationing would begin immediately, though there was plenty of both in storage. The loghouses would bring out their hidden stores of iron weapons and prepare them. The pack would outwait the nomads if possible, hoping that either hunger would move them toward easier prey or the packfast would send help. Hard decisions would await developments.

Hard decisions. Like winnowing the pack by pushing the old and weak and youngest male pups outside the stockade. Marika shuddered.

And then she fell asleep, though she had been determined to stay awake till the last outsider left.

III

With their interest thoroughly piqued, Marika and Kublin visited Machen Cave often. Each time they took advantage of their youth to shake Pohsit, running long circles, often dashing all the way down to the bank of the Hainlin before turning back to cross the hills and woods to where the cavern lay. The sagan could have tracked them by scent, had she the will, but after five miles of ups and downs old muscles gave out. Pohsit would limp back to the packstead, jaw grimly set. There she would grumble and mutter to the Wise, but dared not indict the pups before their dam. Not just for running her to exhaustion. That would be viewed as common youthful insolence.

Pohsit knew they were running her. And they knew she knew. It was a cruel pup's game. And Kublin often repeated his suggestion of escalated cruelty. Marika refused to take him seriously.

Pohsit never discovered that they were running to Machen Cave. Else she would have gone there and waited, and been delighted by what she saw.

That thing that Kublin had sensed first remained in or around the cavern. The sinister air was there always, though the pups never discovered its cause.

Its very existence opened their minds. Marika found herself unearthing more and more inexplicable and unpredictable talents. She found that she could locate anyone she knew usually just by concentrating and reaching out. She found that she could, at times, catch a glimmer of thought when she concentrated on wanting to know what was in the mind of someone she could see.

Such abilities frightened her even though she began using them.

It must be something of the sort that upset Pohsit so, she thought. But why were Pohsit's intentions so deadly?

There was a nostalgic, sad tone to their prowlings that summer, for they knew it was the last when they could run completely free. Adulthood, with its responsibilities and taboos, was bearing down.

After the ground became sufficiently dry to permit tilling, the Degnan began spring planting around their stockade.

Upper Ponath agriculture was crude. The meth raised one grain, which had come north with tradermales only a generation earlier, and a few scrawny, semidomesticated root vegetables. The meth diet was heavy on meats, for they were a species descended of carnivores and were just beginning a transition to the omnivorous state. Their grown things were but a supplement making surviving winter less difficult.

Males and pups did the ground breaking, two males pulling a forked branch plow, the blade of which had been hardened in fire. The earth was turned up only a few inches deep. During the growing season the pups spent much of their time weeding.

Summers were busy for the huntresses, for the upper Ponath meth kept no domesticated animals. All meat came of game.

Their cousins in the south did herd meat animals. Several packs had had tradermales bring breeding stock north, but the beasts were not hardy enough to survive the winters.

Tradermales had suggested keeping the animals in the loghouses during the bitter months. The huntresses sneered at such silliness. Share a loghouse with beasts! Tradermales had shown how to construct a multiple-level loghouse, leaving the lowest level for animals, whose body heat would help warm the upper levels. But that was a change in ways. The meth of the upper Ponath viewed change with deep suspicion.

They suspected the traders of everything, for those males did not conform even remotely to traditional male roles.

Yet one of the high anticipations of spring was the coming of tradermales, with their news of the world, their wild tales, their precious trade goods. Each year they came trekking up the Hainlin, sometimes only a handful carrying their wares in packs on their backs, sometimes a train with beasts of burden. The magnitude of their coming depended upon what the Wise of the packs had ordered the summer before.

The dreamers Marika and Kublin awaited their coming with an anticipation greater than that of their packmates. They plagued the outsiders with ten thousand questions, none of which they seemed to mind. They answered in amusement, spinning wondrous tales. Some were so tall Marika accused them of lying. That amused them even more.

In the year of Machen Cave the anticipation was especially high, for Saettle had ordered a new book brought to the packstead, and much of the winter before the huntresses of Skiljan's loghouse had trapped otec to acquire furs sufficient to pay for it. The snows were gone and the fields were plowed. The greater and lesser moons approached the proper conjunction. The excitement was barely restrained. It was near time for spring rites as well as for the advent of strangers.

But the tradermales did not come.

While they were days late, no one worried. When they were weeks behind, meth wondered, and messengers ran between packsteads asking if tradermales had been seen. There was grave concern among packs which had ordered goods the lack of which might make surviving winter difficult.

They were very late, but they did come at last, without an explanation of why. They were less friendly than in the past, more hurried and harried, lacking in patience. At most packsteads they remained only hours before moving along. There was little spreading of news or telling of tales.

At the Degnan packstead a group nighted over, for the Degnan packstead was known as one of the most comfortable and hospitable. The traders told a few tales by firelight in the square at the center of the packstead, as though in token for their keep. But everyone could tell their hearts were not in the storytelling.

Marika and Kublin cornered an old tradermale they had seen every year they could recall, one who had befriended them in the past and remembered their names from summer to summer. Never shy, Marika asked, "What is the matter this summer, Khronen? Why did you come so late? Why are you all so unhappy?"

This old male was not as grave as the others. One reason

they liked him so was that he was a jolly sort, still possessing some of the mischief of a pup. A bit of that shone through now. "The greater world, pups. The greater world. Odd things are stirring. A taint of them has reached this far."

Marika did not understand. She said so.

"Well, little one, consider our brotherhood as a pack stretching across all the world. Now think about what happens when there is argument between loghouses in your packstead. The loghouses of the brotherhood are at odds. There has been heated division. Everyone is frightened of what it may mean. We are all anxious to finish the season and return, lest something be missed in our absence. Do you see that?"

Both pups understood well enough. Skiljan and Gerrien often allied against other heads of loghouse. Within Skiljan's loghouse itself there was factionalism, especially among the Wise. The old females plotted and skirmished and betrayed one another in small ways, constantly, for the amusement of it. They were too old to be entertained by anything else.

Skiljan joined Marika, Kublin, and the old tradermale. She called him by name and, when the pups were surprised, admitted, "I have known Khronen many years. Since he was only a year older that Kublin."

Khronen nodded. "Since before I joined the traders."

"You are Degnan?" Marika asked.

"No. I was Laspe. Your dam and I encountered one another down by the river when we were your age. She tried to poach some Laspe blackberries. I caught her. It was a grand row."

Marika looked from the male to Skiljan and back. Seldom did she think of her dam having been a pup.

Skiljan growled, "You persist in that lie. After all these years I would think you could admit that you were trespassing on Degnan ground."

"After all these years I could still find my way to that berry patch and show that it is on Laspe ground."

Marika saw her dam was growing angry. She tried to

think of a way to calm her. But Khronen stepped in instead. "That is neither here nor there, now," he said. To Kublin, he added, "She will never grow comfortable with males who do not whimper and cringe when she bares her fangs." Back to Skiljan, "You have something on your mind, old opponent?"

"I overheard what you said to the pups. I suspect that something which so stresses the tradermale brethren might affect the fortunes of my pack. It occurred to me that you might advise us in ways we might serve ourselves as a result."

Khronen nodded. "Yes. There are things I cannot say, of course. But I can advise." He was thoughtful for a time. Then he said, "I suggest you look to your defenses. It may be a harsh winter. I would suggest you invest in the best iron arrowheads, knives, and axes."

"You sell them too dearly."

"I am selling nothing. I am telling you what I believe the wise huntress would do if she were privy to the knowledge I possess. You are free to ignore me, as you so often do. Equally, you are free to buy. Or to make your own arrowheads and whatnot of stone, faithful to the old ways."

"You were always sarcastic, were you not?"

"I have always been possessed of a certain intolerance toward attitudes and beliefs held by the huntresses and Wise of the upper Ponath. Clinging to ways and beliefs obviously false serves no one well."

Skiljan bared her teeth. But Khronen did not submit, as a male of the Degnan might.

The pack's attitudes toward tradermale tools and weapons certainly baffled Marika. They dwarfed the stone in quality, yet seldom were used. Each summer the Wise and huntresses bought axes, arrowheads, knives both long and short, and even the occasional iron plowshare. Whatever they could afford. And almost always those purchases went into hiding and were hoarded, never to be used, deemed too precious to be risked.

What was the point?

Skiljan and Gerrien traded all their otec furs for worked iron that summer.

And so that summer laid another shadow of tomorrow upon Marika's path.

Chapter Three

I

The first enraged tentacles of the blizzard were lashing around the loghouse. Down on the ground floor, the argument persisted still, though now most of the spirit was out of it, most of the outside huntresses had returned to their loghouses, and those who remained did so purely out of perverse stubbornness.

Marika was just wakening, right where she had fallen asleep, when old Saettle left the press and approached the foot of the ladder. She beckoned. "Pups down here. Time for lessons."

"Now?" Marika asked.

"Yes. Come down."

Shivering, those pups old enough for lessons slipped down and eased past the still snarling adults. Saettle settled them on the male side, according to age and learning development, and brought out the books.

There were six of those, and they were the most precious possessions of the loghouse. Some had been recopied many times, at great expense in otec furs. Some were newer.

The pack, and especially those who dwelt in Skiljan's loghouse, was proud of its literacy. Even most Degnan males learned to read, write, and cipher. Though not consciously done as a social investment, this literacy was very useful in helping Degnan males survive once they were sent forth from the packstead. Such skills made them welcome in the other packsteads of the upper Ponath.

Early on Marika had noticed the importance of motivation in learning. Males, when young, were as bored by the lessons as were most of the female pups. But as the males neared adulthood and the spring rites which would see them sent forth from the packstead to find a new pack or perish, their level of interest increased exponentially.

The central thread of pack education was the Chronicle, a record that traced pack history from its legendary founder, Bognan, a rogue male who carried off a female and started the line. That had happened many hundreds of years ago, far to the south, before the long migration into the upper Ponath.

The story, the Wise assured the young, was entirely mythical. A tale wilder than most, for no male would dare such a thing. Nor would any be capable, the sex being less smart, weaker, and emotionally more unstable than the female. But it was a tale fun to tell outsiders, whom it boggled. Every pack had its black forebears. Once they drifted into the mists of time, they became objects of pride.

Six books in Skiljan's loghouse. Almost as many in the rest of the packstead. And the Degnan packstead possessed more than all the other packs of the upper Ponath. Ragged as the packstead was, it was a center of culture and learning. Some summers other packs sent favored female pups to study with the Degnan. Friendships were made and alliances formed, and the Degnan strengthened their place as the region's leading pack.

Marika was proud to have been born into such an important pack.

The lessons were complete and the morning was well

advanced. The angry excitement of the night before had degraded, but the diehards were at it still. Rested huntresses returned from other loghouses. Tempers were shorter than ever.

The prisoner, unable to sustain his terror forever and overcome by exhaustion, had fallen asleep. He lay there ignored, huntresses stepping over and around him almost indifferently. Marika wondered if he had been forgotten.

Some common ground did exist. A watch was established in the watchtower, a task which rotated among the older pups. Most of the less interested adults began preparing for possible siege.

All those precious iron-tool treasures, so long hoarded, came out of hiding. The edges of axes and knives received loving attention. Arrows were mated to iron heads fearsome with many barbs. Marika noted that the heads were affixed to strike horizontally instead of vertically, as hunting arrows were. Meth ribs ran parallel to the ground rather than perpendicular.

More arrows, cruder ones, were made quickly. More spears were fashioned. Scores of javelins were made of sticks with their points hardened in the firepits. The older pups were shown basic fighting techniques. Even the males trained with spears, javelins, tools and knives—when they were not otherwise occupied.

Skiljan, exercising her prerogative as head of loghouse, supported by Gerrien and most of the Degnan Wise, ended the everlasting debate by evicting all outsiders from her loghouse.

The Wise of the pack were more in concert than the huntresses. They issued advices which, because of the near unanimity behind them, fell with the force of orders. What had been preparations made catch-as-catch-can became orderly and almost organized. As organized and cooperative as ever meth became.

They first ordered a short sleep for the cooling of emotions.

Marika wakened from hers uneasy. Kublin was snuggled against her, restless. What was wrong? The psychic atmosphere was electric. There was a stench in it. . . . Pain. And fear. Like that touch when the huntresses were out seeking the source of the scream she had heard.

A true scream ripped up from the ground level. She and Kublin scrambled to the ladder's head, making no friends among pups already crouched there.

They were questioning the prisoner. Pohsit was holding his paw in the huntress's firepit. Another of the Wise sat at his head, repeating a question over and over in a soft voice. He did not repsond, except to howl when Pohsit thrust his paw into the coals again.

The pups were neither upset nor disgusted, only curious. They battled for the best spots around the ladderhead. Marika was sure one would get pushed through the hole.

The torment went on and on. Marika whispered, "They won't get him to tell them anything."

Kublin nodded. He sensed it too.

Marika examined him. His nerves seemed frayed. Hers surely were. While she did not feel the prisoner's pain, she did catch the psychic scent of his fear and distress, the leakover from his scrambled mind. She did not know how to push it away.

Kublin seemed to be feeling all that, too.

Pohsit looked up at them. Her lips pulled back over her teeth in a silent, promising snarl. Kublin inched closer. Marika felt his frightened shiver.

She did not need to touch the sagan's mind to know what she was thinking.

Probuda, Skiljan's second, beckoned. "Down, pups. There is work to do." A massive rock of a female, she stood unmoved as pups tumbled about her, eager to be entrusted with something important. For that was what her tone and phrasing had implied. She had spoken as huntress to huntress.

"Marika. Kublin. You go see Horvat."

"Horvat? But—"

Pobuda's paw bounced off Marika's ear. Marika scooted around the prisoner and his tormentors. He was unconscious. She and Kublin awaited recognition at the edge of Wise territory. Receiving a nod from Saettle, they crossed over to the males' firepit, where Horvat was supervising some sort of expansion project. He was snarling because the hide umbrella, which gathered smoke to send it up a thin pottery flue, was cooked and smoked hard and brittle, and wanted to break rather than bend.

Marika said, "Horvat, Pobuda told us—"

"See Bhlase."

They found the young male, who had come to the pack only two years earlier. "Ah. Good," he said. "Come." He led them to the storage room. "Too dark in there. Kublin. Get a lamp."

Marika waited nervously. She had not visited this end of the loghouse since she was too small to know better. All the usual rules were falling. . . .

Kublin arrived with an oil lamp. Bhlase took it and pushed through the doorskins. It was cold and dark in the storage room. It was more crowded than the loft.

But it was neat—obsessively neat, reflecting Horvat's personality. Bhlase moved about, studying this and that. Marika gawked. The male handed the lamp back to Kublin. Then he started piling leather bags and sealed pottery jars into Marika's arms. "Those go to the firepit."

Though irked by his tone, Marika did as she was told. Bhlase followed with a load of his own. He ordered their plunder neatly, set the pups down, gave Kublin and Marika each a mortar and pestle. He settled between them with his legs surrounding a kettle. He drew a knife.

Marika was astonished. The kettle was copper, the knife iron.

Bhlase opened one leather bag and used a ceramic spoon to ladle dried, crushed leaves into Marika's mortar bowl. "Grind that into powder. I'll need ten more like that."

Marika began the dull task. Bhlase turned to Kublin. More, but different, dried, crushed leaves went into his mortar bowl. These gave off a pungent odor immediately. "Ten from you, too, Kublin."

Marika recalled that Bhlase had been accepted by Skiljan because of his knowledge of herbs and such, which exceeded that of Pohsit.

But what were they doing?

Bhlase had brought several items Marika connected only with cooking. A sieve. A cutting board. A grater. The grater he set into the kettle. He cut the wax seal off one of the jars and removed several wrinkled, almost meth-shaped roots. He grated them into the bowl. A bitter scent rose.

"That is good enough, Marika." He took her mortar bowl, dumped it into the sieve, flung the bigger remains into the firepit. They flashed and added a grassy aroma to the thousands of smells haunting the loghouse. "Nine more will do it. How is yours coming, Kublin? Yes. That is fine. Dump it here. Good. Nine more for you."

"Are you not scared, Bhlase?" Marika asked. He seemed unreasonably calm.

"I have been through this before. When I was a pup, nomads besieged our packstead. They are ferocious but not very smart. Kill a few and they will run away till they have eaten their dead."

"That is awful."

"*They* are awful." Bhlase finished grating roots. He put the grater aside, sieved again, then took up the cutting board. The jar he opened this time contained dead insects the size of the last joint on Marika's smallest finger. He halved each longwise, cut each half crosswise, scraped the results into the kettle. After finishing the insects he opened a jar which at first seemed to contain only a milky fluid. After he poured that into the pot, though, he dumped several dozen fat white grubs onto his cutting board.

"What are we making, Bhlase?" Kublin asked.

"Poison. For the arrowheads and spearheads and jave-lins."

"Oh!" Marika nearly dropped her pestle.

Bhlase was amused. "It is harmless now. Except for

these." He indicated the grubs, which he was dicing with care. "All this will have to simmer together for a long time."

"We have never used poisons," Kublin said.

"I was not here last time nomads came to the Degnan packstead," Bhlase replied. Marika thought she detected a certain arrogance behind his words.

"None of us were," she countered. "That was so long ago Granddam was leader."

"That is true, too." Bhlase broached another jar of grubs. And another after that. Kublin and Marika finished their grinding. Bhlase continued doing grubs till the copper kettle was filled to within three inches of its rim. He took that to a tripod Horvat had prepared, hung it, adjusted it just so over the fire. He beckoned.

"I am going to build the fire just as it must be," he said. "You two keep it exactly the same." He thrust a long wooden spoon into the pot. "And stir it each few minutes. The insects tend to float. The grubs sink. Try not to breathe too much of the steam."

"For how long?" Kublin asked.

"Till it is ready."

Marika and Kublin exchanged pained glances. Pups always got stuck with the boring jobs.

Over by the other firepit, the huntresses and Wise were still trying to get the prisoner to say something useful. He still refused. The loghouse was growing chilly, what with the coming and going of meth from other loghouses.

"Pohsit is enjoying herself," Marika observed, stirring the poison. She kept rehearsing the formula in her mind. She had recognized all the ingredients. None were especially rare. It might become useful knowledge one day.

Kublin looked at Pohsit, gulped, and concentrated on the fire.

II

So time fled. Sharpening of tools into weapons. Making of
crude javelins, spears, and arrows. Males and older pups
drilling with the cruder weapons over and over. The initial
frenzy of preparation faded as nothing immediate occurred.
The lookouts saw no sign of imminent nomad attack. No
sign of nomads at all.

Was the crisis over without actually beginning?

The captive died never having said anything of interest—
as Marika had expected. The huntresses dragged him out
and hurled him off the stockade to lie in the snow before the
gate, mute and mutilated. A warning.

Marika wished she had had a chance to talk with the
prisoner. She knew next to nothing about the lands beyond
the Zhotak.

The huntresses chafed at their confinement, though their
restlessness sprang entirely from their minds. In winter they
often went longer without leaving the packstead. There were
disputes about whether or not the gate should be opened.
Bitter cold continued to devour wood stores.

Skiljan and Gerrien kept the gate sealed.

The weather conspired to support them.

Marika took her turn in the watchtower and saw the
nothing she expected to see. Her watch was not long, but it
was cold. An ice storm had coated everything with crystal.
Footing was treacherous everywhere. Males not otherwise
occupied cleared ice and snow and erected platforms behind
the stockade so huntresses could hurl missiles from their
vantage. A few tried to break stones loose from the pile kept
for use in a possible raid, but they had trouble. The ice
storm had frozen the pile into a single glob.

Kublin called the alarm during his afternoon watch. The

huntresses immediately assumed his imagination had gotten the best of him, he being a flighty pup and male to boot. But a pair of huntresses clambered up the tower, their weight making it creak and sway, as had been done with several earlier false alarms.

Kublin was not a victim of his imagination, though at first he had trouble convincing the huntresses that he was indeed seeing what he saw. His eyes were very sharp. Once he did convince them, they dismissed him. He returned to the loghouse to bask in unaccustomed attention.

"I saw smoke," he announced proudly. "A lot of smoke, far away."

Skiljan questioned him vigorously—"What direction? How far? How high did it rise? What color was it?"—till he became confused and frustrated.

His answers caused a stir.

Marika had less experience of the far countryside than did her elders. It took her longer to understand.

Smoke in that direction, east, at that distance, in that color, could mean only one thing. The packstead of their nearest neighbors, the Laspe, was burning. And packsteads did not burn unless intentionally set ablaze.

The Degnan packstead frothed with argument again. The central question was: to send scouts or not. Skiljan and Gerrien wanted to know exactly what had happened. Many of those who only hours earlier had demanded the gate be opened now wanted it kept closed. Even a large portion of the Wise did not want to risk huntresses if the nomads were that close.

Skiljan settled the question by fiat. She gathered a dozen huntresses of like mind and marched out. She had her companions arm as huntresses seldom did, with an assortment of missile weapons, hatchets and axes, knives, and even a few shields. Shields normally were used only in mock combats fought during the celebrations held at the turning of each season.

Marika crowded into the watchtower with the sentry on duty. She watched her dam's party slip and slide across the

ice-encrusted snowfields till they vanished into the woods
east of the packstead.

When she returned to her loghouse, they gave her the iron
axe her dam had been sharpening, and showed her what to
do. Skiljan had taken it from the nomads she had slain. It
had not been cared for properly. Many hours would be
required to give it a proper edge.

Not far away, Pobuda and several others—Wise, males,
and huntresses who pretended to some skill in metalwork-
ing—were etching the blades of arrowheads and spears.
Bhlase sat in the center of their circle with his pot of poison,
carefully painting a brown, gummy substance into the etch-
ings with a tiny brush. Marika noted that he wore gloves.
The young huntress who carried the finished weapons away
also wore gloves, and racked them out of the reach of the
younger pups.

Marika soon grew bored with grinding the axe's edge. She
had too much energy to sit still all the time. Too many
strange thoughts fled through her mind while she ran the
whetstone over that knicked piece of iron. She tried to
banish the thoughts, to touch her dam.

There were distractions. The touch came and went. She
followed the scouting party peripatetically. Mostly, she
tasted their fear. Kublin kept coming to her with questions
in his eyes. She kept shaking her head till his curiosity
frayed her temper. "Get away!" she snarled. "Leave me
alone! I'll tell you when there's something to tell."

Sometimes she tried to touch Grauel, who carried the
Degnan's message to the packfast. She could not find
Grauel. But she did not worry. Grauel was the best of the
pack in field and forest. If she did not get through, none
could, and there was no hope from that direction.

The scouts returned at dusk, unharmed but grim. Again
Skiljan's loghouse filled with the adult female population of
the packstead. This evening they were more subdued, for
they sensed that the news was bad. Skiljan's report was
terse.

"Nomads attacked the Laspe packstead. They managed

to breach the palisade. They took the stores and weapons and tools, fired the loghouses, and ran away. They did not kill everyone, nor did they take many of the pups. Survivors we talked to said the nomads have taken the Brust packstead and are using it as their base."

End of report. What was not said was as frightening as what was. The Laspe, without stores or tools or weapons, would not survive. The Brust, of course, would all be dead already.

Someone suggested the Laspe pack's huntresses be brought into the Degnan packstead. "Extra paws to bear arms when the nomads come here. And thus the pack name would not die. Come summer they could take new males and rebuild."

Skiljan shook her head. "The nomads are barbarians but not fools. They did slay every female of pupbearing age. The huntresses forced them." She looked at the huntress who had spoken as though *she* were a fool.

That was the meth way—savagery to the last in defense of the pack. Only those too young or too old to lift a weapon would have been spared. The Laspe could be stricken from the roll of upper Ponath packs.

Marika was amazed everyone took the news with such calm. Two packs known obliterated. It had been several generations since even one had been overrun completely. It was a huge disaster, and portended far worse to come.

"What about the nomads?" someone asked. Despite tension, the gathering continued subdued, without snarling or jostling. "How heavy a price did they pay?"

"Not a price dear enough. The Laspe survivors claimed there were ten tens of tens of attackers."

A disbelieving murmur ran through the gathering.

"It does sound impossible. But they left their dead behind. We examined dozens of bodies. Most were armed males." This assertion caused another stir, heavy with distress. "They wore fetishes identifiable as belonging to more than twenty different packs. We questioned a young male left for dead, that the Laspe had not yet tortured. His will

was less strong than that of our recent guest. He had much
to say before he died."

Another stir. Then everyone waited expectantly.

Skiljan said, "He claimed the spring saw the rise of a
powerful wehrlen among the nomads. A rogue male of no
apparent pack, who came out of nowhere and who made his
presence felt throughout the north in a very short time."

A further and greater stir, and now some mutters of fear.

A wehrlen? Marika thought. What was that? It was a
word she did not know. There was so much she did not
know.

At the far end of the loghouse, the males had ceased
working and were paying close attention. They were startled
and frightened. Their fur bristled. They knew, whatever a
wehrlen was.

Murmurs of "rogue" and "male silth" fluttered through
the gathering. It seemed Marika was not alone in not recog-
nizing the word.

"He began by overwhelming the females of an especially
strong and famous pack. Instead of gathering supplies for
the winter, he marched that pack into the territory of a
neighbor. He used the awe of his fighters and his powers to
overcome its huntresses. He added it to the force he had
already, and so on, expanding till he controlled scores of
packs. The prisoner said the news of him began to run
before him. He fired the north with a vision of conquest. He
has entered the upper Ponath, not just because it is winter
and the game has migrated out of the north, but to recap-
ture the Ponath from us, whose foredams took the land from
the ancestors of the nomads. The prisoner even suggested
that the wehrlen one day wants to unite all the packs of the
world. Under *his* paw."

The Wise muttered among themselves. Those who had
opposed the sending of Grauel to the packfast put their
heads together. After a time one rose to announce, "We
withdraw our former objections to petitioning the silth. This
is an abomination of the filthiest sort. There is no option but
to respond with the power of the older abomination."

Only crazy old Zertan remained adamantly against having any intercourse with the packfast.

Skiljan said, "Gerrien and I talked while returning from the Laspe packstead. It is our feeling that another message must be sent. The silth must know what we have learned today. It might encourage them to send help. If not that, they must know for their own sakes."

The motion carried. One of Gerrien's huntresses, Barlog, was selected for the task and sent out immediately. Meth did not enjoy traveling by night, but that was the safer time. By dawn Barlog should be miles ahead of any nomad who might cross her trail.

What could be done had been done. There was nothing more to discuss. The outsiders went away.

Saettle called the pups to lessons.

Marika took the opportunity to ask about the wehrlen. Saettle would not answer in front of the younger pups. She seemed embarrassed. She said, "Such monsters, like grauken, are better not discussed while they are howling outside the stockade."

It was plain enough there were no circumstances under which Saettle would explain. Baffled, Marika retreated to her furs.

Kublin wanted to talk about it. "Zambi says—"

"Zambi is a fool," she snapped without hearing what her other littermate had to say. Then, aware that she was behaving foolishly herself, she called, "Zambi? Where are you? Come here."

Grumbling surlily, her other littermate came out of the far shadows, where he had been clustered with his cronies. He was big for his age. He looked old enough to leave the packstead already. He had gotten the size and strength and endurance that Kublin had been shorted. "What do you want?" he demanded.

"I want to know what you know about this wehrlen thing."

Zamberlin rolled his eyes. "The All forfend. You waste my time. . . ." He stopped. Marika's lips were back, her eyes hot. "All right. All right. Don't get all bothered. All I know is Poogie said Wart said he heard Horvat say a wehrlen is like a Wise meth, only a lot more so. Like a male sagan, I guess, only he don't have to be old. Like a male silth, Horvat said. Only I don't know what that is."

"Thank you, Zambi."

"Don't call me that, Marika. My name is Zamberlin."

"Oh. Listen to the big guy. Go on back to your friends."

Kublin wanted to talk. Marika did not. She said, "Let me go to sleep, Kub." He let her be, but for a long time she lay curled in her furs thinking.

Someone wakened her in the night for a brief stint in the watchtower. She bundled herself and went, and spent her time studying the sky. The clouds had cleared away. The stars were bright, though few and though only the two biggest moons were up, Biter and Chaser playing their eternal game of tag. The light they shed was not enough to mask the fainter stars.

Still, only a few score were visible.

Something strange, that sea of darkness above. Stars were other suns, the books said. So far away that one could not reach them if one walked a thousand lifetimes—if there was a road. According to Saettle's new book, though, the meth of the south knew ways through the great dark. They wandered among the stars quite regularly. . . .

Silth. That name occurred in the new book, though in no way that explained what silth were, or why the Wise should fear them so. It was silth sisters, the book said, who ventured across the ocean of night.

Nothing happened during Marika's watch, as she had expected. Meth did not move by night if they could avoid it. The dark was a time of fear. . . .

How, then, did these silth creatures manage the gulf between the stars? How did they *breathe*? Saettle's book said there was no air out there.

Marika's relief startled her. She felt the tower creak and sway, came back to reality with a guilty start. The nomads could have slipped to and over the palisade without her noticing.

She returned to her furs and lay awake a long time, head aswirl with stars. She tried to follow the progress of the messengers and was startled at how clearly the touch came tonight. She could grasp wisps of their thoughts.

Grauel was far down the river now, traveling by moonlight, and only hours away from the packfast. She had expected to arrive sooner but had been delayed by deep drifts in places, and by having to avoid nomads a few times. Barlog was making better time, gaining on the other huntress. She was thinking of continuing after sunrise.

Emboldened by her success, Marika strayed farther afield, curious about the packfast itself. But she could not locate the place, and there was no one there she knew. There was no familiar resonance she could home in on.

Still curious, she roamed the nearby hills, searching for nomads. Several times she brushed what might have been minds, but without any face she could visualize she could not come close enough to capture thoughts. Once, eastward, she brushed something powerful and hurried away, frightened. It had a vaguely male flavor. This wehrlen creature the Wise were so fussed about?

Then she gave herself a real nightmare scare. She sent her thoughts drifting up around Machen Cave, and there she found that dread thing she had sensed last summer, only now it was awake and in a malevolent mood—and seemingly aware of her inspection. As she reeled away, ducked, and fled, she had a mental image of a huge, starving beast charging out of the cave at some small game unlucky enough to happen by.

Twice in the next few minutes she thought she felt it looking for her, blundering around like a great, angry, stupid, hungry beast. She huddled into her furs and shook.

She would have to warn Kublin.

Sleep finally came.

Nothing happened all next day. In tense quiet the pack simply continued to prepare for trouble, and the hours shuffled away. The huntresses spoke infrequently, and then only in low voices. The males spoke not at all. Horvat drove them mercilessly. The Wise sent up appeals to the All, helped a little, got in the way a lot.

Marika did another turn on watch, and sharpened the captured axe, which her dam deemed a task suitable for a pup her age.

III

Autumn had come. High spirits were less often seen. Huntresses ranged the deep woods, ambushing game already migrating southward. Males smoked and salted with a more grim determination. Pups haunted the woods, gleaning deadwood. The Wise read omens in the flights of flyers, the coloration of insects, how much mast small arboreals stowed away, how deep the gurnen burrowed his place of hibernation.

If the signs were unfavorable, the Wise would authorize the felling of living trees and a second or even third gathering of chote root. Huntresses would begin keeping a more than casual eye on the otec colonies and other bearers of fur, seeing what preparations they made for winter. It was in deep winter that those would be taken for their meat and hides.

As winter gathered its legions behind the Zhotak and the meth of the upper Ponath became ever more mindful of the chance of sudden, deadly storms, time for play, for romping the woods on casual expeditions, became ever more scarce. There was always work for any pair of paws capable of contributing. Among the Degnan even the toddlers did their part.

As many as five days might pass without Marika's getting a chance to run free. Then, usually, she was on firewood detail. Pups tended to slip away from that. Their shirking was tolerated.

That autumn the Wise concluded that it would be a hard winter, but they did not guess half the truth. Even so, the Degnan always put away far more than they expected to need. A simple matter of sensible precaution.

Marika slipped off to Machen Cave for the last time on a day when the sky was gray and the wind was out of the north, damp and chill. The Wise were arguing about whether or not it bore the scent of snow, about who had the most reliable aches and pains in paws and joints. It was a day when Pohsit was lamenting her thousand infirmities, so it seemed she would not be able to rise, much less chase pups over hill and meadow.

Marika went alone. Horvat had Kublin scraping hides, a task he hated—which was why Horvat had him doing it. To teach him that one must do that which one hates as well as that which one enjoys.

It was a plain, simple run through the woods for Marika, a few hours on the slope opposite that where Machen Cave lay, stretching her new sensing in an effort to find the shadow hidden in the earth. Nothing came of it, and after a time she began wandering back toward the packstead, pausing occasionally to pick up a nut overlooked by the tree dwellers. She cracked those with her teeth, then extracted the sweet nutmeat. She noted the position of a rare, late-blooming medicinal plant, and collected a few fallen branches just so it would not seem she had wasted an entire afternoon. It was getting dusky when she reached the gate.

She found Zamberlin waiting there, almost hiding in a shadow. "Where have you been?" he demanded. He did not await an answer. "You better get straight to Dam before anyone sees you."

"What in the world?" She could see he was shaken, that he was frightened, but not for himself. "What's happened, Zambi?"

"Better see Dam. Pohsit claims you tried to murder her."

"What?" She was not afraid at first, just astonished. "She says you pushed her off Stapen Rock."

Fear came. But it was not fear for herself. If someone had pushed Pohsit, it must have been . . .

"Where is Dam?"

"By the doorway of Gerrien's loghouse. I think she's waiting for you. Don't tell her I warned you."

"Don't worry." Marika marched into the packstead, disposed of her burden at the first woodpile, spied her dam, went straight over. She was frightened now, but still much more for Kublin than for herself. "Dam?"

"Where have you been, Marika?"

"In the woods."

"Where in the woods?"

"Out by Machen Cave."

That startled Skiljan. "What were you doing out there?"

"I go there sometimes. When I want to think. Nobody else ever goes. I found some hennal."

Skiljan squinted at her. "You did not pass near Stapen Rock?"

"No, Dam. I have heard what Pohsit claims. Pohsit is mad, you know. She has been trying—"

"I know what she has been trying, pup. Did you decide you were a huntress and would get her before she got you?"

"No, Dam."

Skiljan's eyes narrowed. Marika thought her dam believed her, but also suspected she might know something she would not admit.

"Dam?"

"Yes?"

"If I may speak? I would suggest a huntress of Grauel's skill backtrack my scent."

"That will not be necessary. I am confident that you had nothing to do with it."

"Was she really hurt, Dam? Or just pretending?"

"Half and half. There is no doubt she took a fall. But she was able to walk home and raise a stink. A very inept murder attempt if it was such. I am inclined to think she was clumsy. Though what a meth her age was doing trying to climb Stapen Rock is beyond me. Go now. Stay away from Pohsit for a few days."

"Yes, Dam."

Marika went looking for Kublin immediately. She found him where she had left him. She started to snarl, but before he even looked up he asked, in a voice no one else could hear, "How could you do such a bad job of it, Marika? Why didn't you mash her head with a boulder while she was down, or something?"

Marika gulped. Kublin thought she had done it? Confused, she mumbled something about having had nothing to do with Pohsit's fall. She withdrew.

Not till next day did she become suspicious. By then trails and evidences were impossible to find. And Kublin adamantly denied having had anything to do with it himself, though Marika *was* able to isolate a period when no one had seen him around the packstead. She could establish him no alibi. She did not press, though. For Kublin, a male, even circumstantial evidence would be enough to convict.

In time even Pohsit began to wonder if the whole incident were not a product of her imagination. Imaginary or not, though, she let it feed her hatred, her irrational fear, her determination. Marika began to fear something *would* have to be done about the sagan.

Luckily, more and more of the Degnan were sure Pohsit was slipping into her dotage. Persecution fears and crazy vendettas were common among the Wise.

Marika did her best to stay out of the sagan's way. And when winter brought worse than anyone expected, even Pohsit relented a little, in the spirit of the pack against the outside.

Chapter Four

I

Marika's next night watch was very late, or very early in the morning. The stars had begun to fade as the sun's first weak rays straggled around the curve of the world. She stared at the heavens and daydreamed again, wondering incessantly about things hinted in the new book. What *were* these silth sisters? What were they finding up there among those alien suns? It was a shame she had been born to a pack on the very edge of civilization instead of in some great city of the south, where she might have a chance to enjoy such adventures.

She probed for the messengers again, and again the touch was sharp. Both had reached the packfast. Both were sleeping restlessly in a cell of stone. Other minds moved around them. Not so densely as in a packstead, where there was a continuous clamor of thought, but many nevertheless. And all adult, all old, as if they were all the minds of the Wise. As if they were minds of sagans, for they had that flavor. One was near the messengers, as if watching over them.

Marika tried to touch it more closely, to get the feel of these distant strangers who so frightened the Degnan.

Alarm!

That mind shied in sudden fear, sudden surprise, almost slipping away. Marika was startled herself, for no one ever noticed her.

A countertouch, light for an instant, then hard and sudden like a hammer's blow. Marika whimpered as fractured thought slammed into her mind.

Who are you? Where? What?

There was darkness around the edges of that, and hints of things of terror. Frightened, Marika fled into herself, blanking the world, pinching herself with claws. Pain forced her into her present moment atop the watchtower, alone and cold beneath mocking stars. She stared at Biter's pocked face, so like an old meth Wise female, considering her from the horizon.

What had she done? That old female had been aware of her. Marika's fear redoubled as she recalled all the hints and half-heard talk of her elders that had made her determine to keep her talents hidden. She was certain many of her packmates would be terribly upset if they learned what she could do. Pohsit only suspected, and she wanted to kill. . . .

Had she gone too far, touching that distant female? Had she given herself away? Would there be repercussions?

She returned to her furs and lay a long time staring at the logs overhead, battling fear.

The nomads came next morning. Everyone rushed to the stockade. Even the toddlers, whimpering in their fright. Fear filled the packstead with a stench the north wind did not carry away.

There were about a hundred of the northerners, and they were as ragged as Marika had pictured them. They made no effort to surprise the packstead. That was impossible. They stood off and studied it.

The sky was overcast, but not so heavily that shafts of

sunlight did not break through and sweep over the white earth. Each time a rushing finger of light passed over the nomads, it set the heads of spears and arrows aglitter. There was much iron among them, and not all were as careless of their weapons as had been the owner of the axe Marika had sharpened for so long.

Skiljan went around keeping heads down. She did not want the nomads to get a good estimate of numbers. The packstead looked small because its stockade had been built close to the loghouses. Let them think the packstead weaker than it was. They might do something foolhardy and find their backs broken before they learned the truth.

Marika did not find that reasonable thinking. The nomad leaders would have questioned meth from captured packsteads, wouldn't they? Surely they would have learned something about the Degnan packstead.

She gave them too much credit. They seemed wholly ignorant. After a few hours of watching, circling, little rushes toward the stockade by small groups trying to draw a response, a party of five approached the gate slowly, looking to parlay. An old male continued a few steps more after the other four halted. Speaking with an accent which made him almost incomprehensible, he called out, "Evacuate this packstead. Surrender your fortunes to the Shaw. Become one with the Shaw in body and wealth, and none of you will be harmed."

"What is he talking about?" huntresses asked one another. "What is this 'Shaw'?"

The old male stepped closer. More carefully, trying to approximate the upper Ponath dialect more closely, he repeated, "Evacuate the packstead and you will not be harmed."

Skiljan would not deign to speak with a rogue male. She exchanged a meaningful glance with Gerrien, who nodded. "Arrows," Skiljan ordered, and named the five best archers among the Degnan huntresses. "Loose!" An instant later the nomads were down. "That is five we do not have to fight," Skiljan said, as pragmatic as ever.

The crowd on the field sent up a terrible howl. They surged forward, their charge a disorganized, chaotic sweep. The Degnan sent arrows to meet them. A few went down.

"They have ladders," Marika said, peeping between the sharpened points of two stockade logs. "Some of them have ladders, Dam."

Skiljan boxed her ear, demanded, "What are you doing out here? Get inside. Wise! Get these pups cleared off the stockade. Marika. Tell Rechtern I want her."

Rechtern was the eldest of all the Degnan Wise, a resident of Foehse's loghouse. The All had been kind to her. Though she had several years on the next oldest of the Wise, her mind remained clear and her body spry.

Marika scrambled down and, rubbing her ear, went looking for the old female. She found her watching over the pups of Foehse's loghouse as they fled inside. She said, "Honored One, the huntress Skiljan requests you come speak with her." The forms required one to speak so to the Wise, but, in fact, Skiljan's "request" amounted to an order. The iron rule of meth society was stated bluntly in the maxim "As strength goes."

Marika shadowed Rechtern back to the stockade, heard her dam tell the old female, "Arm the males. We may not be able to hold them at the stockade." Only the Wise could authorize arming the males. But a huntress such as Skiljan or Gerrien could order the Wise. There were traditions, and rules, and realities. "As strength goes."

Marika waited in the shadows, listening, shaking, irked because she could not see what was happening. There were snarls and crashes above and outside. There were cries of pain and screams of rage and the clang of metal on metal. The nomads were trying to scale the stockade. The huntresses were pushing them back. On the platforms behind the inner circle of the palisade, old females still able to bend a bow or hurl a javelin sped missiles at any target they saw.

A female cried out overhead. A body thumped down beside Marika, a nomad female gravid but skeletally thin. A long, deep gash ran from her dugs to her belly. Her entrails leaked out, steaming in the cold. A metal knife slipped from her relaxing paw. Marika snatched it up.

Another body fell, barely missing her. This one was an old female of the Degnan. She grunted, tried to rise. A howl of triumph came from above. A huge, lank male leapt down, poised a stone-tipped spear for the kill.

Marika did not think. She hurtled forward, buried the knife in the nomad's back. He jerked away, heaved blood all over his dead packmate. He thrashed and made gurgling sounds for half a minute before finally lying still. Marika darted out and tried to recover the knife. It would not come free. It was lodged between ribs.

Another nomad dropped down, teeth bared in a killing snarl. Marika squeaked and started to back away, eyeing the spear her victim had dropped.

The third invader pitched forward. The old Degnan female who had fallen from the palisade had gotten her feet under her and leapt onto his back, sinking her teeth in his throat. The last weapon, meth called their teeth. Marika snatched up the spear and stabbed, stabbed, stabbed, before the nomad could shake the weak grasp of the old female. No one of her thrusts was a killer, but in sum they brought him down.

Yet another attacker came over the stockade. Marika ran for her loghouse, spear clutched in both paws. She heard Rechtern calling the males out.

More nomads were over the stockade in several other places. A dozen were looking for someone to kill or something to carry away.

The males and remaining old females rushed upon them with skinning knives, hatchets, hammers, hoes, and rakes. Marika stopped just outside the windskins of her loghouse, watched, ready to dart to safety.

More nomads managed to cross the stockade. She thought them fools. Badly mistaken fools. They should have cleared the defenders from the palisade before coming inside. When the huntresses there—few of them had been cut down—no longer faced a rush from outside, they turned and used their bows.

There was no mistaking a nomad struck by an arrow on which Bhlase's poison had been painted. The victim went into a thrashing, screaming, mouth-frothing fit, and for a few seconds lashed out at anyone nearby. Then muscles cramped, knotted, locked his body rigidly till death came. And even then there was no relaxation.

The males and old females fled into the loghouses and held the doorways while the huntresses sniped from the palisade.

The surviving invaders panicked. They had stormed into a death trap. Now they tried to get out again. Most were slain trying to get back over the stockade.

Marika wondered if her dam had planned it that way, or if it was a gift from the All. No matter. The attack was over. The packstead had survived it. The Degnan were safe.

Safe for the moment. There were more nomads. And they could be the sort who would deem defeat a cause for blood feud.

Seventy-six nomad corpses went into a heap outside the stockade. Seventy-six leering heads ended up on a rack as a warning to anyone else considering an attack upon the packstead. Only nineteen of the pack itself died or had to be slain because of wounds. Most of those were old females and males who had been too weak or too poorly armed. Many fine weapons were captured.

Skiljan took a party of huntresses in pursuit of those nomads who had escaped. Many of those were injured or had been too weak to scale the stockade in the first place. Skiljan believed most could be picked off without real risk to herself or those who hunted her.

The Wise ruled that the Mourning be severely truncated. There was no wood to spare for pyres and no time for the elaborate ritual customary when one of the Degnan rejoined the All. It would take a week to properly salute the departure of so many. And they in line behind the three who had fallen near Stapen Rock, as yet unMourned themselves.

The bodies could be stored in the lean-tos against the stockade till the Degnan felt comfortable investing time in the dead. They would not corrupt. Not in weather this cold.

It occurred to Marika that they might serve other purposes in the event of a long siege. That the heaping of dead foes outside was a gesture of defiance with levels of subtext she had not yet fully appreciated.

So bitterly was she schooled against the grauken within that her stomach turned at the very thought.

She volunteered to go up into the tower, to watch Skiljan off.

There was little to see once her dam crested the nearest hill, hot on the tracks of the nomads. Just the males cutting the heads off the enemy, building racks, and muttering among themselves. Just the older pups tormenting a few nomads too badly wounded to fly and poking bodies to see if any still needed the kiss of a knife. Marika felt no need to blood herself.

She had done that the hard way, hadn't she?

But for the bloody snow it could have been any other winter's day. The wind grumbled and moaned as always, sucking warmth with vampirous ferocity. The snow glared whitely where not trampled or blooded. The trees in the nearby forest snapped and crackled with the cold. Flyers squawked, and a few sent shadows racing over the snow as they wheeled above, eyeing a rich harvest of flesh.

Where there is no waste, there is no want. So the Wise told pups more times than any cared to hear or recall.

The old females ordered a blind set in the open field, placed two skilled archers inside, and had several corpses dragged out where the scavengers would think they were safe. When they descended to the feast, the archers picked them off. Pups scampered in with the carcasses. The males let them cool out, then butchered them and added them to the larder.

There was a labor to occupy, but not to preoccupy. One by one, some with an almost furtive step, the Degnan went to the top of the palisade to gaze eastward, worrying.

Skiljan returned long after dark, traveling by Biter light, burdened with trophies and captured weapons. "No more than five escaped," she announced with pride. "We chased them all the way to Toerne Creek, taking them one by one. We could have gotten them all, had we dared go farther. But the smoke of cookfires was heavy in the air."

Again there was an assembly in Skiljan's loghouse. Again the huntresses and old females, and now even a few males deemed sufficiently steady, debated what should be done. Marika was amazed to see Horvat speak before the assembly, though he said little but that the males of the loghouse were prepared to stand to arms with the rest of the pack. As though they had any choice.

Pobuda rose to observe, "There are weapons enough now with those that have been taken, so that even pups may be given a good knife. Let not what happened today occur again. Let none of the Degnan meet a spear with a hoe. Let this plunder be distributed, the best to those who will use it best, and be so held till this crisis has passed."

Pobuda was Skiljan's second. Marika knew she spoke words Skiljan had put into her mouth, for, though fierce, Pobuda never had a thought in her life. Skiljan was disarming a potential squabble over plunder before it began—or at least putting it off. Let the bickering and dickering be delayed till the nomad was safely gone from the upper Ponath.

None of the heads of loghouse demurred. Not even Logusz, who bore Skiljan no love at all, and crossed her often for the sheer pleasure of contrariness.

Skiljan said, "Pobuda speaks wisely. Let it be so. I saw that several shields were taken. And a dozen swords. Let those be given huntresses on the outer stockade." A snarl of amusement stretched her lips. "They will make life difficult and death easy for the climbers of ladders." She held up a sword, did a brief battle dance in which she pretended to strike down a nomad coming at her from below.

Marika stared at the sword and was amazed. She had not seen the long knife during the fighting. It flickered in the light from the firepit, scattering shards of red light. She shivered.

It was the first weapon she ever saw which had no purpose other than the killing of members of her own species. Every other had as its primary function use in the hunt.

"But these new weapons will not be enough," Skiljan said. "Not nearly enough. There is much blood in this thing now. We have dared destroy those sent to destroy us. This wehrlen of the nomads, this ruler over many packs, if he is as mad as they say, will not let this lie. He cannot, for even a small defeat must reflect upon his power. He cannot have that firm a grip upon the huntresses who follow him. He cannot fail and survive. So we will see nomads again, tomorrow or the day after. He will come himself. And he will come in great strength, perhaps with his whole horde."

A mutter of anger and of fear rippled through the assembly. Skiljan stood aside so the Wise might speak their minds.

"I wish we knew about this wehrlen," Kublin whispered to Marika. "I wish we did not have to be enemies. It would be interesting to discover who he is, what he is trying to do really, why he is not content, like huntresses, just to take what he needs and go."

Marika gave him a baffled look. What was this?

Rechtern was first of the Wise to speak. She said, "I have little to tell. But a question to ask. Where did Zhotak nomads acquire swords? Eh? Twelve swords were taken, all were borne by huntresses in their prime. They were swords of quality, too. Yet we here, between the north and the cities where such things are made, have never seen such blades. In fact, we know of swords only from hero stories told us by such as Saettle. The question again: Where did nomads acquire weapons of such quality, meant only for the slaying of meth?"

The entire performance was rhetorical, Marika realized. No one could answer knowledgeably, or even speculatively. The old female merely wished to raise an issue, to plant a seed against the return of summer.

There were no smiths among the meth of the upper Ponath. Nor were there any known to be among the nomads. All things of metal came from the cities of the south, and were sold by tradermales.

There would be hard questions asked when the tradermales appeared again.

After Rechtern almost all the Wise rose to speak in turn, including many who had nothing to say. That was the way of the old females. They talked long and long, harkening to ancient times to find something to compare with what had happened that day. Looking to precedent for action and response was second nature to the Wise.

The normal raid went nothing like what had happened. Seldom was a packstead destroyed, and then only in bloodfeud, after a surprise attack. The last such in the upper Ponath had occurred in Zertan's time. Meth just did not go in for wholesale slaughter.

The pack were awed by the scale of the killing, but not sickened. Death was. Killing was. Their confusion arose from enemy behavior, which was, it seemed, based on reasoning entirely outside their ken. Though hunger drove them, the nomads now lying dead outside the stockade had not come to the packstead simply to take food by force.

There were lessons. Saettle, even wounded, allowed no respite from the lessons. Marika asked for a reading about something similar to what had happened.

"Nothing resembles what happened here, pup. It is unprecedented in our books. Perhaps in the chronicles of the silth, who practice darkwar and whose written memories stretch back ten thousand years. But you are not here to talk over what has been talked over for so many hours. You are here to learn. Let us get on with our ciphers."

"What is darkwar? What are the silth?" Marika asked. But her questions fell on deaf ears. The Wise could not be moved once their minds were set. She would be neither seen nor heard while she persisted. She abandoned the effort quickly.

Behind the students, arguments over tactics continued.

Before them, and on the male side, weapons passed from paw to paw, being sharpened, being painted with poison once more. Both activities went on till well after Marika went to her furs and fell asleep despite all her curiosities and fears.

Once she wakened to what she felt might be a touch, panicky. But it did not come again. Restless, she reached toward the packfast, searching for the Degnan messengers. They were not in the place of stone.

She found them on the path homeward, hurrying by moonlight. Hope surged, but soon fell into the grasp of despair. Drawing closer to Grauel's thoughts, she saw that only three from the packfast accompanied them. Aching, frightened, she reached for Kublin and snuggled. He murmured in his sleep, but did not waken.

II

The stir below caused a stir above. The gouge of elbows and toes and paws as pups clambered over her wakened Marika. Kublin was gone from her side.

It was the middle of the night still. Other slow pups were rubbing their eyes and asking what was happening. Marika crawled to the head of the ladder, where Kublin had gotten himself a good vantage point. Marika squeezed in beside him, oblivious to the growls of those she pushed aside. "What is it?" she asked.

"I don't know. Somebody from Gerrien's loghouse came. The huntresses are getting ready to go out."

He was right. The huntresses were donning their heaviest furs. As if they expected to be out a long time. The males watched quietly from their end. Likewise the Wise, though Marika's granddam was holding forth in a subdued voice, ignored by everyone. Pohsit, too, was speaking, but seemed to be sending prayers up to the All.

Pobuda began checking weapons.

Something stirred in shadows where nothing should be moving. Startled, Marika stared at the storage area along the west wall, right were male territory met Wise. She saw nothing.

But now she caught a similar hint of motion from shadows along the base of the east wall. And again when she looked there was nothing there.

There had to be, though. She sensed something on that same level where she sensed the distant messengers and the dread within Machen Cave. Yes. It was something like that. But not so big or terrible.

Now she could almost see it when she looked at it. . . .

What was happening?

Frightened, Marika crawled back to her furs. She lay there thoughtfully for a while, recovering. Then she began considering how she might get out and follow the huntresses. But she abandoned that notion quickly. If they were leaving the packstead, as their dress and weaponry implied, it would be folly for a pup to tag along.

The grauken was out there.

Skiljan strode about impatiently, a captured sword in paw, a bow and quiver across her back.

Something had happened, and something more was about to happen.

Marika pulled her boots on.

Below, the huntresses began leaving the loghouse.

Marika pushed through the pups and descended the ladder. Kublin's whisper pursued her. "Where are you going?"

"Outside." She jumped as a paw clasped her shoulder. She whirled, found Pobuda's broad face just inches from her own.

"What are you doing, pup?"

"I was going outside. To the tower. To watch. What is going on?"

Perhaps if she were not Skiljan's pup, Pobuda would not have answered. But, after a moment's reflection, the loghouse's second huntress said, "A nomad encampment has been spotted in the woods. Near Machen Cave. They are going to raid it."

Marika gaped.

"The tower, then. No farther, or I will chew your ears off and feed you to Skiljan when she gets back."

Marika gulped, dispensed with the last thread of her notion about following the huntresses. Pobuda made no idle threats. She hadn't the imagination.

Marika donned her otec coat under Pobuda's baleful eye. Pobuda wanted to go hunting with the others. But if Skiljan went out, she had to remain. She was not pleased. Skiljan never delegated the active roles.

Marika pulled her hat down over her ears and ducked through the windskins before anyone could call her back.

Pohsit sped a look of hatred after her.

The packstead was cold and dark. Only a few of the lesser moons were up, shedding little light. The last of the expedition were slipping into the exit spiral. Other huntresses were on the stockade, shivering and bouncing to keep warm. Most of the huntresses were going out. It must be an important raid.

Marika started climbing the tower. A face loomed above, unrecognizable. She ignored it. Her thoughts turned to the sky. It was clear again tonight. Why had the weather been so good lately? One ice storm and a few flurries. That probably meant the next storm would be especially brutal, charged as it would be with all the energies pent during the good days.

The sentinel proved to be Solfrank. They eyed one another with teeth bared. Then Solfrank backed away from the head of the ladder, unable to face her down. She scrambled into the precarious wicker basket. Out on the snowfields, the huntresses were spreading out and moving northward, dark, silent blotches against trampled white.

"There," Solfrank said, pointing. There was pride in his voice. He must be the cause of all the activity.

There was a glow in the forest in the direction of Machen

Cave. A huge glow, as of a fire of epic proportion. A gout of sparks shot skyward, drifted down. Marika was astonished.

It must be some nomad ceremony. One did not build fires that could be seen for miles, and by potential foes, just to keep warm.

"How long has that been going on?"

"Only a little while. I spotted it right after I came on watch. It was just a little glow then. They must be burning half the forest now."

Why, Marika wondered, was Skiljan risking exposing so many huntresses? Hundreds of nomads would be needed to build such a conflagration. Those wild meth could not be so foolish as to presume their fire would not be seen, could they?

She became very worried, certain her dam had made a tactical mistake. It must be a trap. A lure to draw the Degnan into an ambush. She wanted desperately to extend her touch. But she dared not while Solfrank was there to watch her. "How long do you have left?"

"Only a few minutes."

"Do you want me to take over?"

"All right." He went over the side of the basket before she could change her mind.

Solfrank, Marika reflected, was impressed by nothing but himself. That fire out there had no meaning except as a small personal triumph. It would get him some attention. He was possessed of no curiosity whatsoever.

Fine. Good.

The tower stopped shaking to his descent. She watched him scurry toward the warmth of Gerrien's loghouse. The moment he entered, Marika faced north again and tried sensing her dam.

The touch was the strongest ever it had been. It seemed she was riding behind Skiljan's eyes, seeing what she saw, though she could not capture her dam's thoughts. Yet those became apparent enough when she directed the huntresses who accompanied her, for Marika could then see what they did, and even heard what they and her dam said part of the time.

Almost immediately the huntresses scattered to search out any nomad scouts who might be watching the packstead. They found none. They then filtered through the woods toward Machen Cave. They moved with extreme care, lest they alert sentinels.

Those did not materialize either. Marika sensed in her dam a growing contempt for the intelligence of the northerners.

Skiljan did not permit contempt to lessen her guard. She probed ahead carefully, lest she stumble into some trap.

But it was no trap. The nomads simply had not considered the possibility their bonfire might be seen from the Degnan packstead.

The fire lay on the south bank of the creek. It was huge. Marika was awed. Skiljan and her companions crouched in brush and watched as nomads piled more wood upon the blaze. The thunk of axes came from the opposite slope.

They were clearing the hill around the cave.

Hundreds of nomads hugged the fire's warmth.

Skiljan and Gerrien whispered together. Marika eavesdropped.

"What *are* they doing?" Skiljan asked. Scores labored upon the slopes. One particular nomad moved among them, giving orders that could not be heard. Little could be told of that person at a distance, except that it was someone the nomads considered important.

There were shouts. Boulders rumbled downhill. Nomads scrambled out of their path.

"The cave," Gerrien replied. "They're clearing the mouth of the cave. But why baffles me."

Back of all the other racket were the sounds of log drum and tambor and chanting. The nomad Wise were involved in some sort of ceremony.

"They would not be trying to draw the ghost, would they?" Skiljan asked.

"They might be. A wehrlen . . . They just might be. We have to stop that."

"Too many of them."

"They do not know we are here. Maybe we can panic them."

"We will try." The two separated. During the next several minutes Skiljan whispered to each of the huntresses on her side of the hill. Then she returned to center. Gerrien arrived seconds later.

Skiljan and her companions readied their bows. Marika's dam said, "Shout when you are ready."

Gerrien closed her eyes for half a minute, breathed deeply. Then she opened them, nodded, laid an arrow across her bow, rose. Skiljan rose beside her.

An ululating howl ripped from Gerrien's throat. In an instant it was repeated all across the slope. Arrows stormed downhill. Nomads squealed, shrieked, shouted. Dozens went down.

Skiljan's shafts, Marika noted, all flew toward the nomad Wise. And many found their marks.

Gerrien arced her arrows toward the meth leader on the far slope. It was a long flight in tricky light, and meth with shields had materialized around that one. None of Gerrien's shafts reached their mark.

A wild-eyed meth in bizarre black clothing suddenly materialized a few paces from Skiljan. She pointed something like a short, blunt spear. Skiljan and Gerrien were astonished by the apparition's appearance.

The meth cursed in a strange dialect and glared at the thing in her paws. She hefted it as a club. A pair of poisoned arrows ripped into her chest.

Gerrien then charged downhill. All the huntresses joined her. Javelins arced ahead of them. Nomads ran in circles. Already some were scattering into the darkness up the opposite slope. Only a handful dared counterattack. Their charge was met by huntresses with captured swords, and hurled back.

The panic among the nomads heightened. On the slope

opposite, the leader screamed in dialect, trying to stiffen resistance.

Gerrien carried the charge two thirds of the way to the creek, then halted. Sheer numbers of nomads promised to make further going too difficult. After some bloody sword-play, spearplay, and javelin throwing, she loosed another ululating howl and withdrew.

Confused, terrified, the nomads did not press.

The Degnan huntresses loosed their remaining arrows. Every shaft that touched a nomad killed, for each was poisoned.

Once their last arrows flew, the Degnan ran. They left more than a hundred nomads slaughtered. Awe at what they had done would not touch them for some time, for they were too involved with fighting and surviving. But battle and slaughter were not meth customs. There was no precedent for this in the upper Ponath. Fighting in the mass meant holding the stockade against northern raiders, not taking death to the nomads before they struck.

Marika sensed the elation of the huntresses. They had done the nomads great damage while suffering no harm themselves. Perhaps this would compel them to seek easier looting. Now the Degnan needed do nothing but outrun their enemies.

Marika scrambled down the tower, ran to the loghouse. "Pobuda," she gasped. "They are coming back. The nomads are chasing them."

Pobuda asked no questions. Not then. She alerted the rest of the packstead. Everyone capable, males included, hurried to reinforce the palisade.

And found there was nothing to see.

Marika got up the tower again and tried to remain invisible. When she did look down she spied Pobuda staring up, paws on hips, looking angry.

A shout rolled out of the distance. Gerrien and Skiljan. Marika could not tell which. As if to offset its earlier perfection, the touch would not open at all. Perhaps she was too excited.

Those on the stockade heard. Weapons came to the ready. Dark shapes appeared on the snowfields, running toward the gate. The Degnan huntresses came in a compact group, with the strongest to the rear, skirmishing with a scatter of nomads darting around their flanks. The nomads were having no luck. But scores more now were pouring from the woods. It looked as though Skiljan and Gerrien would be caught against their own stockade.

Arrows reached out. Nomads went down. Those most imperiled held up. Skiljan and Gerrien faced their huntresses around and retreated more slowly, backing into the now open gateway. Well-sped poisoned arrows kept the pursuit at bay. Marika saw that her dam carried the club that had been wielded by the strange meth in black.

Skiljan was last inside. She slammed the gate. Gerrien barred it. The home-come huntresses rushed around the spiral and took their places upon the stockade, hurling taunts at the nomads.

The enemy made one ragged rush. It fell apart before it reached the foot of the palisade. The survivors fled ignobly. From a safe distance nomads who had taken no part howled ferocious threats and promises.

Marika abandoned the watchtower while all attention was concentrated elsewhere. She hastened to her loghouse and to her sleeping furs, where she tried to make herself vanishingly small against Kublin.

III

It was late fall, but not as late as the incident of Pohsit and Stapen Rock. The skies were graying and lowering with the promise of what was to come. The creeks often ran raging with runoff from small but virulent storms. All the portents were evil.

But a spirit of excitement filled the Degnan packstead. Runners from other packs came and went hourly. Wide-ranging huntresses brought in reports which Degnan just out of puphood sped off to relay to neighboring packs.

No sighting, said the reports. No sighting. No sighting. But each negative message only heightened the anticipation.

Marika was more excited than any of her packmates. This was a landmark autumn. This would be the first of her apprentice runs with the hunting pack.

"Soon, now. Soon," the Wise promised, reading the portents of wind and sky. The herds must be on the move by now. Another day. Another two days. The skies are right. The forerunners will appear."

Up in the Zhotak a month or more ago, the kropek would have begun to gather. The young would be adolescent now, able to keep up during the migration south. The nomads would be nipping the flanks of the herds, but they seldom cooperated enough to take sufficient game to see themselves through their protracted winter.

The autumn kropek hunt was the major unifying force of the settled upper Ponath culture. Some years there were fairs. Occasionally two, three, even four packs gathered to observe an important festival. But only during the kropek hunt did the Degnan, Greve, Laspe, and other packs operate in unison—though they might not see one another at all.

The herd had to be spotted first, for it never followed the same route southward. Then an effort had to be made to guide it, to force it into a course that would allow a maximal harvest beneficial to all the Ponath packs.

Ofttimes the post-hunt, when the packs skinned and butchered and salted and smoked, became a gigantic fair of sorts. Sometimes tradermales arrived to take advantage of the concentration of potential customers. Frequently, charitable dams made arrangements on behalf of favored male offspring, saving them the more dangerous search for a new pack.

The kropek was not a large beast, but it was stubborn and difficult prey. Its biggest specimens stood three feet high at the shoulder. The animal had stubby legs and a stiff gait, and was built very wide. It had a thick skin and a massive head. Its lower jaw was almost spadelike. The female developed fearsome upthrust tusks as she matured. Both sexes were fighters.

In summer the kropek ran in small, extended-family herds just below the tundra, subsisting on grubs and roots. But the kropek was a true omnivore, capable of eating anything that did not eat it first. They did not hunt, though, being lazy as a species. Vegetables neither ran nor fought back. The only adventure in a kropek's life was its long vernal and autumnal migrations.

The meth of the upper Ponath hunted kropek only in the fall. In the spring, for the months bracketing the mating season, kropek flesh was inedible. It caused vomiting and powerful stomach cramps.

A young huntress raced into the packstead. The forerunners of the migration had been spotted in the high Plenthzo Valley, following that tributary of the east fork of the Hainlin. The near part of that valley lay only twenty miles east of the Degnan packstead. Excitement reached new heights. The kropek had not passed down Plenthzo Valley in generations. The good broad bottomland there made travel easy but gave meth room to maneuver in the hunt. There were natural formations where the migration could be brought under massed missile fire, the hunters remaining safe from counterattack.

Kropek were feisty. They would charge anything that threatened them—meaning mainly meth, for the meth were their most dangerous natural enemy. A meth caught was a meth dead. But meth could outrun and outsmart kropek.

Most of the time.

Huntresses double-checked weapons held ready and checked a dozen times since the season began. Messengers went out to the neighbors, suggesting meeting places. Males shouldered packs and tools. Pups being taken out to watch and learn scooted around, chattering at one another, trying to stay out of sight of those who ordered chores.

Skiljan finally gave Marika the light bow she had been hoping was meant for her. "You stay close, pup. And pay attention. Daydream around the kropek and you will find yourself dreaming forever. In the embrace of the All."

"Yes, Dam."

Skiljan wheeled on Kublin. "You stay close to Bhlase. Hear me? Do not get in the huntresses' way."

"Yes, Dam."

Marika and Kublin exchanged glances behind Skiljan's back, meaning they would do what they wanted.

A paw slammed against Marika's ear. "You heard your dam," Pobuda said. Her teeth were bared in amusement. "Put those thoughts out of your mind. Both of you."

Damned old Pobuda, Marika thought. She might be wide and ugly, but she never forgot what it was like to be young. You could not get away with anything with her around. She always knew what you were thinking.

Skiljan, and Barlog from Gerrien's loghouse, led the way. They set a pace the pups soon found brutal. Marika was panting and stumbling when they reached the Laspe pack-stead, where the Laspe huntresses joined the column. Marika did not, as she usually did, study the odd structure of the Laspe stockade and wonder why those meth did things so differently. She hadn't the energy. She had begun to realize that carrying a pack and bow made all the difference in the world.

Pobuda trotted by, mocking her with an amused grunt. Though Pobuda's pack weighed thrice what Marika's did, the huntress was as frisky as a pup.

Marika glanced back at Kublin, among the males. Her littermate, to her surprise, was keeping pace with Zambi. His face, though, betrayed the cost. He was running on pure will.

The pace slackened as they went up into the hills beyond the Laspe packstead. The scouts raced ahead, carrying only their javelins. The huntresses moved in silence now, listening intently. Marika never heard anything.

An hour later the Degnan and Laspe joined three packs coming up from the south. The enlarged party continued eastward on a broad front, still listening.

Marika finally surrendered to curiosity and asked why.

Skiljan told her, "Because kropek were spotted in the Plenthzo Valley does not guarantee that that is the route to be followed by the main herd. It could come some other way. Even over these hills. We do not want to be caught off guard." After walking some dozens of yards, she added, "You always hear the herd before you see it. So you always listen."

The pace remained slow. Marika recovered from her earlier strain. She wanted to drop back and lend encouragement to Kublin, but dared not. Her place was with the huntresses now.

The day began to fail as the packs descended toward the floodplain of the Plenthzo. Scouts reported other packs were in the valley already. The main herd was still many miles north, but definitely in the valley. It would be nighting up soon. There would be no hunting before tomorrow.

They came to the edge of the floodplain in the last light of day. Marika was amazed to see so much flat and open land. She wondered why no packstead stood on such favorable ground.

Only Pobuda felt inclined to explain. "It looks good, yes. Like a well-laid trap. Three miles down, the river enters a narrows flanked by granite. When the snows melt and the water rushes down, carrying logs and whatnot, those narrows block. Then the water rises. This land becomes one great seething brown flood, raging at the knees of those hills down there. Any packstead built on the plain would be drowned the first spring after it was built."

Marika saw the water in her mind, and the image suddenly became one of angry kropek. She began to comprehend the nervousness shown by some of the huntresses.

She did not sleep well. Nor did many huntresses, including her dam. There was much coming and going between packs, plotting and planning and negotiating. Messengers crossed the river, though meth disliked swimming intensely. Packs were in place on the far bank, too, for it was not known which way the kropek would follow, and those beasts had no prejudices against water.

Dawn arrived with unexpected swiftness. Pursuant to Skiljan's instructions, Marika placed her bedroll in a tree and memorized its location. "We will be running the herd," her dam said.

Marika expressed her puzzlement.

"The herd leaders must be kept moving. If we let them stop, the herd stops. Then there is no cutting individuals out or getting to those we might drop with arrows. They would not let us near enough."

The packs with which they had traveled moved out. Since first light scores of huntresses and males had been at work some distance down the plain, erecting something built of driftwood, deadwood, and even cut logs. Marika asked her dam about that.

"It is to scatter the herd. Enough for huntresses to dart in and out of the fringes, planting javelins in the shoulders of the beasts, or hacking at hamstrings." Skiljan seemed impatient with explanations. She wanted to listen, like the others. But her duty as dam was to relay what she knew to her young.

"They are coming," Pobuda said.

And a moment later Marika heard them, too. More, she felt them. The ground had begun to tremble beneath her feet.

The noise swelled. The earth shuddered ever more. And Marika's excitement evaporated. Her eagerness went away, to be replaced by growing apprehension. That sound grew and grew like endless thunder. . . .

Then she spied the herd, a stain of darkness that spanned most of the plain.

"Both sides of the river," Pobuda observed. "Not running yet."

"The wind is with us," Skiljan replied. "Thank the All."

Pobuda spied Marika's nervousness, despite her effort to conceal it. She mocked, "Nothing to it, pup. Just dash up beside a male, leap onto his shoulders, hold on with your legs while you lift his ear, and slide a knife in behind it. Push it all the way to the brain, though. Then jump clear before he goes down."

"Pobuda!" Skiljah snapped.

"Eh?"

"None of that. Not from anyone of my loghouse. We have nothing to prove. I want everyone able to carry meat home. Not one another."

Pobuda frowned, but did not argue.

"Do they do that?" Marika asked her dam.

"Sometimes," Skiljan admitted. "To show courage. Behind the ear *is* a good spot, though. For an arrow." Skiljan cocked her head, sniffed the breeze. A definite, strong smell preceded the kropek. "Only place an arrow will kill one of them. Not counting a low shaft upward into the eye."

"Why use bows, then?"

"Enough hits will slow them down. It will be stragglers mostly, that we get. The old, the lame, the stupid, the young that get confused or courageous or foolish." She looked at Marika with meaning. "You stay outside me. Understand? Away from the herd. Use your bow if you like. Though that will be difficult while running. Most important, make plenty of noise. Feint at them when I do. It is our task to keep them running." As an afterthought, "There are some advantages to hunting in the forests. The trees do keep them scattered."

Skiljan had to speak loudly to be heard over the kropek. Marika kept averting her gaze from the brown line. So many of them!

The tenor of the rumble changed. The herd began moving faster. Faintly, over the roar, Marika heard the ululation of meth hunting.

"Ready," Skiljan said. "Just after the leaders come abreast of us. And do what I told you. I will not carry you home."

"Yes, Dam." All those venturesome thoughts she had had back at the packstead had abandoned her. Right now she wanted nothing more than to slink off with Kublin, Zambi, and the males.

She was scared.

Pobuda gave her a knowing look.

The roar of hooves became deafening. The approaching herd looked like a surge in the surface of the earth, green becoming sudden brown. Lean, tall figures loped along the near flank, screaming, occasionally stabbing with javelins.

"Now," Skiljan said, and dashed toward the herd.

Marika followed, wondering why she was doing such a foolish thing.

The Degnan rushed from the woods shrieking. Arrows arced in among the herd leaders, who put on more speed. Skiljan darted in, jabbed a male with her javelin. Marika made no effort to follow. At twenty feet she was as close as ever she wanted to be. The eyes of the ugly beasts held no fear. They seemed possessed of an evil, mocking intelligence. For a moment Marika feared that the kropek had plans of their own for today.

Distance fled. With speed came quick weariness. The meth who had been running the herd fell away, their hunting speed temporarily spent. They trotted while they regained their breath. The kropek seemed incapable of tiring.

There was endurance and endurance, though. Meth could move at the quick trot indefinitely, though they were capable of only a mile at hunting speed.

A male feinted toward Skiljan. Pobuda and Gerrien were there instantly, ready to slip between it and the herd if it gave them room. It moved back, ran hip to shoulder with another evil-eyed brute. Marika shuddered, imagining what would become of someone unlucky enough to fall in their path.

Another male feinted. Again huntresses darted in. Again the beast faded back.

Marika tried launching an arrow. She narrowly missed one of the huntresses. Her shaft fell with no power behind it, vanished in the boil of kropek. She decided not to try again.

Her lungs began to burn, her calves to ache. And she was

growing angry with these beasts who refused to line up and die.

A third male feinted. And she thought, *Come out of there, you! Come out here where I can—*

It wheeled and charged her, nearly falling making so sudden a turn.

She did not stop running, but neither did she try to evade its angry, angling charge. She froze mentally, unable to think what to do.

Pobuda flung past, leaping over the kropek. She planted her javelin in its shoulder as she leapt. A second later Gerrien was on the beast's opposite flank, planting her own javelin as the kropek staggered and tried to turn after Pobuda. It tried to turn on Gerrien, then. Barlog jabbed it in the rear. It sprang forward, ran farther from the herd.

Then it halted and swung around, right into Marika. She had no choice but to jump up, over, as a big, wide mouth filled with grinding teeth rose to greet her.

She leapt high enough. Just barely high enough. Her toes brushed its snout.

"Keep running!" Skiljan yelled.

Marika glanced back once. The kropek stood at bay, surrounded.

Did I do that? Did I bring it out? she wondered. *Or was it coincidence?*

So try it again. But there was no time. They were approaching the obstacles built that morning. Marika watched her dam closely.

Skiljan slowed and turned away from the herd, to give the flood room to break around the barriers.

But the herd did not swing. It drove straight ahead at full speed, into the obstacles.

How many tons of kropek flesh in that raging tide? More than could be calculated. The barriers collapsed. Kropek climbed over kropek. The air filled with squeals of anger and agony.

Beyond, scores of huntresses were in flight. They had expected the herd to break up and pass around them. Now they used their speed advantage to angle away from that unstoppable wave. Most of them made it.

Skiljan did not pick up the pace again. When the Degnan came even with the barricade, they stopped, well away from the flow. Skiljan said, "There will be many stragglers here once the main herd passes."

Marika thought about loosing an arrow. Pobuda read her mind. "You would be wasting your shafts, pup. Save them."

It seemed hours before the last of the herd passed.

Skiljan was right. There were many stragglers, though those kropek that had gone down early were now little more than bloody stains in the trampled earth. The pack moved in, began the slaughter.

The stragglers clumped up in a compact mass. The heavily tusked females faced outward, held the line while the quicker, more agile males awaited a chance to leap upon their tormentors.

Down the valley the herd became congested at the narrow place. It had to force its way through a storm of missiles hurled by scores of huntresses safely perched atop high rocks. Over the next few days most of the wounded kropek would be run down and finished.

Marika tried luring one forth from the group encircled at the broken barrier. She had no luck.

Her talent—if such it was, and not a curse—was terribly unreliable.

The huntresses began picking on the more volatile males among the stragglers, one at a time. Tormented sufficiently, the beast would launch a furious charge that would expose it to attack from all sides. That made for slow work, but the number of animals dragged away for cooling out and butchering increased steadily.

There was no mercy in the huntresses, and seemingly no end to the hunt. With nightfall the males built fires from the remains of the barricades. Their light reflected redly from the eyes of the kropek still besieged. None of those rushed forward now. Which made it a standoff for the time being, though missiles kept arcing in, doing some damage. Very limited damage. Striking from head on, most just bounced off.

Fires burned all along the valley. Everywhere, on both sides of the river, meth were butchering, and gorging on organ meats. Marika thought her stomach would burst.

From the end of the floodplain came the continued squeal and rumble of kropek trying to force the narrows.

Skiljan finally allowed Marika to retrieve her bedroll, then to go settle down with the other pups, where she found Kublin in a state of exhaustion so acute she was frightened. But he did not complain. In that he was becoming something more admirable than Zamberlin, who carped about everything, though nature had equipped him far better to take it.

Before Marika parted from her dam, though, Skiljan said, "Think on what you have seen today. Reflect carefully. For meth sometimes behave very much like kropek. They develop momentum in a certain direction and nothing will turn them."

Marika reflected, but she would not understand the whole lesson for a long time.

Chapter Five

I

Marika was in the watchtower when the nomads returned the morning after her dam's night raid. She got no chance to descend.

Perhaps two hundred advanced toward the packstead, coming from the direction of the Laspe packstead. They halted beyond the reach of bows, howled, brandished weapons and fetishes. Their Wise moved among them, blessing. The huntresses among them carried standards surmounted by the skulls of meth and artfs, and the tails of kirns. Kirns were huge omnivores of the Zhotak, supposed by the nomads to be holy. Their ferocity and cunning and perseverance were legend. Thus the significance of their tails.

A big young male came forward, teeth bared as he stepped over and around bodies left from the night before. He shouted, "Abandon the stead and you will be forgiven all. Resist and your pups will be eaten."

A bold one for a male, Marika thought. He must be the rogue the Wise called the wehrlen. What other male would be so daring?

Skiljan sped an arrow. She was good, and should not have missed, yet her shaft drifted aside. A breeze, Marika supposed.

But her dam missed twice more, a thing unprecedented. No adjustment brought her nearer her mark. The nomads cheered. The mad male howled mockingly and offered his back. He stalked away slowly.

He had his answer.

Skiljan shouted, "Rogue! You dare the wrath of the All, flouting the laws of our foredams. If you truly believe yourself chosen, meet me in bloodfight."

A murmur of horror ran around the stockade. Was Skiljan mad too? Meet a *male* in bloodfight? Unheard of. Unprecedented. Disgusting. The creatures were not to be taken seriously.

Marika understood instantly, though. It was a ploy to weaken the wehrlen in the sight of his followers. They would believe him a coward if he refused. His position had to be precarious, for males did not lead and packs did not unite. Marika recalled the kropek hunt. Was this something like that, the nomads joining in the face of extremity?

The threat the wehrlen posed could be disrupted with a few well-chosen words, or by the proposed duel, the outcome of which could not be in doubt. No male could stand against a huntress of Skiljan's speed, ferocity, and skill.

The wehrlen turned, bared his teeth in mockery, bowed slightly, then walked on.

The ploy had failed. The nomads could not hear Skiljan's challenge.

The wehrlen reached them, took a spear from one, leaned upon it. After a moment he waved a languorous paw in the direction of the packstead.

The two hundred howled and charged.

The Degnan were better prepared today. All the archers faced the rush. Poisoned shafts stormed into the horde. Scores fell before the charge reached the stockade. Skiljan had placed half the archers where the rush could not reach them till it had crossed the outer stockade. Those huntresses kept speeding arrows once close fighting had been joined.

Old females still capable of bending bows were perched atop the loghouses. The females on the stockade were disposed so that those nomads who got over would find some paths easier than others. These paths concentrated them for the older archers. Skiljan had all the captured swords up front, and those were put to deadly use.

Nomads seized places on the shelf behind the stockade. They used their ladders to span the gap to the inner stockade, scrambled across. Many were hit and fell into the gap between barriers.

The armed males and older pups crouched in shadow under the inner platform. When nomads jumped down they attacked the invaders from in back. A great many nomads died there, and those who survived that found the loghouses sealed against them. When they turned on the males and pups, the archers atop the loghouses shot them down.

It was a great slaughter. Marika's heart hammered as she saw hope rising. They could do it again! Already over half the attackers were down. The others would flee, probably, as soon as they realized they had been set up for killing.

Hope died.

A horde of nomads came howling out of the forest from the direction of Machen Cave. They numbered several times the party which had attacked already. They were coming against the north wall, and the Degnan had concentrated at the point of assault on the east.

Marika screamed at her dam and pointed. Skiljan looked. Her face went slack. A nomad nearly got her before she recovered her equilibrium.

These new attackers surged up to the stockade, scarcely touched by arrows. They boiled around its base like maggots in an old carcass. Their ladders rose. Up they came, seized a foothold. Parties advanced along the platforms to right and left. Some spanned ladders across to the second circle. Others began chopping through the gate, seeking to penetrate the packstead by the traditional route.

That scores of them were dying under the hail of poisoned
arrows seemed not to bother them at all.

There were so many. . . .

Scores reached the interior unscathed. They hurled themselves upon the pups and males. Scores more died. Every
weapon, no matter how crude, had been treated with the
poison.

The old females atop the loghouses sped arrows as fast as
they could bend their bows—and could do nothing to stem
the endless flood. For a moment Marika recalled the kropek
sweeping over the barricades in Plenthzo Valley. This was
the same thing. Madness unstoppable.

Here, there, nomads tried to claw their way up the slick
ice on the loghouses, to get at the old archers. At first they
had no luck.

Marika whimpered. The stockade was almost bare of
defenders. It would be but a matter of minutes. . . . Terror
filled her. The grauken. The cannibal. The wehrlen had
promised to devour the pups. And she could do nothing from
her vantage. Nothing but wait.

She saw Gerrien go down under a pile of savages, snarling
till the last, her teeth sunk in an enemy throat. She watched
her dam fall a moment later in identical fashion, and wailed
in her grief. She wanted to jump down, to flee into the
forest, but she could not. Nomads surrounded the base of
the watchtower.

No one was going to escape.

She watched Zamberlin writhe out his life, screaming, on
a nomad spear. She saw Solfrank die after wielding an axe
as viciously as any huntress. Three nomads preceded him
into the embrace of the All. She watched the old females
atop the loghouses begin falling to thrown axes and spears.
These nomads carried no bows, little difference though that
made now.

She saw Kublin race out from under a platform, side open
in a bloody wound. He was trying to reach his dam's
loghouse. Two slavering nomads pursued him.

Black emotion boiled inside Marika, hot and furious.

Something took control. She saw Kublin's pursuers through a dark fog, moving in slowed motion. For a time it was as though she could see through them, see them without their skins. And she could see drifting ghosts, like the ghosts of all her foredams, hovering over the action. She willed a lethal curse upon the hearts of Kublin's pursuers.

They pitched forward, shrieking, losing their weapons, clawing their breasts.

Marika gaped. What? Had she done that? Could she kill with the touch?

She tried again. Nothing happened this time. Nothing at all. Whimpering, she strained to bring up that hot blackness again, to save what remained of her pack. It would not come.

The nomads began assaulting the loghouse doors. They broke through Gerrien's. In moments the shrieks of the very old and very young filled the square. A nomad came out carrying a yearling pup, dashed its brains out against the doorpost. Others followed him, also carrying terrified pups. Broken little bodies went into a heap. More nomads poured inside. Some brought out loot. Some brought torches. They began trying to fire the other loghouses—not an easy task.

The fighting soon dwindled to a single knot of huntresses clumped near Skiljan's door. Only two old females remained atop the roofs, still valiantly sending arrows. Nomads began to lose interest in battle. Some bore plunder out of loghouses already breached, or began squabbling over food. Others started butchering the pups taken from Gerrien's loghouse. Some prepared a huge bonfire of captured firewood. The victory celebration began before the Degnan were all slain.

And Marika saw it all from her watchtower trap.

A nomad came up the ladder. She drove her knife into his eye. He stiffened as the poison surged through him, plunged back down. His fellows below cursed her, threw stones and spears, harmed her not at all. The wicker of the stand turned their missiles.

She looked at the wehrlen, standing alone, leaning upon his spear, smug in victory. And the blackness came up without her willing it. It came so fast she almost missed her chance to shape it. She saw him naked of flesh, saw ghosts, and, startled, willed his heart to burst. Through the darkness she saw him leap in agony—then her thrust recoiled. It turned and struck back. She tried to dodge physically, crouched, whimpered.

Whatever happened, it did her no harm. It only terrified her more. When she rose and peeped over the wicker, she saw the wehrlen still rooted, clinging to his spear for support. She had not destroyed him, but she had hurt him. Badly. Only a powerful will kept him erect.

Gamely, Marika began seeking that blackness again.

The last defenders of Skiljan's doorway went down. Someone seized Kublin and hurled him away to fall among the countless bodies bloodying the square. He moved a little, tried to drag himself away. Marika screamed silently, willing him to lie still, to pretend he was dead. Maybe the cannibals would overlook him. He stopped moving.

The nomads began using axes on doors that would not yield to brute force. The door to Skiljan's loghouse boomed like a great drum. As each stroke fell, Marika jumped. She wondered how soon some nomad would realize that an axe was the tool to bring her down.

The door to Skiljan's loghouse went. Marika heard both Pohsit and Zertan shriek powerful curses. Her granddam sprang out with vigor drawn from the All knew where, slashing with claws painted with poison. She killed three before she went down herself.

Marika did not see what became of Pohsit. The tower began to creak ominously.

She sent up a prayer to the All and clutched her bloody knife. One more to go with her into the dark. Just one more.

II

Marika surveyed her homeland. This was what she would leave behind. To the north, forests and hills which rose in time to become the low mountains of the Zhotak. Beyond, tiaga, tundra, and permanent ice. That was the direction from which winter and the grauken came.

Below, they were roasting pups already. The smell of seared meth flesh made Marika lose her breakfast. The nomads circling her tower cursed her.

Eastward lay rolling hills white with snow, looking like the bare bones of the earth. Beyond the Plenthzo Valley the hills rose higher and formed the finest otec territory.

Southward, the land descended slowly to the east branch of the Hainlin, then in the extreme distance rose again to wooded hills almost invisible because the line between white earth and pale gray cloud could not be distinguished. Marika never had traveled beyond the river. She knew the south only through stories.

The west was very like the east, except the rolling hills were mostly bare of trees and there were no higher hills looming in the far distance. In fact, the hills descended. The land continued a slow drop all the way to the meeting of rivers where the stone packfast stood so many days away.

Thought of the packfast made her recall the messengers, Grauel and Barlog. The messengers bringing help that would arrive too late.

She felt a hint of a touch.

For a moment she thought it just the tower vibrating to the pounding blows of the axes below.

Another hint.

This was the thing itself.

She spun, looked at the wehrlen. He had recovered somewhat. Now he was moving toward the packstead, using his spear like a crutch. He seemed totally oblivious to all the bodies and the racks of heads which his followers had overturned. Four fifths of this meth had been slaughtered. Did he not care?

She noted his enfeeblement and gloried in what she had done. In what the Degnan had accomplished. There would be no more nomad terror in the upper Ponath.

A touch, though. If not from him, then who?

She recalled the messengers once more, and the response she had elicited from the old meth in the packfast. How close were Grauel and Barlog and their paltry aid? Maybe she had enough of this bizarre talent to at least speed them warning about the nomad.

She opened out, and reached out, and was astonished.

They were close. Very close. That way . . . She looked more closely at the land. For a moment she saw only the scrubby conical trees which dotted the snowscape. Then she realized that a few of those trees were different. They stood where no trees had stood before. And they were moving toward the packstead in short bursts.

Not trees at all. Three meth in black. Meth very like the one dam had slain near Machen Cave. Their clothing was like hers, like nothing Marika had ever seen, loose, voluminous, whipping in the wind. They came toward the packstead like the advance of winter, inexorable, a tall one in the middle, one of normal height to either side.

Behind them hundreds of yards, Marika now distinguished Grauel and Barlog crouched near a true tree. The two huntresses from Gerrien's loghouse had realized the magnitude of the disaster before them. They were too shaken to come ahead.

The axe kept slamming against the leg of the tower. They were taking long enough, Marika thought. Were they intentionally trying to torment her? Or was it just that the axe was in abominable condition?

The three black figures were two hundred yards away now, no longer making any effort to conceal their approach. A nomad spotted them, shouted, and pointed. Dozens more nomads clambered onto the platforms behind the stockade.

The male chopping at the watchtower stopped for a moment.

The three dark figures halted. The one in the middle raised both paws and pointed forefingers at the palisade.

Marika saw nothing. It was nothing physical. But her mind reeled away from an impact as strong as the wehrlen's counterattack. And nomads began screaming and falling off the stockade, clawing at their chests just the way Kublin's attackers had.

The screaming ended. A deep silence filled the packstead. Nomads looked at nomads suddenly dead. The male below the tower dropped his axe. Mouths opened but nothing came forth.

Then an excited babble did break out. More nomads mounted the stockade.

This time all three dark meth raised their arms, and every nomad on the palisade fell, shrieking and clawing their chests.

Nomads boiled through the spiral, clambered over the stockade, all rushing the three, murder in their hearts and eyes. A handful besieged the wehrlen, who seemed to have halted to regain his breath. Marika could not guess what confused tale he heard, but did see him shudder and, as if by pure will, pull himself together.

Those nomads who chose to attack the meth in black died by the score. Not one got closer than a dozen feet.

The meth in black began circling round the stockade, toward the mouth of the spiral.

The wehrlen watched them come into view. He did something. One of the three mouthed a faint cry and dropped. The others halted. The taller did something with her fingers. The wehrlen stiffened. Marika felt his surprise. Rigid as old death, he fell slowly forward.

Nomad witnesses howled in despair. They ran. It did them no good. The fastest and last to fall covered no more than twenty yards.

The two in black knelt over the third. Marika saw the tall one's head shake. They rose and walked the spiral into the packfast. A few dozen nomads remained inside. They scaled the stockade, trying to flee.

It was all very baffling to Marika.

The two entered the packstead's interior. A last few nomads died before they could hurl spears. Of the scores and scores of fallen, not one showed any sort of wound.

The dark two strode to the heart of the square, stepping over but otherwise ignoring the dead. There they halted, turned slowly, surveyed the carnage. They seemed aware of Marika but indifferent to her presence in the tower. The taller said something. The shorter went to the door of Logusz's loghouse. A moment later, inside, nomads began screaming. She moved across to Foehse's loghouse. Screams again. She then seemed satisfied.

Marika finally shook her knotted muscles into motion. Terror had left her so shaky she nearly fell twice getting down. She grabbed the axe from the male who had been chopping the tower leg, rushed toward the place where she had seen Kublin last.

Kublin was the only one of her blood who might still be living.

She had to dig him out from under a heap of nomads. He was breathing still, and bleeding still. She held him close and wept, believing, though she had neither healer's knowledge nor skill, that nothing could be done.

Somehow it all became concentrated in Kublin. All the grief and loss. The blackness welled within her. She saw ghosts all around her thickly, as though the spirits of the dead were reluctant to leave the place of battle. She looked inside Kublin, through Kublin, as though he were transparent. She saw the depth of his bruises and wounds. Angrily, she willed him health instead of death.

Kublin's eyes opened momentarily. "Marika?"

"Yes, Kublin. I'm here, Kublin. Kublin, you were so brave today."

"You were in the tower, Marika. How did you get down?"

"Help came, Kub. We won. They're all dead. All the nomads. The messengers came back in time." A lie. In time for what? Of all the Degnan other than the messengers themselves, only she and Kublin remained alive. And he was about to die.

Well, at least he could go into the arms of the All thinking something had been accomplished.

"Brave," Kublin echoed. "When it was time. When it counted. It was easier than I thought, Marika. Because I didn't have to worry."

"Yes, Kublin. You were a hero. You were as great as any of the huntresses today."

He rewarded her with that big winning look he got that made her love him above all her other siblings, then he relaxed. When she finally decided that he had stopped living, she wept.

Seldom, seldom did a meth female shed tears, unless in ritual. The two who wore black turned to stare at her, but neither made any move to approach her. They exchanged the occasional word or two while they watched.

The messengers came into the packstead. At last. Numb from shock, they surveyed the carnage. Grauel let out one prolonged, pained howl of torment. Barlog came to Marika, gently scratched the top of her head, as one did with infants in pain or distress. Marika wondered what had become of her hat. Why hadn't she felt the cold nipping at her ears?

Having collected herself, Grauel joined the two meth who wore black.

III

They sheltered the night in Skiljan's loghouse, which, having held the longest, had been damaged least. Marika could not get the stench of roast pup out of ther nostrils. She kept shaking and hugging herself and slinking into shadows, where she closed into herself and watched ghosts bob through the loghouse walls. For a long time she was not very sane. Sometimes she saw meth who were not there and

spoke with them as though they were. And then she saw one
meth who might have been there, and she did not believe
what she saw.

The messengers forced her to drink an infusion of chaphe,
which finally pushed her down into a deep, long, dreamless
sleep.

Nevertheless, in the deep hours of the night, she either
wakened partially or dreamed she overheard the two in
black. Grauel and Barlog and a tumble of ragged skins that
might have contained a third body were scattered around
one firepit. The outsiders sat by the other.

The taller said, "She is the one who touched us at Akard.
Also the one who struck twice during the fighting. A strong
one, well-favored by the All."

The rag-skin pile stirred.

"But untrained," the second outsider countered. "These
ones who find themselves on their own are difficult to discipline. They never really fit in."

This meth was very old, Marika realized. She had not
noticed before. She had not looked at these intruders closely
at all. This one had to be older than her granddam. Yet she
remained spry enough to have made a long journey in a
forced march, traveling without rest, and then had had
energy left to help drive away or kill hundreds of nomads.
What manner of meth was she? What sort of creatures were
these meth of the packfast?

"Silth bitches," she heard her dam murmur, as though
she were still alive and crouching before the firepit, muttering about all the things she hated in her world. But at least
Marika did not *see* her crouching there. Her mind was
beginning to recover.

"We must take her back. That was, after all, the purpose
of the expedition. To find the source of that touch."

"Of course. Like it or not. Fear it or not. Khles, I have a
foreboding about this one. A name comes to me again and
again unbidden, and I cannot shake it. Jiana. Nothing good
will come of her. She has that air of doom about her. Do you
not sense it?"

The other shrugged. "Perhaps I am not sufficiently Wise. What of the others?"

"The old one is useless. And mad. But the huntresses we will take, too. While they remain in shock, unready yet to race into the wilds to avenge their pack and get themselves killed in the avenging. We never have enough help, and they have no other pack to turn to. Myself, I foresee them becoming far more useful than the pup."

"Perhaps. Perhaps. Labor does have its value. Ho! Look there. See the little eyes glow in the firelight. She is a strong one, pushing back the chaphe sleep. Sleep, little silth. Sleep."

Behind the two strange meth the pile of rag skins stirred once again. Almost seethed, Marika thought.

The taller outsider extended a paw toward Marika. Fingers danced. Moments later sleep came, though she fought it with all her will, terrified. And when she wakened she remembered, but could not decide if what she recalled had been dream or fact.

The Wise made little distinction anyway. So what did it matter? She would accept all that as fact, though what she had heard made no sense.

Chapter Six

I

Morning came. Marika awakened disoriented. Where were the noises of a loghouse beginning its day? The clatter, the chatter, the bickering were absent. The place was as still as death. Marika remembered. Remembered and began to whine.

She heard footsteps. Someone stopped behind her. She remained facing the wall. What a time to spend her first night in huntress's territory!

A paw touched her. "Pup? Marika?"

She rolled, looked into Grauel's face. She did not like Grauel. The huntress from Gerrien's loghouse had no pups of her own. She was very short with others' young. There was something indefinably wrong about her.

But this was a different Grauel, a changed Grauel, a Grauel battered by events. A Grauel shocked into gentleness and concern. "Come, Marika. Get up. It is time to eat. Time to make decisions."

Barlog was doing the cooking. Marika was amazed.

She surveyed her home. It seemed barren without the

jostle and snarl. All outsiders surrounding the firepit. How many outsiders had ever eaten here? Very few.

And a huntress cooking. Times were odd, indeed.

The food was what one might expect of a huntress who had cooked only a few times in her life, and then in the field. A simple stew. But Marika's mouth watered anyway. She had not eaten since dawn the day before. Yet she did not gobble what Barlog handed her. She ate slowly, reluctant to get to what must follow. Yet the meal did end. Marika clasped her hands across her full stomach as Grauel said, "We three must decide what we will do now."

Barlog nodded.

Last of the Degnan. Last of the richest pack of the upper Ponath. Some things did not have to be said. They could not wait for summer, then take new males and begin breeding back up. Especially as Grauel could not bear pups. There were no Wise to teach, no males to manage the packstead. Of food and firewood and such there was such a plentitude that that wealth was a handicap in itself.

Times were hard. If the nomads themselves did not come first, some pack left in tight straits by them would discover the wealth here and decide to plunder. Or move in. Two huntresses and a pup could not hold the palisade. Not unless the silth from the packfast stayed. And did so for years.

Marika suspected even a few days were out of the question.

Silently, she cursed the All. She stared into the embers at the bottom of the firepit, thinking of the wealth in iron and stores and furs that would be lost simply because the Degnan could not defend them.

Neighbors or nomads. There were plenty of both who would commit murder gladly now. Winter was ahowl and the grauken was loose in the world.

A few nomads had escaped the massacre yesterday. Marika did not doubt that there were others scattered about the upper Ponath. Were they gathering? Might their scouts be at Stapen Rock, watching, knowing the packstead could be taken easily once the strangers departed?

That was the worst of it. Thinking the nomads might get everything after all.

Grauel was speaking to her. She pricked up her ears. "What? I was thinking."

"I said the sisters offered us a place in their packfast." Loathing under strict control tautened Grauel's voice. These meth were the silth whom Marika's dam and granddam and Pohsit had so hated.

But why?

Grauel continued, "We have no choice if we wish to survive. Barlog agrees. Perhaps we can take new males and begin the line afresh when you have reached mating age."

Marika shook her head slowly. "Let us not lie to ourselves, Grauel. The Degnan are dead. Never will we grow strong enough to recover this packstead from those who claim it."

She had wanted to see the stone packfast inhabited by these meth called silth. But not at this price. "Run to the Laspe, Grauel," she said. "Tell them. For a while, at least, let our wealth aid someone who shares our misery. They will have a better chance of holding it. And they will become indebted, so we would have a place to return one day."

The silth, seated a short distance away, were paying no attention. Indeed, they seemed preoccupied with the male end of the loghouse. They whispered to one another, then did pay attention, as if very much interested in the huntresses' response to Marika's suggestion.

Grauel and Barlog were startled by the notion. It had not occurred to them, and probably could not have. Two packs sharing a stead was not unheard of, but it was rare.

Grauel nodded reluctantly. Barlog said, "She is as smart as her dam was." She rose.

Grauel snapped at her. For a moment they argued over who would carry the message.

Marika realized that both wanted to get away from the packstead and its uncompromising reminders of disaster.

"Both of you go. That will be safer. There are nomads around still."

The huntresses exchanged looks, then donned their coats. They were gone in moments.

For a long time the silth did nothing but sit staring into the firepit, as though trying to read something in the coals. Marika collected the eating utensils. As she cleaned them and stowed them away, the silth kept glancing at her. Occasionally, one whispered to the other. Finally, the tall one said, "It is time. She has not sensed it." She came and got one of the bowls Marika had cleaned, filled it from the pot, carried it to the trap closing the cellar belonging to the loghouse males. She set the bowl down, opened the trap, blew aroma into the darkness below. Then she retreated, looking amused.

Marika stopped working, wondering what was happening.

A wrinkled, meatless, gray old paw appeared. Marika frowned. Not even Horvat . . .

A head followed the paw fearfully.

"Pohsit!" Marika said.

Pure venom smoldered in the sagan's eyes. She snatched the bowl and started to retreat into the cellar.

"Stop," the tall silth ordered. "Come out."

Pohsit froze. She retreated no farther, but neither did she do as directed.

"Who is this, pup?"

"Pohsit," Marika replied. "Sagan of this loghouse."

"I see." The silth's tone said more than her words. It said that the feeling the sagan had for those of the packfast was reciprocated. "Come out of there, old fraud. Now."

Shaking, Pohsit came up. But she stopped when her feet cleared the cellar stair. She stared at the silth in stark terror.

For an instant Marika was amused. For the first time in her young life, she saw the sagan at a genuine disadvantage. And yet, there Pohsit stood, even while shaking, with her paw making slow trips from bowl to mouth with spoonfuls of stew.

"That is the male end of the loghouse, is it not, pup?" the taller silth demanded.

"Yes," Marika replied in a small voice. Pohsit was looking at her still, still poisonous with promise.

The sagan staggered. Her bowl and spoon slipped from her paws. Those flew to her temples. She screamed, "No! Get out of my head! You filthy witches. Get out."

The screaming stopped. Pohsit descended like a dropped hide, folding in upon herself. And for a moment Marika gaped. That was the exact rag pile she had seen during the night when she was not sure whether or not she was dreaming.

Had Pohsit been up here then? But the silth seemed surprised by her presence. Seemed to have discovered her only recently.

No sense here. . . .

But she had seen her dam, too, hadn't she? And Pobuda. And many others who could not have been there because they were all dead. Or was that a dream?

Marika began to shake, afraid that she had begun to lose her grip on reality.

The alternative, that at times she was not quite firmly anchored in the river of time, she pushed out of mind the instant it occurred. That was too frightening even to contemplate.

"Just as I thought," the taller silth said. "Terror. Pure cowardice. She hid down there thinking the savages would not look for her there."

Hatred smoldered in the eyes that peeped out of the skin pile.

Marika sensed an opportunity to repay all the evil Pohsit had tried to do her. She had only to appeal to these meth. But Pohsit was Degnan. Crazy, malicious, poisonous, hateful, but still closer than any outsiders.

Grauel and Barlog would be pleased to learn that one of the Wise, and a sagan at that, had survived.

As though touching her thoughts, the older silth asked, "What shall we do with her, pup?" Marika now knew them for the creatures her elders had muttered against, but still did not know what silth were.

"Do? What do you mean, do?" She wished they would give names, so she could fix them more certainly in mind. But when she asked, they just evaded, saying their names were of no consequence. She got the feeling they were not prepared to trust her with their names. Which made no sense at all. The only other outsiders she had met, the wandering tradermales, insisted on giving you their names the moment they met you.

"We have looked into this one's mind. We know it as we know our own now." A whine escaped Pohsit. "We know how she tormented you. We know she would have claimed your life had she the chance. How would you requite such malice?"

The question truly baffled Marika. She did not want to do anything, and they must understand that. One did not demand vengeance upon the Wise. They were soon enough in the embrace of the All.

The older silth whispered, "She is too set in savage ways." But Marika overheard.

The other shrugged. "Consider the circumstances. Might we not all forgive our enemies in a like situation?"

There was something going on that Marika could not grasp. She was not sure if that was because she was yet too young to understand, or because these silth were too alien to comprehend.

She had been convinced that Pohsit was mad for at least a year. Now the sagan delivered final proof.

Pohsit hurled herself out of the rag pile at Marika. An iron knife flashed, its brightness dulled by traceries of Bhlase's poison. Marika made a feeble squealing sound and tried to crawl out of the way. Her effort was ineffective.

But Pohsit did not strike. She continued forward, bent at the waist, upper body way ahead of her feet. Her legs did not work right. Marika was reminded of a marionette one of the tradermales used to demonstrate at the night fire after the day's business was complete. The sagan had that same goofy, flailing gait.

It carried her the length of the loghouse and into the wall a few feet to one side of the doorway.

Marika watched the old meth rise slowly, a whimper sliding between her teeth. She faced around and met the cold stares of the silth, thinking of trying again. In a moment she put the thought out of mind.

Pohsit's behavior made no more sense than ever.

"What shall we do with her, pup?"

Still Marika would offer the sagan no harm. She shook her head. "Nothing. . . . I do not understand her. I do not hate her. Yet she hates me."

"That is the way of the false when faced with the true. You know you will not be safe while she lives."

Fear animated Pohsit now, and Marika suddenly knew the silth were right: she had hidden in the male fane out of cowardice. "Pohsit. Pohsit. What do you fear? You are so old death must be a close friend."

A spark of hatred for a moment glimmered through Pohsit's terror. But she did and said nothing more. Marika turned her back. "Let her do what she will. It is all the same to me."

The silth began ignoring Pohsit as studiously as did Marika. After a time the sagan quietly donned a coat—someone else's, way too big for her—and slipped out of the loghouse. Marika saw the tall silth nod slightly to the older.

She did not understand that till much later.

II

The silth questioned Marika about her talent. How had she grown aware that she was unusual? How had her talent manifested itself? They seemed convinced it would have caused her grave troubles had she let it become known.

"Your dam should have brought you to the packfast years ago. You and your littermates. As all pups are to be brought. It is the law."

"I know little about the packfast and the law," Marika replied. "Except that not many meth pay attention to either here in the upper Ponath. I have heard many jests made at the expense of that law. And I have heard our teacher, Saettle, say we came into the Ponath to escape the law."

"No doubt." The taller silth was extremely interested in Machen Cave. She kept returning to that. She asked Marika to be more specific about her experiences. Marika related each in as much detail as she could recall.

"You seem a little uncertain about something. As though there is more that you are afraid to tell."

"There is more," Marika admitted. "I just do not know if you will believe me."

"You might be surprised, pup. We have seen things your packmates would deny can exist." This was the older silth. Marika was not entirely comfortable with that one. In her way, she had a feel very like Pohsit. And she evidently had the power to be as nasty as Pohsit wished *she* could be.

"The last time I was there I really was not there. If you see what I mean."

The tall silth said, "We do not see. Why do you not just tell it?"

"The other night. When dam and the others went out to raid the nomads. They were up at Machen Cave with a big bonfire and all their Wise doing some kind of ceremony. Anyway, I followed dam through the touch. It was stronger than ever. I could see and hear everything she saw and heard." She choked on her words, eyed the silth oddly.

"You have remembered something."

"Yes. There was one of your kind there. With the nomads. . . ."

Both silth rose suddenly. The tall one began pacing. The other hovered over Marika, staring down intently.

"Did I say something wrong? Did I offend?"

"Not at all," the tall one said. "We were startled and distressed. A sister like ourselves, you say? Tell us more."

"There is little to tell. Dam and Gerrien attacked the nomads. Most of them panicked and fled. But suddenly this one meth, dressed like you almost, appeared out of nowhere, and—"

"Literally?"

"Excuse me?"

"She materialized? In fact? She did not just step from behind a tree or something?"

"No. I do not think so. She just appeared right in front of dam and Gerrien. She pointed something at them, then cursed it. It seemed like it was supposed to do something and did not. Then she tried to club them with it. Dam and Gerrien killed her. It was a strange weapon. All of metal."

The silth exchanged glances. "All of metal, eh? Where is this Machen Cave? I think we would be very interested in this metal club."

"Machen Cave is north. Several hours. But you do not have to go there. Dam brought the club home."

Excitement sparked between the silth. "Indeed? Where is it now, then?"

"I will have to find it. Dam put it away somewhere. She said she would trade the metal to the tradermales. Or maybe we could fashion tools from it."

"Find it, please."

While she talked Marika had begun setting the inside of the loghouse in order. When she kept paws and mouth busy, she did not have to think about what lay outside the loghouse. She continued distracting herself by searching for Skiljan's trophy. "Here it is."

The tall meth took it. Both sat down, facing one another, the metal club between them. They passed it back and forth, examined it minutely, even argued over a few small writing characters stamped into one side. They did so, though, in a language Marika did not understand. By the cautious way they handled the thing, Marika decided it was a dangerous something they had seen but never before touched.

"It is very important that you recall every detail about this meth you saw. The one who carried this club. It is certain she was our enemy. If we can identify her pack, by her clothing, say, we will be better equipped to protect our own. There should be no silth with the nomads."

"There should be no wehrlen either," said the older silth. "A wehrlen come out of nowhere, with skills as advanced as our own, or nearly so. This is an impossibility."

The taller meth was thoughtful a moment. "That is true." She looked at Marika intently. "Where does this Machen Cave lie again?" And Marika felt something brush her mind, a touch far lighter than that she had experienced the night the far silth had responded to her probing of the packfast. "Ah. So. Yes. Sister, I am going to go there after all. To see if the bodies remain. You learn what you can from the wehrlen."

The older silth nodded. She went out of the loghouse immediately.

The other dallied a moment, looking at Marika, saying nothing. Finally, she too departed, scratching Marika behind the ear lightly as she went. "It will all work out, pup. It will all work out."

Marika did not respond. She sat down and stared into the coals in the firepit. But she found no clues there.

III

She straightened the inside of the loghouse a bit more, moving in a daze. When she could find nothing more to preoccupy her there, she donned her coat. She had to go outside sometime and face the truth. No sense putting it off any longer.

It was every bit as terrible as she remembered, and worse. The carrion eaters had gathered. It would be a fat winter for them.

Though it was pointless, she began the thankless task of cleaning the packstead. One by one, straining her small frame to its limits, she dragged the frozen corpses of her packmates into the lean-to sheds. They would be safe from the carrion eaters there. For a time.

Near the doorway to Gerrien's loghouse she came on something that made her stop, stand as still as death for a long time.

Pohsit. Dead. Sprawled, one arm outstretched as if beseeching the loghouse, the other at her heart, her paw a claw. When Marika finally tore her gaze away she saw the elder silth in the mouth of the stockade spiral, watching.

Neither said a word.

Marika bent and caught hold of Pohsit's arm and dragged her into a lean-to with the others. Maybe, just a little, she had begun to understand what "silth" meant, and why her elders cursed and feared them.

Sometimes she could not reach her packmates because they were buried beneath dead nomads. Those she dragged around the spiral to the field outside, where she left them to the mercy of the carrion eaters. The wehrlen, she noted, had been both moved and stripped. The elder silth had searched him thoroughly.

There was no end to the gruesome task. So many bodies. . . . When her muscles began to protest, she rested by gathering fallen weapons instead, moving them near the doorway of her dam's loghouse, laying them out neatly by type, as if for inventory. She had tried to strip the better furs from the dead, too, but that had proven too difficult. The bodies would have to be thawed first.

Always the carrion eaters surrounded her. They would not learn to remain outside the stockade. They flapped away, squawking, only when she came within kicking distance. She sealed her ears to their bickering over tidbits. Listening might have driven her mad.

She was more than a little mad anyway. She drove herself mercilessly, carrying out a task without point.

After a time the taller silth returned, loping gracefully and easily upon the dirtied snow. She carried a folded garment similar to her own. She joined the other silth, and the two watched Marika, neither speaking, interfering, nor offering to help. They seemed to understand that an exorcism was in progress. Marika ignored them and went on. And went on. And went on till her muscles cried out in torment, till fatigue threatened to overwhelm her. And still she went on.

She passed near the silth often, pretending they did not exist, yet sometimes she could not help overhearing the few words they did exchange. Mostly, they talked about her. The older was becoming concerned. She heard herself called smart, stubborn, and definitely a little insane.

She wondered what the tall silth had learned around Machen Cave. They did not discuss that. But she was not interested enough to ask.

The sun rode across the sky, pursued by the specks of several lesser moons. Marika grew concerned about Grauel and Barlog. They had gone long enough to reach the Laspe packstead and return. Had they fallen foul of nomad survivors? Finally, she scaled the watchtower, which threatened to topple off its savaged legs. She barely had the energy to complete the climb. She saw nothing when she did and looked toward the neighboring packstead.

She dug around inside herself, seeking her ability to touch, with increasing desperation. It just was not there! She had to reach out and make sure Grauel and Barlog were all right! The All could not claim them too, leaving her alone with these weird silth! But it was hopeless. Either she had lost the ability or it had gone dormant on her in her shock and fatigue.

She told herself there was no point worrying. That worry would do no good, would change nothing. But she worried. She stood there studying the countryside, unconsciously resting, till the wind penetrated her furs and her muscles began to stiffen, then she climbed down and lost herself in labor again.

She did not know, consciously, what she was doing, but she was avoiding grief, because it was a grief too great to bear. Even toughened Grauel and Barlog had needed something to occupy them, to allow some of the pressure to leak off unnoted, to give some meaning to having survived. How much more difficult for a pup not yet taught to keep emotion under tight control.

The silth understood grief. They stayed out of her way, and did nothing to discourage her from working herself into an exhausted stupor.

The shadows were long and the carrion eaters almost too overfed to fly. Marika had dragged most all of her pack-mates into the lean-tos. Suddenly she realized that she had not found Kublin. Zambi had been there, right where she remembered him falling, but not Kub. Kub should have been one of the first she reached, because she had left him atop one of the heaps of dead. Hadn't she?

Had she dragged him away and not noticed? Or had she forgotten? The more she tried to remember, the more she became confused. She became locked into a lack of movement, in complete indecision, just standing in the square while a rising wind muttered and moaned about her.

The sky above threatened new snow. A few random flakes danced around, dashed in to melt upon her nose or to sting her eyeballs. The several days' break in winter's fury would end soon. The white would come and mask death till spring pulled the shroud aside.

One of the silth came and led her into Skiljan's loghouse, settled her near a freshened fire. The other was building up the fire at the male end of the loghouse and setting out pots and utensils in preparation for a meal far too large for three. Neither spoke.

Grauel and Barlog arrived with the darkness, leading the Laspe survivors. They numbered just a few over three score, and all fit comfortably into the one loghouse. The silth dished up stew silently, watched while the Laspe ate greed-ily. After a time they prepared an infusion of chaphe and insisted Marika drink it. As she faded away, barely aware of them wrapping her in furs, she murmured, "But I wanted to hear about what you found at Machen Cave."

"Later, little silth. Later. Rest your heart now. Rest your heart."

* * *

She wakened once in the deep hours. The fire crackled
nearby, sending shadows dancing. The taller silth sat beside
the firepit, motionless as stone except when dropping
another piece of wood into the flames. Her eyes glowed in
the firelight as she stared at Marika.

A touch, gentle as a caress. Startled, Marika recoiled.

*Easy, little one. There is nothing to fear. Go back to
sleep.*

Something enwrapped her in warmth, comfort, reassur-
ance. She fell asleep immediately.

Morning found the packstead blanketed with six inches of
new snow. The remaining bodies in the square had become
vague lumps seen through slowly falling snowflakes. The air
was almost still, the new flakes large, and the morning
deceptively warm. It seemed one could go out and run
without a coat. Grauel and Barlog rose early and went out to
take up where Marika had left off. A few of the Laspe
survivors joined them. There was little talk. The snowfall
continued, lazy but accumulating quickly. It was a very wet
snow.

Noon came. The silth made everyone come inside and eat
a huge meal. Marika watched the Laspe Wise cringe away
from the two in black, and wondered why. But she did not
ask. She did not care enough about anything to ask questions just then.

Marika and Grauel were first to go back outside. Almost
the instant they stepped into the snowfall the huntress
snapped Marika's collar and yanked her down, clapped a
paw over her mouth before she could speak. Holding
Marika, she pointed.

Vague figures moved through the snowfall around Gerrien's loghouse. Nomads! And they could not be ignorant of
the fact that the packstead was inhabited still, for Skiljan's
loghouse was putting out plenty of smoke.

Marika wriggled her way back through the doorway.
Grauel slid inside behind her. Once she was certain she

would not be heard outside, the huntress announced, "We have company outside. Nomads. I would guess only a few, trying to steal whatever they can under cover of the snow."

The silth laid down their ladles and bowls, closed their eyes. In a moment the taller nodded and said, "There are a dozen of them. Quietly taking food."

Marika listened no more. Barlog had snatched up a bow and was headed for the door, not bothering to don a coat. Marika scampered after her, tried to restrain her. She failed, and in an instant was out in the snow again, still trying to hold the huntress back.

Her judgment was better than Barlog's. As the huntress pushed outside, an arrow ripped past her ear and buried itself in the loghouse wall.

Barlog drew her own arrow to her ear, let fly at a shadow as another arrow streaked out of the falling snow. The latter missed. Barlog's brought a yip of pain.

The door shoved against Marika's back. Grauel pushed outside, cursing Barlog for her folly. She readied her own bow, crouched, sought a target.

Marika flopped onto her belly. Barlog, too, crouched. Arrows whipped overhead, stuck in or bounced off the loghouse. They heard confused shouting in dialect as the nomads debated the advisability of flight. A shaft from Grauel's bow found a shadow. That settled the matter for the nomads. They hefted their wounded and ran. They were not about to stay in a place so well known to death.

Where were the silth? Marika wondered. Why didn't *they* do something?

Grauel and Barlog made fierce noises and chased after the nomads—making sure they did not catch up. Marika followed, feeling foolish as she yipped around the spiral.

The nomads vanished in the snowfall. Grauel and Barlog showed no inclination to pursue them through that, where an ambush could so easily be laid. Grauel held Marika back. "Enough, pup. They are gone."

During all the excitement Marika never felt a hint of touch. The silth had done nothing.

She challenged them about it the moment she returned to the loghouse.

The taller seemed amused. "One must think beyond the moment if one is to be silth, little one. Go reflect on why it might be useful to allow some raiders to escape."

Marika did as she was told, sullenly. After her nerves settled, she began to see that it might indeed be beneficial if word spread that the Degnan packstead was defended still. Beneficial to the remaining Laspe anyway.

She began to entertain second thoughts about emigrating to the silth packfast.

That afternoon the silth gave her another infusion of chaphe to drink. They made Grauel and Barlog drink of it and rest, too. And when night fell and Biter rose to scatter the world with her silvery rays, the two females said, "It is time to leave."

Between them, Marika, Grauel, and Barlog found a hundred reasons for delaying. The two females in black might have been stone, for all they were moved. They brought forth travel packs which they had assembled while the three Degnan slept. "You will take these with you."

Marika, too stupefied to argue much, went through hers. It contained food, extra clothing, and a few items that might come in handy during the trek. She found a few personal possessions also, gifts from Kublin, Skiljan, and her granddam that had meant much to her once and might again after time banished the pain. She eyed the silth suspiciously. How had they known?

Resigned, Grauel and Barlog began shrugging into the coats. Marika pulled on her otec boots, the best she owned. No sense leaving them for Laspe scavengers.

A thought hit her. "Grauel. Our books. We cannot leave our books."

Grauel exchanged startled glances with Barlog. Barlog nodded. Both huntresses settled down with stubborn expressions upon their faces.

"Books are heavy, pup," the taller silth said. "You will tire of carrying them soon. Then what? Cast them into the river? Better they stay where they will be appreciated and used."

"They are the treasure of the Degnan," Marika insisted, answering the silth but speaking to the huntresses. "We have to take the Chronicle. If we lose the Chronicle, then we really are dead."

Grauel and Barlog agreed with a fervor that startled the silth.

Few wilderness packs had the sense of place in time and history that had marked the Degnan. Few had the Degnan respect for heritage. Many had no more notion of their past than the stories of their oldest Wise, who erroneously told revised versions of tales passed down by their own granddams.

Grauel and Barlog were embarrassed. It shamed them that they had not thought of the Chronicle themselves. So long as it existed and was kept, the Degnan would exist somewhere. They became immovably stubborn. The silth could not intimidate them into motion.

"Very well," the taller said, ignoring the angry mutter of her companion. "Gather your books. But hurry. We are wasting moonlight. The sky may not stay clear long. The north spawns storms in litters."

The two huntresses took torches and left Skiljan's loghouse, made rounds of all the other five. They collected every book of the pack that had not been destroyed. Marika brought out the six from the place where Saettle had kept those of Skiljan's loghouse. When all were gathered, there were ten.

"They are right," she admitted reluctantly. "They *are* heavy."

They were big, hand-inscribed tomes with massive wood and leather boards and bindings. Some weighed as much as fifteen pounds.

Marika set the three volumes of the Chronicle aside, looked to the huntresses for confirmation. Grauel said, "I could carry two."

Barlog nodded. "I will carry two also."

That made four. Marika said, "I think I could carry two, if they were light ones." She pushed the massive Chronicle volumes toward the huntresses. Grauel took two, Barlog the other. No more than two would be lost if one of them did not reach the packfast.

Three books had to be selected from the remaining seven. Marika asked the huntresses, "Which do you think will be the most useful?"

Grauel thought for a moment. "I do not know. I am not bookish."

"Nor am I," Barlog said. "I hunt. We will have little real use for them. We just want to save what we can."

Marika exposed her teeth in an expression of exasperation.

"You choose," Grauel said. "You are the studious one."

Marika's exasperation became more marked. A decision of her own, a major one, as though she were an adult already. She was not prepared mentally.

On first impulse she was tempted to select those that had belonged to her own loghouse. But Barlog reminded her that Gerrien's loghouse had possessed a book on agriculture that, once its precepts had been accepted, had improved the pack's yields, reducing the labor of survival.

One of the silth said, "You will have no need of a book about farming. You will not be working in the fields. Leave it for those who will have more need."

So. A choice made.

Marika dithered after rejecting only one more book, a collection of old stories read for the pleasure of small pups. There would be no need of that where they were going.

The older silth came around the fire, arrayed the books before Marika after the manner of terrac fortune plaques, which the sagans so often consulted. "Close your eyes, Marika. Empty your mind. Let the All come in and touch you. Then you reach out and touch books. Those shall be the ones you take."

Grauel grumbled, "That is sheer chance."

Barlog added, "Witch's ways," and looked very upset. Just the way the Wise did whenever talk turned to the silth.

They were afraid. Finally, Marika began to realize what lay at the root of all their attitudes toward the silth. Sheer terror.

She did exactly as she was told. Moments later her paw seemed to move of its own accord. She felt leather under her fingers, could not recall which book lay where.

"No," said the older silth. "Keep your eyes closed."

Grauel grumbled something to Barlog.

"You two," the old silth said. "Pack the books as she chooses them. Place the others in the place where books are stored."

Marika's paw jerked to another book. For a moment it seemed something had hold of her wrist. And on the level of the touch, she sensed something with that darkshadow presence she associated with the things she called ghosts.

Again, and done.

The old silth spoke. "Open your eyes, pup. Get your coat. It is time to travel."

Unquestioning, Marika did as she was told. Coat on, she raised her pack and snugged it upon her shoulders the way Pobuda had shown her, finally, coming back from the hunt in Plenthzo Valley. She felt uncomfortable under the unaccustomed weight. Recalling the march to and from the hunt, and the deep, wet snow, she knew she would become far more uncomfortable before she reached the silth packfast.

Maybe she *would* end up discarding the books.

Maybe the silth had been trying to do her a favor, trying to talk her out of taking the books.

There were no farewells from or for the Laspe, who watched preparations for departure with increasing relief. As they stepped to the windskins, though, Marika heard the Laspe Wise begin a prayer to the All. It wished them a safe journey.

It was something.

As she trudged around the spiral of the stockade, the new snow dragging at her boots, Marika asked the silth ahead,

"Why are we leaving now? Could we not travel just as safely in the daytime?"

"We are silth, pup. We travel at night."

The other, from behind Marika, said, "The night is our own. We are the daughters of the night and come and go as we will."

Marika shivered in a cold that had nothing to do with the wind off the Zhotak.

And around her, in the light of many moons, all the world glimmered black and bone.

BOOK TWO
AKARD

Chapter Seven

I

There was nothing to compare with it in Marika's brief experience of life. Never had she been so totally, utterly miserable, so cold, so punished. And the first night of travel was only hours old.

She knew how Kublin must feel—must have felt, she reminded herself with a wince of emotion—when trying to keep up with Zambi and his friends.

The new, wet snow was a quicksand that dragged at her boots every step, though they had placed her next to last in the file, with only Barlog behind her to guard their backs. Her pack was an immense dead weight that, she was sure, would crush her right down into the earth's white shroud and leave her unable, ever, to rise to the surface again. The wind off the Zhotak had risen, flinging tatters of gray cloud across the faces of the moons, gnawing at her right cheek till she was sure she would lose half her face to frostbite. The temperature dropped steadily.

That was a positive sign only in that if it fell enough they could be reasonably sure they would not face another blizzard soon.

All that backbreaking labor, trying to clear the packstead of bodies, came back to haunt her. She ached everywhere. Her muscles never quite loosened up.

Grauel was breaking trail. She tried to keep the pace down. But the silth pressed, and it was hard for the huntress to slack off when the older of the two could keep a more rigorous pace.

Once, during the first brief rest halt, Grauel and the taller silth fell into whispered argument. Grauel wanted to go more slowly. She said, "We are in enemy territory, sister. It would be wiser to move cautiously, staying alert. We do not want to stumble into nomads in our haste."

"It is the night. The night is ours, huntress. And we can watch where you cannot."

Grauel admitted that possibility. But she said, "They have their witchcrafts, too. As they have demonstrated. It would not be smart to put all our trust into a single—"

"Enough. We will not argue. We are not accustomed to argument. That is a lesson you will learn hard if you do not learn it in the course of this journey."

Marika stared at the snow between her feet and tried to imagine how far they had yet to travel. As she recalled her geography, the packfast lay sixty miles west of the packstead. They had come, at most, five miles so far. At this pace they would be three or four nights making the journey. In summer it could be done in two days.

Grauel did not argue further. Even so, her posture made it obvious she was in internal revolt, that she was awed by and frightened of the silth, yet held them in a certain contempt. Her body language was not overlooked by the silth either. Sometime after the journey resumed Marika caught snatches of an exchange between the two. They were not pleased with Grauel.

The elder said, "But what can you expect of a savage? She was not raised with a proper respect."

A hint of a snarl stretched Marika's lips. A proper

respect? Where was the proper respect of the silth for a huntress of Grauel's ability? Where was a proper respect for Grauel's experience and knowledge? Grauel had not been arguing for the sake of argument, like some bored Wise meth with time to kill.

It did not look that promising a future, this going into exile at the packfast. No one would be pleased with anyone else's ways.

She was not some male to bend the neck, Marika thought. If the silth thought so, they would find they had more trouble than they bargained for.

But defiance was soon forgotten in the pain and weariness of the trek. One boot in front of the other and, worse, the mind always free to remember. Always open to invasion from the past.

The real pain, the heart pain, began then.

More than once Barlog nearly trampled her, coming forward in her own foggy plod to find Marika stopped, lost within herself.

The exasperation of the silth grew by the hour.

They were weary of the wilderness. They were anxious to return home. They had very little patience left for indulging Degnan survivors.

That being the case, Marika wondered why they did not just go on at their own pace. They had no obligation to the Degnan, it would seem, in their own minds from the way they talked. As though the infeudation to which Skiljan and Gerrien had appealed for protection was at best a story with which the silth of the packfast justified their robberies to packs supposedly beholden to them. As though the rights and obligations were all one-sided, no matter what was promised.

Marika began to develop her own keen contempt for the silth. In her agony and aching, it nurtured well. Before the silth ordered a day camp set in a windbreak in the lee of a monstrous fallen tree, Marika's feeling had grown so strong the silth could read it. And they were baffled, for they had found her more open and unprejudiced than the older

Degnan. They squattted together and spoke about it while
Grauel and Barlog dug a better shelter into the snow drifted
beneath the tree.

The taller silth beckoned Marika. For all her exhaustion,
the pup had been trying to help the huntresses, mainly by
gathering firewood. They had reached a stretch where tall
trees flanked the river, climbing the sides of steep hills.
Oddly, the land became more rugged as the river ran west,
though from the plateau where the Degnan packstead lay it
did not seem so, for the general tendency of the land was
slowly downward.

"Pup," the taller silth said, "there has been a change in
you. We would try to understand why overnight you have
come to dislike us so."

"This," Marika said curtly.

"This? What does 'this' mean?"

Marika was not possessed of a fear the way the huntresses
were. She did not know silth, because no one had told her
about them. She said, "You sit there and watch while
Grauel and Barlog work not only for their own benefit but
yours. At the packstead you contributed. Some. In things
that were not entirely of the pack to do." Meaning remove
bodies.

The elder silth did not understand. The younger did, but
was irked. "We did when there was none else to do. We are
silth. Silth do not work with their paws. That is the province
of—"

"You have two feet and two paws and are in good health.
Better health than we, for you walk us into the earth. You
are capable. In our pack you would starve if you did not do
your share."

Fire flashed in the older silth's eyes. The taller, after
another moment of irritation, seemed amused. "You have
much to learn, little one. If we did these things you speak of,
we would not be seen as silth anymore."

"Is being silth, then, all arrogance? We had arrogant
huntresses in our pack. But they worked like everyone else.
Or they went hungry."

"We do our share in other ways, pup."

"Like by protecting the packs who pay tribute? That is the excuse I have always heard for the senior huntresses traveling to the packfast every spring. To pay the tribute which guarantees protection. This winter makes me suspect the protection bought may be from the packfast silth, not from killers from outside the upper Ponath. Your protection certainly has done the packs no good. You have saved three lives. Maybe. While packs all over the upper Ponath have been exterminated. So do not brag to me of the wonderful share you do unless you show me much more than you have."

"Feisty little bitch," the taller silth said, aside to the elder.

The older was at the brink of rage, an inch from explosion. But Marika had stoked her own anger to the point where she did not care, was not afraid. She noted that Grauel and Barlog had stopped pushing snow around and were watching, poised, uncertain, but with paws near weapons.

This was not good. She had best get her temper cooled or there would be difficulties none of them could handle.

Marika turned her back on the silth. She said, "As strength goes." Though this seemed a perversion of that old saw.

She won a point, though. The tall silth began pitching in after, just long enough to make it appear she was not yielding to a mere pup.

"Be careful, Marika," Grauel snapped when they were a distance away, collecting wood. "Silth are not known for patience or understanding."

"Well, they made me mad."

"They make everyone mad, pup. Because they can get away with doing any damned thing they want. They have the power."

"I will watch my tongue."

"I doubt that. You have grown overbold with no one to slap your ears. Come. This is enough wood."

Marika returned to their little encampment wondering at Grauel. And at Barlog. The agony of the Degnan did not, truly, seem to have touched them deeply.

II

Neither Grauel nor Barlog said a word, but the covert looks they cast at the fire made it clear they did not consider it a wise comfort. Smoke, even when not seen, could be smelled for miles.

The silth saw and understood their discomfort. The taller might have agreed with them, once the cooking was finished, but the elder was in a stubborn mood, not about to take advice from anyone.

The fire burned on.

The huntresses had dug a hollow beneath the fallen tree large enough for the five of them, and deep enough to shelter them from the wind entirely. As the sun rose, the silth crept into the shelter and bundled against one another for warmth. Marika was not far behind. Only in sleep would she find surcease from aches both physical and spiritual. Grauel followed her. But Barlog did not.

"Where is Barlog?" Marika asked, half asleep already. It was a morning in which the world was still. There was no sound except the whine of the wind and the crackle of frozen tree branches. When the wind died momentarily, there was, too, a distinct rushing sound, water surging through rapids in the river. Most places, as Marika had seen, the river was entirely frozen over and indistinguishable from the rest of the landscape.

"She will watch," Grauel replied.

The silth had said nothing about setting a watch. Had, in fact, implied that even asleep they could sense the approach of strangers long before the huntresses might.

Marika just nodded and let sleep take her.

She half wakened when Barlog came to trade places with

Grauel, and again when Grauel changed with Barlog once more. But she remained completely unaware of anything the next time Barlog came inside. She did not waken because that was when she was ensnarled in the first of the dreams.

A dark place. Stuffy. Fear. Weakness and pain. Fever and thirst and hunger. A musty smell and cold dampness. But most of all pain and hunger and the terror of death.

It was like no dream Marika had ever had, and there was no escaping it.

It was a dream in which nothing ever happened. It was a static state of being, almost the worst she could imagine. Nightmares were supposed to revolve around flight, pursuit, the inexorable approach of something dread, tireless, and without mercy. But this was like being in the mind of someone dying slowly inside a cave. Inside the mind of someone insane, barely aware of continued life.

She wakened to smoke and smells and silence. The wind had ceased blowing. For a while she lay there shuddering, trying to make sense of the dream. The Wise insisted dreams were true, though seldom literal.

But it slipped away too quickly, too soon became nothing more than a state of malaise.

Grauel had a fresh fire blazing and food cooking when Marika finally crawled out of the shelter. The sun was well on its way down. Night would be along soon after they ate, packed, and took care of personal essentials. She settled beside Grauel, took over tending the fire. Barlog joined them a moment later, while the silth were still stretching and grumbling inside the shelter.

"They are out there," Barlog said. Grauel nodded. "Just watching right now. But we will hear from them before we reach the packfast."

Grauel nodded again. She said, "Do not bother our superior witches with it. They know most all there is to know. They must know this, too."

Barlog grunted. "Walk warily tonight. And stay close. Marika, stay alert. If something happens, just get down into the snow. Dive right in and let it bury you if you can."

Marika put another piece of wood onto the fire. She said nothing, and did nothing, till the taller silth came from the shelter, stretched, and surveyed the surrounding land. She came to the fire and checked the cook pot. Her nose wrinkled momentarily. Travel rations were not tasty, even to huntresses accustomed to eating them.

She said, "We will pass the rapids soon after nightfall. We will walk atop the river after that. The going will be easiest there."

Aside, Barlog told Marika, "So we traveled coming east. The river is much easier than the forest, where you never know what lies beneath the snow."

"Will the ice hold?"

"The ice is several feet thick. It will hold anything."

As though the silth were not there, Grauel said, "There are several wide places in the river where we will be very exposed visually. And several narrow places ideal for an ambush." She described what lay ahead in detail, for Marika's benefit.

The silth was irked but said nothing. The older came out of the shelter and asked, "Is that pot ready."

"Almost," Grauel replied.

Rested, even the older silth was more cooperative. She began moving snow about so that their pause here would be less noticeable after their departure.

Grauel and Barlog exchanged looks, but did not tell her she was wasting her time. "Let them believe what they want to believe," Barlog said.

The taller silth caught that and responded with a puzzled expression. None of the three Degnan told her they thought the effort pointless because the nomads knew where they were already.

Biter rose early that night, full and in headlong flight from Chaser, which was not far behind. The travelers reached the river as that second major moon rose, setting their shadows aspin. Once again the silth wanted to push hard. This time Grauel and Barlog refused to be pushed. They moved at their own pace, weapons in paw, seeming to study every step before they took it. Marika sensed that they were very tense.

The silth sensed it too, and for that reason, perhaps, they did not press, though clearly they thought all the caution wasted.

And wasted it seemed, for as the sun returned to the world it found them unscathed, having made no contact whatsoever with the enemies Grauel and Barlog believed were stalking them.

But the huntresses were not prepared to admit error. They trusted their instincts. Again they set a watch during the day.

Again nothing happened during the day. Except that Marika dreamed.

It was the same, and different. All the closeness, pain, terror, darkness, hunger were there. The smells and damp and cold were there. But this time she was a little more conscious and aware. She was trying to claw her way up something, climbing somewhere, and the mountain in the dark was the tallest mountain in the world. She kept passing out, and crying out, but no one answered, and she seemed to be making no real ground. She had a blazing fever that came and went, and when it was at its pitch she saw things that could not possibly be there. Things like glowing balls, like worms of light, like diaphanous moths the size of loghouses that flew through earth and air with equal ease.

Death's breath was winter on the back of her neck.

If she could just get to the top, to food, to water, to help.

One of her soft cries alerted Grauel, who wakened her gently and scratched her ears till shuddering and panting went away.

The temperature rose a little that day and stayed up during the following night. With the temperature rise came more snow and bitter winds that snarled along the valley of the east fork, flinging pellets of snow into faces. The travelers fashioned themselves masks. Grauel suggested they hole up till the worst was past. The silth refused. The only reason they would halt, storm or no, was to avoid getting

lost. There was no chance of that here. If they strayed from
the river they would begin climbing uphill. They would run
into trees.

Marika wished she could come through by day instead of
by night in snow. What little she could see suggested this
was impressive country, far grander than any nearer home.

There was no trouble with nomads that night either, nor
during the following day. Grauel and Barlog insisted the
northerners were still out there, though, tracking the party.

Marika had no dreams. She hoped the horror was over.

The weather persisted foul. The taller silth said, as they
huddled in a shelter where they had gone to ground early,
"We will be in trouble if this persists. We have food for only
one more day. We are yet two from Akard. If we are delayed
much more we will get very hungry before we reach home."
She glanced at the older silth. The old one had begun
showing the strain of the journey.

Neither huntress said a word, though each had suggested
pushing too hard meant wasting energy that might be
needed later.

Marika asked, "Akard? What is that?"

"It is the name of what you call the packfast, pup."

She was puzzled. Was Akard the name of the silth pack
there?

The storm slackened around noon. The travelers clung to
their shelter only till shadows began gathering in the river
canyon. The sun fell behind the high hills while there were
yet hours of daylight left.

The silth wanted to make up lost time. "We go now," the
taller said. And the older hoisted herself up, though it was
obvious that standing was now an effort for her.

Marika and the huntresses were compelled to admire the
old silth's spirit. She did not complain once, did not yield to
the infirmity of her flesh.

Again Grauel and Barlog would not be rushed. Both went
to the fore, and advanced with arrows across their bows,
studying every shadow along the banks. Their noses wriggled as they sniffed the wind. The silth were amused. They

said there were no nomads anywhere near. But they humored the huntresses. The old one could not move much faster anyway. The taller one covered the rear.

Marika carried her short steel knife bared. She was not that impressed with silth skills, for all she knew them more intimately than did Grauel or Barlog.

It happened at twilight.

The snow on one bank erupted. Four buried savages charged. The silth were so startled they just stood there.

Grauel and Barlog released their arrows. Two nomads staggered, began flopping as poison spread through their bodies. There was no time for second arrows. Barlog ducked under a javelin thrust and used her bow to tangle a nomad's legs. Grauel smacked another across the back of the neck with her bow.

Marika flung herself onto the back of the huntress Barlog tripped, driving her knife with all her weight. It was a good piece of iron taken from her dead dam's belt. It slid into flesh easily and true.

Barlog saw that nomad down, whirled to help Grauel, dropping her bow to draw her sword.

Javelins rained down. One struck the older silth but did not penetrate her heavy travel apparel. Another wobbled past Marika's nose and she remembered what she had been told to do if they were attacked. She threw herself into the snow and tried to burrow.

A half dozen huntresses streaked toward the stunned silth. Grauel and Barlog floundered toward them. Grauel still held her bow. She managed to get off two killing shafts.

The other four piled onto the silth, not even trying to kill them, just trying to rip their packs off their backs, trying to wrest the iron club away from the taller. Barlog hacked at one with her sword. The blade would not slice through all the layers of clothing the nomad wore.

Marika got herself up again. She started toward the fray. Javelins intercepted her, drove her back.

There were more nomads on the bank now. At least

another half dozen. The cast was long for them, so they seemed intent on keeping her from helping.

Then she heard sounds from the other bank. She looked, saw more nomads.

For the first time since the fighting started she was afraid.

One of the nomads got the iron club away from the tall silth and started toward the south bank, howling triumph.

Marika reeled. There was an instant of touch, wrenchingly violent. Screams echoed down the canyon, to be muted quickly by sound-absorbent snow. In moments the nomads were all down, clawing their chests. Marika's own heart fluttered painfully. She scrambled nearer Grauel and Barlog to see if the touch had affected them, too.

For all the violence, only the older silth was badly injured. She made no complaint, but her face was grim with pain.

Curses in dialect rolled off the slopes.

"There are more of them," Marika told the taller silth. "Do something."

"I have no strength left, pup. I cannot reach that far."

There was a rattling *pop-pop-pop* from way up on the southern side of the canyon. Some things like insects buzzed around them. Some things thumped into the snow. The taller silth cursed softly and dragged Marika down.

The older gritted out, "You had better find some strength, Khles."

The tall silth snarled at Grauel and Barlog, "Get the old one to the bank. Get her behind something. All of you, get behind something." She closed her eyes, concentrated intently.

The popping went on and on.

"What is that?" Marika asked as she and the huntresses neared the north bank with their burden.

A new sound had entered the twilight, a grumble that started softly and slowly and built with the seconds, till it overpowered the popping noise.

"Up there!" Grauel snarled, pointing to the steepest part of the southern slope.

That entire slope was in motion, trees, rocks, and snow.

"Move!" the tall silth snapped. "Get as far as you can. The edge of it may reach us."

Her tone did more to encourage obedience than did her words.

The popping stopped.

The snow rolled down. Its roar sounded like the end of the world to a pup who had never heard anything so loud. She crouched behind a boulder and shivered, awed by the majesty of nature's fury.

She looked at the silth. Both seemed to be in a state of shock. The old one, ignoring her injuries, kept looking at the nearest dead nomads in disbelief. Finally, she asked, "How did they do that, Khles? There was not a hint that they were there before they attacked."

Without looking her way, Grauel said, "They have been with us since the first night, haunting the ridges and trails, waiting for an opportunity. Waiting for us to get careless. We almost did." She poked a nearby corpse. "These are the best-fed nomads I ever saw. Best dressed, too. And most inept. They should have killed us all three times over." She eyed the silth.

They did not respond. The tall one continued to stare up the slope whence the avalanche had come. There were a few calls in dialect still, but from ever farther away.

Barlog was shaking still. She brushed snow off her coat. A dying finger of the avalanche had caught her and taken her down.

The tall silth asked Grauel, "Were any of you hurt?"

"Minor cuts and bruises," Grauel said. "Nothing important. Thank you."

That startled the tall one. She nodded. "We will have to carry the old one. I am no healer, but I believe she has broken ribs and a broken leg."

Barlog made her own examination. "She does."

She and Grauel used their swords to cut poles from which they made a travois. They placed the old silth and their packs upon it, then took turns pulling. The tall silth took her turn, too. It was no time for insisting upon prerogatives.

Marika helped later, when the going became more difficult and the travois had to be carried around obstacles.

Grauel and Barlog believed there were no nomads watching anymore.

"How did they sneak up on you?" Marika asked, trudging in the tracks of the tall silth.

"I do not know, pup." She searched the darkness more diligently than ever the huntresses had. Marika realized suddenly that the silth was afraid.

III

Nomads were no further problem. Enemies were not needed. Weather, hunger, increasing weakness due to exposure and short rations, those were enough to make the trek a misery. Marika took the travel better than her companions. She was young and resilient and not spending much energy pulling the travois.

Thus, when it came time to take shelter, the duty fell upon her. Grauel and Barlog were so exhausted they could do little but tend the fire and stir the pot—the pot that had so little to fill it. They snarled at one another for not having had sense enough to loot the nomads. The tall silth's pointing out that the nomads had carried nothing but weapons did not soften the dispute.

Meth did not withstand hunger well. Already Marika felt the grauken stirring within her. She looked at the others. If it came to that desperate moment, upon whom would they turn? Her or the old silth?

They had been five days making a two-day journey. Marika asked the tall silth, "How far must we travel yet? Surely we must be very close."

"Fifteen miles more," the silth said. "A quarter of the way yet. The worst quarter. Five miles down we have to leave the river for the trails. There are many rapids where the river will not be frozen over."

Fifteen miles. At the rate they had been progressing since the old one got hurt, that might mean three more days.

"Do not despair, pup," the silth said. "I have put aside my pride and touched those who watch for us in Akard. They are coming to meet us."

"How soon?" Grauel asked, her only contribution to the conversation.

"They are young and healthy and well fed. Not long."

Not long proved to be a day and a half. Every possible thing that could go wrong did, including an avalanche which destroyed the trail and compelled a detour. The grauken looked out of every eye, needing only a nudge to tear free. But meet those other silth they did, eight miles from the packfast, and they celebrated with what for Marika was the feast of her young life.

After that the cold and snow should have been mere nuisances. A meth with a full belly was ready to challenge anything. But not so. They had been too long hungry and exposed. The slide toward extinction continued.

Marika did not see Akard from outside on arriving, for they approached the stone packfast under a heavily clouded sky at a time when no moons were up. The only hints of size and shape came from lights glimpsed only momentarily. But by then she was not interested in the place except as journey's end. She half believed she would never make it there.

The journey from the Degnan packstead took ten nights, most spent covering the last twenty miles. For all she had food in her belly, Marika was exhausted, being half carried by the silth who had come to the rescue. And she was in better shape than any of her companions. She hoped that never again would she have to travel in winter.

They carried her into a place of stone and she collapsed. She did not think how much more terrible it had become for her companions, all of them having been carried the past few days, lingering on the frontiers of death. She thought of nothing but the all-enveloping warmth of her cell, and of sleep.

Sleep was not without its unpleasantness, though. She dreamed of Kublin. Of Kublin alone and terrified and injured and abandoned, surrounded by strange and unfriendly faces. It was not a dream that made sense. She began to whimper in her sleep and did not rest at all well.

For days no one paid Marika any heed. She was a problem the silth preferred to ignore. She ate. She slept. When she recovered enough to feel curious, she began roaming the endless halls of stone, by turns amazed, baffled, awed, frightened, disgusted, lost. The place was a monster loghouse—of stone, of course—surrounded by a high palisade of stone. Its architecture was alien, and there was no one to tell her why things were the way they were. The few meth her own age she encountered all were hurrying somewhere, were busy, or were just plain contemptuous of the savage among them.

The packfast was a tall edifice built upon limestone headland overlooking the confluence of the forks of the Hainlin. The bluffs fell sixty feet from the packstead's base. Its walls rose sixty feet above their foundations. They were sheer and smooth and in perfect repair, but did have a look of extreme age. There was a wide walkway around their top, screened by a stone curtain which looked like a lower jaw with every other tooth missing. The whole packfast was shaped like a big square box with an arrowhead appended, pointing downriver. There were huntresses upon the walls always, though when Marika asked them why, they did admit that Akard had seen no trouble within living memory.

"Still," one with more patience than most said, "it has been a hard winter, and the northerners are not known for their brains. They may yet come here."

"They are not completely stupid," Marika said. "They may come, indeed. They will look, and then they will go away. Packsteads are easier prey."

"No doubt. There have been rumors that nomads have been seen in the upper Ponath already."

Marika took a step back. She cocked her head in incredulity. "Rumors? Rumors? Do you not know why the huntresses and I came here?"

"You were brought because you have the silth talent."

"I came because I had nowhere else to go. The nomads destroyed all my pack but the two huntresses who came with me. As they destroyed several other packs and packsteads before ours. Within walking distance of ours. There are tens of hundreds of them in the upper Ponath. Ten tens of tens died at our packstead."

The huntress's disbelief was plain. "The sisters would not permit that."

"No? They did not do anything positive that I saw. Oh, they did finish the wehrlen leading the nomads, and they killed those who were plundering our packstead when they got there, but they did not go on to free the rest of the upper Ponath of invaders."

"Wehrlen," the huntress murmured. "You said wehrlen?"

"Yes. A very strong one. The silth said he was as powerful and well trained as they." Warmed to her story, Marika added, "And there were silth with the nomad horde. My dam slew one. The tall sister, that the other called Khles sometimes, brought back her robe and weapon."

Marika suddenly turned to stare up the valley of the east fork. She had been baffled as to why the nomads had pursued them toward the packfast when they carried so little that was worth taking. Unless . . . The tall silth had acted as though that club and robe were great treasures.

Perhaps they were. For reasons she did not understand. The nomads *had* directed their attention toward the club and the taller silth's pack.

Already she knew life among the silth would be more complicated than it had been at the packstead. Here *everyone* seemed to be moved by motives as shadowed as Pohsit's.

The huntresses who patrolled the walls and watched the

snows called themselves sentries. It was a word new to Marika.

She learned many new words, hearing them almost too fast to assimilate them. "Fortress" was another. Akard was what its meth called a fortress, a bastion which maintained the claim of a silth order called the Reugge, which had its heart in a far southern city called Maksche.

Marika was inundated with more new words when she discovered the communications center.

At the downstream tip of the fortress, at the point of the arrowhead, there was a great tall tree of metal. Marika discovered that her second day of roving. It looked like something drawn by a disastrously twisted artist trying to represent a dead tree. It had a dozen major branches. Upon those sat wire dishes with bowls facing south, each backed be a larger dish of solid metal. There were many smaller branches, seedling size, growing straight up from the main branches. Every inch of metal gleamed in the sunshine. Snow did not stick on the metal branches the way it did on the trees of the forest.

Below and in front of that mad tree there was one huge dish which faced the heavens above the southern horizon. Sometimes that dish moved the way a head did when the eye was following fast game.

What in the world? Very baffling for a pup from the upper Ponath, who found so much metal put to such inexplicable use criminal at the least. She wondered if Grauel or Barlog knew what was going on here. They had been to the packfast before. Surely they had unraveled some of its mysteries. She would have to become more insistent about being shown where they were recuperating.

Grauel and Barlog were sequestered apparently. She had not seen them since entering the packfast. No one would tell her where they were being treated. When she tried to use her own remarkable senses to locate them, something blocked her.

She did not think she was going to like the packfast Akard.

She knew she did not like the way the fortress's hunt-resses cringed and cowered around the silth. She knew there would be a confrontation of epic proportion the day the silth demanded that of her.

She went down to where the metal tree was and roamed around. But she could find nothing that explained what she saw. Or what she felt. While she was there she became dizzy and disoriented. It took all her concentration to overcome the giddiness and confusion long enough to find her way to a distance sufficient to reduce both.

Her secret senses seemed all scrambled. What had hap-pened? Had she stumbled into some of the great magic for which the silth were so feared?

Chapter Eight

I

Marika could not stay away from that strange part of the packfast where her brain and talent scrambled. Three times that day of discovery she returned. Three times she reeled away, the third time so distressed her stomach nearly betrayed her.

There had been a true qualitative difference that last time, the strangeness being more intense.

She leaned against a wall and tried to hold her dinner down, panting, letting the chill north wind suck the sudden fever from her face. Finally, she pulled herself together enough to move on.

She ducked into the first doorway she encountered. The vertigo was less intense inside.

She halted. She heard odd voices ahead. Strange lights flickered around her. Lights without flame or much heat when she passed a finger near them. Quiet lights, constant in their burning, hard to the touch when she did rest a finger upon them. What witchery was this?

She became very nervous. She had been told she could go

wherever she wanted and see anything she wanted. Yet the silth must have their ritual places, like the males and huntresses of the packstead, and those certainly would be off limits. Was this such a place? She dreaded the chance she would interrupt the silth at their black rites. They had begun to seem as dark as her packmates had feared.

Curiosity overcame fear. She moved forward a few steps, looked around in awe. The room was like nothing she had ever imagined. Some yards away a female in a blue smock moved among devices whose purposes Marika could not pretend to fathom. Some had windows that flickered with a ghostly gray light. The voices came from them. The female in the blue smock did not respond.

Devils. The windows must open on the underworld, or the afterworld, or . . . She fought down the panic, moved forward a few more steps toward the nearest of those ghostly portals.

She frowned, more confused than ever. A voice came through the window, but there was no one on the other side. Instead, she saw squiggles arranged in neat columns, like a page from a book in reversed coloration.

Flicker. The page changed. A new set of squiggles appeared. Some of those altered while she watched. She gasped and stepped closer again, bent till her nose was almost against the window.

The meth finally noticed her presence. "Hello," she said. "You must be the new sister."

Marika wondered if she ought to flee. "I do not know," she replied, throat tight. She was confused about her status. Some of the meth of the packfast did call her sister. But she did not know why. No one had taken time to explain. She did know that the word "sister" did not mean what it might have at home: another pup born of the same dam. None of these meth seemed to be related by blood or pack.

The society was nothing like that of a pack. Hierarchies and relationships were confusing. So far she had figured out for sure only that those who wore black were in charge and everyone else deferred to them in a curious set of rituals which might never make sense.

"What is this place?" Marika asked. "Is it holy? Am I intruding?"

"This is the communications center," the female replied, amused. "It is holy only to those hungry for news from the south." It seemed she had made a great jest. And was sorry to have wasted it on a savage unable to appreciate it. "You are from the stead in the upper Ponath that the nomads destroyed, are you not?"

Marika nodded. That story had gotten around fast once she had told the sentry. Many of the meth who wore colors other than black wanted to know all about the siege of the Degnan packstead. But when Marika told them the story, it made them unhappy. For themselves, not for the meth of the upper Ponath.

"Nomads running together in thousands. Ruled by a wehrlen. Times are strange indeed. What next?"

Marika shrugged. Her imagination was inadequate to encompass how her life could turn worse than it had already.

"Well, you are from the outside, so all this will be new to you. The upper Ponath is as backward a region as can be found on this world, bar the Zhotak, and deliberately so. That is the way the sisterhood and the brethren want it kept. Come. There is nothing here to fear. I will show you. My name is Braydic, by the way. Senior Koenic is my truesister, though blood means nothing here."

"I am Marika." Marika moved to the female's side.

Braydic indicated the nearest gray window. "We call this a vision screen. A number of things can be done with it. At the moment this one is monitoring how much water we have stored behind each of the three dams on the Husgen. That is what you call the west fork of the Hainlin. For us the east fork continues to be the Hainlin and the west fork becomes the Husgen. If you have been up on the ramparts at all, you must have seen the lower dam and its powerhouse."

Marika feared she might have walked into a trap quite

unlike the one she had suspected. Meth did not chatter. They became very uncomfortable with those who did. Talkers were suspected of being unbalanced. Generally, they were just lonely.

Braydic poked several black lozenges among the scores ranked before the vision screen. Each lozenge had a white character inscribed upon it. The squiggles left the screen. A picture replaced them. After a moment Marika realized it represented a view up the west fork of the Hainlin, the branch Braydic called the Husgen. It portrayed structures about which Marika had been curious but had felt too foolish to ask.

"This is the powerhouse. This is the dam. The dam spans the river, forming a wall that holds back the water. The water comes down to the powerhouse through huge earthenware pipes, where it turns a wheel." Braydic poked lozenges again. Now the screen portrayed a big wooden wheel turning slowly as water from a pipe poured down upon blades. "The wheel in turn turns a machine which generates the power we use."

Marika was baffled, of course. What power? Did the silth generate the touch artificially?

Braydic recognized her confusion. "Yes. You would not understand, would you?" She stepped to a wall, touched something there. All the lights, except those near the vision screens, went out. Then on again. "I meant the power that works the lights and vision screens and such. I am monitoring the water levels behind the dams because the spring thaw will begin before long. We have to estimate how much to let water levels drop so the three lakes will be able to absorb meltoff without risk of overflow."

Marika remained lost. But she nodded, pretending to understand. If she did that, maybe Braydic would keep talking instead of sending her away.

She was lonely, too.

At home adults got impatient when you did not understand. Except for the studies in books, which said nothing of things like this, you were expected to learn by watching.

"Do not be afraid to say you do not know," Braydic told her. "Nor ashamed. If you do not admit ignorance, how are you to learn? No one will bother teaching you what you pretend to know already."

Marika studied the black lozenges. They were marked with the characters and numbers of the common symbology, but there were a dozen characters she did not recognize, too. Braydic pressed a larger lozenge which lay to one side. The vision screen went blank.

"Do you read or write, little sister?"

She wanted to say she was Degnan. Degnan were educated. But that seemed a fool's arrogance here. "I read. I do not write very well, except for ciphers. We had very little chance to practice writing, except when we made clay tablets or bark scrolls and could use a stick stylus or piece of charcoal. Pens, inks, and papers are all tradermale goods. They are too dear for pup play."

Braydic nodded. "I see. Think of a written word, then. All right? You have one?"

"Yes."

"Pick out the characters on the keyboard. Press them in the order you would write them. Top to bottom, the way you would read them."

Tentatively, Marika touched a lozenge. The first character of her name appeared on the vision screen. She pressed another and another, delighted. Without awaiting permission she pecked out her dam's name, and Kublin's.

"You should place a blank space between words," Braydic said. "So the reader knows where one ends and the next begins. To do that you press this key." Swiftly, all her fingers tapping at once, she repeated what Marika had done. "You see?"

"Yes. May I?"

"Go ahead."

Marika tapped out more words. She would have tried every word she knew, but one of the silth interrupted.

Braydic changed. She became almost craven. "Yes, mistress? How may I please you?"

"Message for Dhatkur at the Maksche cloister. Most immediate. Prepare to send."

"Yes, mistress." Braydic tapped lozenges swiftly. The vision screen blanked. A single large symbol took the place of Marika's doodlings. It looked like two comets twining around one another, round and round, spiraling outward from the common center. "Clear, mistress."

"Continue."

Braydic tapped three more lozenges. The symbol vanished. A face replaced it. It said a few words that Marika did not understand.

She gasped, suddenly stricken by the realization that the vision screen was portraying the image of a meth far away. This was witchcraft, indeed!

The silth spoke with that far meth briefly. Marika could not follow the exchange, for it was in what must be a silth rite tongue. Still, it sounded trivial in tone. More important the wonders surrounding her. She gazed at Braydic in pure awe. This witch ruled all this and she wasn't even silth.

The silth sister finished her conversation. She laid a paw on Marika's shoulder. "Come, pup. At your stage you should not be exposed to too much electromagnetic radiation."

Baffled, Marika allowed herself to be led away. She glanced back once, surprised a look on Braydic's face which said she would be welcome any time she cared to return.

So maybe she had found one meth here who could become a friend.

The silth scooted Marika through the door, then turned back to Braydic. In an angry voice she demanded of the meth in blue, "What are you doing? That pup came out of a Tech Two Zone. You are giving her Tech Five knowledge. Gratuitously."

"She is to be educated silth, is she not?" Braydic countered, with some spirit.

"We do not yet know that." The silth shifted from accented common speech to that she had used while speaking through the vision screen. She became very loud. Her temper was up. Marika decided to get away from there before that wrath overtook her.

II

They took her before the taller silth who had brought her out of the upper Ponath. That one, whom they all called Khles here, was confined to bed yet. Her one leg, only lightly wounded in the nomad attack, had begun to mortify during the long struggle to reach the packfast. She had spoken neither of the wound nor infection during the journey.

The sisters who brought Marika chattered among themselves beforehand, gossiping about the possibility that Khles's leg would have to be amputated. The healer sisters were having trouble conquering the infection.

"So," the tall one said, "they all forgot or ignored you, yes?" She seemed grimly amused. "Well, nothing lasts forever. The easy days are over."

Marika said nothing. The days had not been easy at all. They had been lonely and filled with the self-torment brought by memories of the packstead. They had been filled with the deep malaise that came of knowing her entire pack was going into the embrace of the All without a Mourning. And there was nothing she, Grauel, or Barlog could do. None of them knew the rites. Ceremonies of Mourning were the province of the Wise. The last of the Degnan Wise had perished—Marika was morally certain—through the agency of the silth.

When she slept, there were dreams. Not as intense, not as long, not as often, but dreams still edged with madness, burning with fever.

"Pay attention, pup."

Marika snapped out of a reverie.

"Your education will begin tomorrow. The paths of learning for a silth sister are threefold. Each is a labor in itself. There will be no time for daydreaming."

"For a silth sister? I am a huntress."

"You belong to the Reugge sisterhood, pup. You are what the sisterhood tells you you are. I will warn you once now. For the first and last time. Rebellion, argument, backtalk are not tolerated in our young. Neither are savage habits and customs. You are silth. You will think and act as silth. You are Reugge silth. You will think and act as Reugge silth. You have no past. You were whelped the night they brought us through the gates of Akard."

Marika responded without thinking. "Kropek shit!" It was the strongest expletive she knew.

As strength goes.

The silth was on her own ground now and not inclined to be charitable, understanding, or forgiving. "You will change that attitude. Or you will find life here hard, and possibly short."

"I am not silth," Marika insisted. "I am a huntress to be. You have no other claim upon me. I am here by circumstance only, not by choice."

"Even among savages, I think, pups do not argue with their elders. Not with impunity."

That did reach Marika. She had to admit that her lack of respect left much to be desired. She stared at the stone floor a pace in front of her toes.

"Better. Much better. As I said, your education will follow a threefold path. You will have no time to waste. Each path is a labor in itself."

The first path of Marika's education was almost a continuation of the process she had known at the packstead. But it went on seven hours every day, and spanned fields broader than any she could have imagined before becoming a refugee.

There was ciphering. There was reading and writing, with ample materials to practice the latter. There was elementary science and technology, which expanded her amazed mind to horizons she could hardly believe, even while sensing that her instructors were leaving vast gaps. That such wonders existed, and she had never known . . .

There was geography, which astounded her by showing her the true extent of her world—and the very small place in it held by the upper Ponath. Her province was but a pinprick upon the most extreme frontier of civilization.

She learned, without being formally taught, that her world was one of extreme contrasts. Most meth lived in uttermost poverty and savagery, confined to closed or semi-closed Tech Zones. Some lived in cities more modern than anything she saw at the packfast, but the lot of the majority was little better than that of rural meth. A handful, belong-ing to or employed by the sisterhoods, lived in high luxury and were free to move about as they pleased.

And there were the rare few who lived the dream. They could leave the planet itself, to venture among the stars, to see strange worlds and stranger races. But there was little said of that in the early days. Just enough to whet her appetite for more.

The second pathway of learning resembled the first, and paralleled it, but dealt only with the Reugge sisterhood itself, teaching the sisterhood's history, its primary rituals, its elementary mysteries. And mercilessly pounded away at the notion that the Reugge sisterhood constituted the axis of the meth universe. Marika tired of that quickly. The mes-sage was too blatantly self-serving.

The third course . . .

In the third pathway Marika learned why her dam had feared and hated silth. She learned what it meant to be silth. She studied to become silth. And that was the most demand-ing, unrelenting study of all.

Her guide in study, her guardian within the packfast, was named Gorry.

Gorry was the elder of the females who had brought her from the packstead. She never quite recovered from that journey. She blamed her enfeebled health upon Marika. She was a hard, unforgiving, unpleasant, and jealous instruc-tress.

Marika preferred her to the one called Khles, though. The healer sisters did have to take her leg. And after that loss she became embittered. Everyone avoided her as much as possible.

Still they would not allow Marika to see Grauel or Barlog. She began to understand that they were trying to isolate her from any reminder of her origins.

She would not permit that.

III

Marika stood at the center of a white stone floor in a vast hall in the heart of Akard fortress. The floor around her was inlaid with green, red, and black stone, formed into boundaries and symbols. High above, glass windows—one of the marvels of the packstead—admitted a thin gray light come through a frosting of snow. That light barely illuminated the pillars supporting an all-surrounding balustrade forty feet above. The pillars were green stone, inlaid with red, black, coral, and white. Shadows lurked behind them. The glory of that hall ended at the columns, though. The stone of the wall back behind them was weathered a dark brownish gray. In places lichens patched it.

The white floor was a square forty feet to a side. The symbol at its center was that of the entwined comets, in jet and scarlet, three feet across. Marika stood upon the focus of the mandala.

There were no furnishings and no lighting in that chamber. It stirred with echoes constantly.

Marika's eyes were sealed. She tried to control her breathing so no sound would echo anywhere. She strove under Gorry's merciless gaze. Her instructress leaned on the rail of the balustrade, motionless as stone, a dark silhouette hovering. All the light leaking through the windows seemed to concentrate on Marika.

Outside, winter flaunted its chill and howl, though the

spring melt should have begun. It was time trees were budding. Snowflowers should have been opening around the last branch-shaded patches of white. But, instead, another blizzard raged into its third day and third foot of gritty powder snow.

Marika could not put that out of her mind. It meant continued hard times in the upper Ponath. It meant late plantings, poor hunting, and almost certain trouble with nomads again next winter, no matter how mild.

Very little news from the upper Ponath reached the packfast. What did come was grim. The nomads had decimated several more packsteads, even without their wehrlen to lead them. Other packsteads, unable to sustain a winter so long, had turned grauken.

Civilization had perished in the upper Ponath.

Summer would not be much of a respite, for there would be little game left after a winter so cruel.

There had been no word from the Degnan packstead. The fate of the Laspe remained a mystery.

There were silth out now, young ones, hunting nomads, trying to provide the protection Akard supposedly promised. But they were few, unenthusiastic, and not very effective.

Something whispered in the shadows under the balustrade. Something moved. Marika opened her eyes. . . .

Pain!

Fire crackled along her nerves. A voice within her head said, calmly, *See with the inner eye.*

Marika sealed her eyes again. They leaked tears of frustration. They would not tell her what to do. All they did was order her to do it. How could she, if she did not know what they wanted?

The sound of movement again, as of something with claws moving toward her stealthily. Then in a sudden rush. She whirled to face the sound, her eyes opening.

A fantastic beast leapt toward her, its fang-filled jaws opened wide. She squealed and ducked, grabbing at a knife no longer at her waist. The beast passed over her. When she turned, she saw nothing. Not even a disturbance in the dust on the floor.

Pain!

Frustration welled into anger. Anger grew into seething blackness. Ignoring the throbbing agony, she stared up at old Gorry.

Then she saw ghosts drifting through the shadows.

The old silth wavered, became transparent. Marika snatched at the pulsing ruby of her heart.

Gorry cried out softly and fell away from the railing.

Marika's pain faded. The false sounds went with the pain. She breathed deeply, relaxing for the first time that day. For a moment she felt very smug. That would show them that they could not—

Something touched her for an instant, like the blow of a dark fist. There was no pain but plenty of impact. She staggered off the center of the mandala, fell to her knees, disoriented and terrified.

She did not seem to be in control of herself. She could not make her limbs respond. What were they doing to her? What were they going to do to her?

More sounds. These genuine. Hurried feet moved above.

The paralysis relaxed. She regained her feet. Excited whispers filled the chamber. She looked up. Several silth surrounded Gorry. One pounded the old silth's chest, then listened for a heartbeat. "In time. Got to her in time."

The tall one who had come to the packstead, who now had only one leg, leaned her crutches on the railing and glared down at Marika. She was very, very angry. "Come up here, pup!" she snapped.

"Yes, Mistress Gibany."

Much to her embarrassment, Marika had discovered that Khles was not a name but a title. It marked Gibany as having a major role in Akard silth ritual. What that role was Marika did not yet know. She had not yet been admitted to any but the most basic rites.

* * *

In her own loghouse neither defiance nor the inclination to debate would have occurred to Marika. But here in the packfast, despite repeated warnings, she felt little of her customary reserve. These silth had not yet earned her respect. Few she saw seemed deserving of respect. She met Senior Koenic's eye and snapped, "Because she hurt me."

"She was teaching you."

"She was not. She was torturing me. She ordered me to do something I do not know how to do. I do not yet know what it was. Then she tortured me for not doing it. She taught me nothing. She showed me nothing."

"She was teaching you by forcing you to find the way for yourself."

"That is stupid. Even beasts are shown what they must do before their trainer rewards or punishes them. This way is neither reasonable nor efficient." She had thought out this speech many times. It rolled out almost without thought, despite her fright.

She believed what she said. Her elders in the Degnan pack had been impatient enough with pups, but they had at least demonstrated a thing once before becoming irritable.

"That is Gorry's way."

"It being her way makes it no less stupid and inefficient."

The senior was in a surprisingly tolerant mood, Marika reflected, as the fear-driven engine of her rage began to falter. Few adult meth would so long endure so much backtalk.

"It separates the weak from the strong. When you came here you understood—"

One more spark of defiance. "When I came I understood nothing, Senior. I did not even ask to be brought. I was brought blind, thinking I would become a huntress for the packfast, willing to come only because of circumstance. I never heard of silth before my dam sent messengers to ask you for help. All I know about silth I have learned since I have been here. And I do not like what I have learned."

The senior's teeth gleamed angrily in the lamplight. Her patience was about exhausted. But Marika did not back down, though now her courage was entirely bravado.

What would she do if she made them angry enough to push her out the gate?

The senior controlled herself. She said, "I will grant you that Gorry is not the best of teachers. However, self-control must be the first lesson we learn as sisters. Without discipline we are nothing. Field-workers, technicians, and guardians behave as you have. Silth do not. I think you had better learn to control your temper. You are going to continue in Gorry's tutelage. With this between you."

"Is that all?"

"That is all."

Marika made parting obsequies, as taught. But as she reached the heavy wooden door to the senior's quarters, the silth called, "Wait."

Marika turned, suddenly terrified. She wanted to get away.

"You must appreciate your obligation to your sisterhood, Marika. Your sisterhood is all. Everything your pack was, and your reason for living, too."

"I cannot appreciate something I do not understand, Senior. Nothing I see here makes sense. Forgive a poor country pup her ignorance. Everything I see implies this sisterhood exists solely to exploit those who do not belong. That it takes and takes, but almost never gives."

She was thinking of the feeble effort to combat the invasion of the nomads.

"You see beyond the first veil. You are on the threshold of becoming silth, Marika. With all that that implies. It is a rare opportunity. Do not close the door on yourself by clinging stubbornly to the values of savages."

Marika responded with a raised lip, slipped out, dashed downstairs to her cell. She lighted a candle, thinking she would lose herself in one of the books they had given her to study. "What?"

The Degnan Chronicle was stacked upon her little writing desk.

The next miracle occurred not ten minutes later.

Marika responded to a tentative scratching at her door. "Grauel!" She stared at the huntress, whom she had not seen since the trek to Akard.

"Hello, pup. May I?"

"Of course." Marika made way for her to enter. There was not much room in her cell. She returned to the chair at her writing desk. Grauel looked around, finally settled on Marika's cot.

"I cannot become accustomed to furniture," Grauel said. "I always look for furs on the floor first."

"So do I." And Marika began to realize that, for all she had been desperate to see either Grauel or Barlog for weeks, she really did not have much to say. "Have they treated you well?"

Grauel shrugged. "No worse than I expected."

"And Barlog? She is well?"

"Yes. I see they brought you the Chronicle. You will keep it up?"

"Yes."

For half a minute there did not seem to be anything else to say. Then Grauel remarked, "I hear you are in trouble." And, "We try to keep track of you through rumor."

"Yes. I did a foolish thing. I could not even get them to tell me if you were alive."

"Alive and fit. And blessing the All for this wondrous gift of snow. You really tried to kill your instructress? With witchcraft?"

"If that is what you call it. Not kill, though. Just hurt back. She asked for it, Grauel." Then, suddenly she broke down and poured out all her feelings, though she suspected the senior had sent Grauel round to scold her. "I do not like it here, Grauel." For a moment she was so stressed she slipped into the informal, personal mode, which among the Degnan was rarely used except with littermates. "They aren't nice. Can't you make them stop?"

Then Grauel held her and comforted her clumsily, and she abandoned the false adulthood she had been wearing as a mask since her assault on Gorry. "I don't *understand*, Grauel."

In a voice unnaturally weak for a grown female, Grauel told her, "Try again, Marika. And be patient. You are the only reason *any* of the Degnan—if only we—survive."

Marika understood that well enough, though Grauel was indirect. Grauel and Barlog were in Akard on sufferance. For the present their welcome depended upon hers.

She was not old enough to have such responsibility thrust upon her.

She could not get out of the more intimate speech mode, though she knew it made Grauel uncomfortable. "What are the silth, Grauel? Tell me about them. Don't just make warding signs and duck the question the way everybody did at home. Tell me what you know. *I* have to know."

Grauel became more uncomfortable. She looked around as though expecting to find someone lurking in the little cell's shadows.

"Tell me, Grauel. Please? Why do they want me?"

Grauel found her courage. She was one of the bravest of the Degnan, a huntress Skiljan had wanted by her when hunting game like kagbeast. She so conquered herself she managed to slip into the informal mode, too.

"They're witches, Marika. Dark witches, like in the stories. They command the spirit world. They're strong, and they're more ruthless than the grauken. They're the mistresses of the world. We were lucky in the upper Ponath. We had almost no contact with them, except at the annual assizes. They say we're too backward for the usual close supervision up here. This is just a remote outpost maintained so the Reugge sisterhood can retain its fief right to the Ponath. Tales tradermales bring up the Hainlin say they are much stronger in the south, where they hold whole cities as possessions and rule them with the terror of their witchcraft, so that normal meth dare not speak of them even as we do now. Tradermales say that in some cities meth dare not admit they exist even though every move and decision must be made with an eye to propitiating them. As though they were the All in Render's avatar. Those who displease them die horribly, slain by spirits."

"What spirits?"

Grauel looked at her oddly. "Surely you know that much? Else how did you hurt your instructress?"

"I just got angry and wished her heart would stop," Marika said, editing the truth. Her voice trailed off toward the end. She realized what she was doing. She recalled all those instances when she thought she was seeing ghosts. Were those the spirits the silth commanded? "Why are they interested in me?"

"They say you have the silth's secret eye. They say you can reach into the spirit world and shape it."

"Why would they take me even if that were true?"

"Surely by now you know that sisterhoods are not packs, Marika. Have you seen any males in the packfast? No. They must find their young outside. In the Ponath the packsteads are supposed to bring their young of five or six to the assizes, where the silth examine them and claim any touched by the silth talent. The females are raised as silth. The males are destroyed. Males with the talent are much rarer than females. Though it is whispered that if such sports ever die out completely, then there will be no more females of talent born either." One frantic glance around, and in a barely audible, breathy whisper, "Come the day."

"The wherlen."

"Yes. Exactly so. They turn up in the wilds. Few of the Ponath packs and none of the nomads go along with the system. Akard is not strong enough to enforce its will throughout the Ponath. There are no silth on the Zhotak. Though there have been few talents found in the Ponath anyway."

"Dam suspected," Marika mused. "That is why none of my litter ever went to the assizes."

"Perhaps. There have been other pups like you, capable of becoming silth, but who did not. It is said that if the talent is not harnessed early, and shaped, it soon fades. Had this winter not been what it was, and brought what it did, in a few years you would have seen whatever you have as a pup's imagination." There was a hint, almost, that Grauel spoke with sure knowledge.

"I'm not sure its *isn't* imagination," Marika said, more to herself than to Grauel.

"Just so. Now, in the cities, they say, they do it differently. Tradermales say the local cloisters screen every pup carefully and take those with the talent soon after birth. Most sisters, including those here, never know any life but that of silth. They question the ways of silth no more than you questioned the ways of the Degnan. But our ways were not graven by the All. Tradermales bring tales of others, some so alien as to be incomprehensible."

Marika reflected for half a minute. "I still don't understand, Grauel."

Grauel bared her teeth in an expression of strained amusement. "You were always one with more questions than there are answers, Marika. I have told you all I know. The rest you will have to learn. Remember always that they are very dangerous, these witches, and very unforgiving. And that these exiled to the borderlands are far less rigid than are their sisters in the great cities. Be very careful, and very patient."

In a small voice, Marika managed to say, "I will, Grauel. I will."

Chapter Nine

I

In unofficial confinement, Marika did not leave her cell for three days. Then one of Akard's few novice silth brought a summons from Gorry.

Marika put aside her flute, which she had been playing almost continuously, to the consternation of her neighbors, and closed the second volume of the Chronicle. Already that seemed removed from her, like a history of another pack.

The messenger, whose name Marika did not recall and did not care about, looked at the flute oddly. As if Marika might look at a poisonous grass lizard appearing unexpectedly while she was loafing on a hillside, painting portraits in the clouds. "You have a problem?" Marika asked.

As strength goes. The other youngsters were afraid of her even before the Gorry incident. She was a savage, and clearly a little mad. And tough, even if smaller and younger than most.

"No. I never saw a female play music before."

"There are more wonders in the world than we know." She quoted a natural science instructress who was more than a little dotty and the target of the malicious humor of half the younger silth. "How fierce is her mood?"

"I am not supposed to talk to you at all. None of us are till you develop proper attitudes."

"The All has heard my prayers after all." She looked up and sped a uniquely Degnan *Thanks-be* heavenward. And inside wondered why she was so determined to irk everyone around her. She had always been a quiet pup, given to getting in trouble for daydreaming, not for her mouth.

"You will make no friends if you do not stop that kind of talk."

"My friends are all ghosts." She was proud of being able to put a double meaning into a sentence in the silth low speech, which she had been learning so short a time.

The novice did not speak again, in the common speech or either of the silth dialects. She led Marika to Gorry's door, then marched off to tell everyone about the savage's bad manners.

Marika knocked. A weak voice bid her enter. She did so, and found herself in a world she did not know existed.

The senior did not live so well.

There was more comfort, and more wealth, in that one chamber than Marika had seen in her entire life at the Degnan packstead.

Gorry was recuperating upon a bed of otec furs stuffed with rare pothast down. The extremities of the room boasted whole ranks of candles supplementing the light cast by the old silth's private fire. Fire and candles were tended by a nonsilth pup of Marika's own age.

Marika saw many things of rich cloth such as tradermales brought north in their wagons, to trade for furs and the green gemstones sometimes found in the beds of streams running out of the Zhotak. There were metals in dazzling abundance, most not in the form of tools or weapons at all. Marika's head spun. It was a sin, that power should be so abused and flaunted.

"Come here, pup." The candle tender helped prop Gorry

up in her bed. The old silth indicated a wooden stool placed nearby. "Sit."

Marika went. She sat. She was as deferential as she knew how to be. When the rage began to bubble she reminded herself that Grauel and Barlog depended upon her remaining in good odor.

"Pup, I have been reviewing our attempts to provide you with an education. I believe we have approached it from the wrong direction. This is my fault principally. I have refused to acknowledge the fact that you have grown up outside the Community. I have not faced the fact that you have many habits of thought to unlearn. Until you have done that, and have acquired an appropriate way of thinking, we cannot reasonably expect you to respond as silth in an unfamiliar situation. Which, I now grant, all of this is. Therefore, we will set a different course. But be warned. You will be expected to adhere to sisterhood discipline once it has been made clear to you. I shall be totally unforgiving. Do you understand?"

Marika sensed the tightly controlled rage and hatred seething within the silth. The senior must have spoken to her. "No, Mistress Gorry."

The silth shuddered all over. The candle tender wrung her paws and looked at Marika in silent pleading. For a moment Marika was frightened for the old meth's health. But then Gorry asked, "What is it that you do not understand, pup? Begin with the simplest question."

"Why are you doing this to me? I did not ask—"

"Did your dam and the females of your pack ask if you wanted to become a huntress?"

"No, mistress," Marika admitted. "But—"

"But you are female and healthy. In the upper Ponath a healthy female becomes a huntress in the natural course. Now, however, it develops that you have the silth talent. So it is the natural course that you become silth."

Marika was unable to challenge that sort of reasoning. She did not agree with Gorry, but she did not possess the intellectual tools with which to refute her argument.

"There is no choice, pup. It is not the custom of the sisterhood to permit untrained talents liberty within the Community demesne."

Oblique as that was, Marika had no trouble understanding. She could become silth or die.

"You are what you are, Marika. You must be what you are. That is the law."

Marika controlled her temper. "I understand, Mistress Gorry."

"Good. And you will pursue your training with appropriate self-discipline?"

"Yes, Mistress Gorry." With all sorts of secret reservations.

"Good. You will resume your education tomorrow. I will inform your other instructresses. Henceforth you will spend extra time learning the ways of the Community, till you reach a level of knowledge of those ways appropriate to a candidate of your age."

"Yes, Mistress Gorry."

"You may go."

"Yes, Mistress Gorry." But before Marika departed she paused for a final look around. She was especially intrigued by the books shelved upon the one wall beside the fireplace. Of all the wealth in that place, they impressed her most.

Sleep became a stranger. But just as well. There was so much to do and learn. And that way there were fewer of the unhappy dreams.

She was sure her haunt was Kublin's ghost, punishing her for not having seen the Degnan Mourned. She wondered if she ought not to discuss her dreams with the silth. In the end, she did not. As always was, what was between her and Kublin—even Kublin passed—was between her and Kublin.

II

The dreams continued. Spotted, random dreams unrelated to any phenomenon or natural cycle that Braydic could identify. They occurred unpredictably, as though at the behest of another, which convinced Marika that she was the focus of the anger of her dead. Ever more of her nights were haunted—though she now spent less time than ever asleep. There was too much to learn, too much to do, for her to waste time sleeping.

Braydic told her, "I think your dreams have nothing to do with your dead. Except within your own mind. You are just rationalizing them to yourself. I believe they are your talent venting the pressure of growth. You were too long without guidance or training. Many strange things befall pups who reach your age without receiving guidance or instruction. And that among the normally talented."

"Normally talented?" Marika suspected Braydic was brushing the edge of the shadow that had pursued her since she had noticed that something had passed among Akard's meth. All treated her oddly. The pawful of pups inhabiting the fortress not only, as expected, disdained her for her rude origins; they were afraid of her. She saw fear blaze up behind evasive eyes whenever she cornered one long enough to make her talk.

Only Braydic seemed unafraid.

Marika spent a lot of time with the communicator now. Braydic helped her with her language lessons, and let her pretend that she was not alone in her exile. Seldom did she see Grauel or Barlog, and when she did it was by sneakery and there was no time to exchange more than a few hasty words.

"Gorry has much to say about you to my truesister, Marika. And little of it good. Some reaches my humble ears." Nervously, Braydic set fingers dancing upon a keyboard, calling up data she had scanned only minutes before. Her shoulders straightened. She turned. "You have a glorious future, pup. If you live to see it."

"What?"

"Gorry knows pups and talents. She was once important among those who teach at Maksche. She calls you the greatest talent-potential Akard has yet unearthed. Maybe as remarkable a talent as any discovered by the Reugge this generation."

Marika scoffed. "Why do you say that? I do not feel remarkable."

"How would you know? At your age you have only yourself as comparison. Whatever her faults, Gorry is not given to fanciful speaking. Were I in your boots I would guard my tail carefully. Figuratively and even literally. A talent like yours, so bright it shines in the eyes of the blind, can become more curse than gift of the All."

"Curse? Danger? What are you saying?"

"As strength goes, pup. I am warning you. Those threatened by a talent are not shy about squashing one— though they will act subtly."

Again Braydic tapped at a keyboard. Marika waited, and wondered what the communicator meant. And wondered that she no longer felt so uncomfortable around the communications center. Perhaps that was another manifestation of the talent that so impressed Braydic. The communicator did say she was dealing instinctively with the electromagnetic handicap that others never overcame.

Braydic yanked her attention back to what she was saying. "It is no accident that most of the more important posts in most of the sisterhoods are held by the very old. Those silth were only a little smarter and a little stronger when they were pups. They did not attract attention. As they aged and advanced, they looked back for those who might overtake them and began throwing snares into the paths of the swifter runners."

What Pohsit would have done had she had the chance.

"They did not press those older than they."

Marika responded with what she thought would be received as a fetchingly adult observation. She was a little calculator often. "That is no way to improve the breed."

"There is no breed to improve, pup. The continued existence of all silthdom relies entirely upon a rare but stubbornly persistent genetic recessive floating in the broader population."

Marika gaped, not understanding a word.

"When a silth is accepted as a full sister, her order passes her through a ritual in which she must surrender her ability to bear pups."

Marika was aghast. That went against all survival imperatives.

In the packs of the upper Ponath, reproductive rights were rigorously controlled by, and often limited to, the dominant females. Such as Skiljan. Mating freely, meth could swamp the local environment in a very few years.

The right to reproduce might be denied, but never the ability. The pack might need to produce pups quickly after a wild disaster.

"A true silth sister must not be distracted by the demands of her flesh, nor must she be possessed of any obligation beyond that to her order. A female in heat has no mind. A female with newly whelped pups is neither mobile nor capable of placing the Community before her offspring. Nature has programmed her."

Braydic shifted subject suddenly, obviously in discomfort. "You have one advantage, Marika. One major safety. You are here in Akard, which has been called The Stronghold of Ambition's Death. None here will cut you in fear for themselves. They are without hope, these Akard silth. They are those who were kicked off the ladder, yet were deemed dangerous enough to demand lifelong exile. The enemies you are making here hate you because they fear your strength, and for less selfish reasons. Gorry dreads what you may mean to the Community's future. Long has she claimed to snatch glimpses of far tomorrows. Since your coming her oracles have grown ever more hysterical and dark."

Marika had assumed a jaw-on-paw attitude of rapt attention guaranteed to keep Braydic chattering. She did not mind the communicator's ceaseless talk, for Braydic gladly swamped the willing ear with information the silth yielded only grudgingly, if at all.

"The worst danger will come when you capture their attention down south. And capture it you will, I fear. If you are half what Gorry believes. If you continue in the recalcitrant character you have shown. They will have to pay attention." Braydic toyed with the vision screen. She seemed uneasy. "Given six or seven years unhindered, learning as fast as you have, the censure of the entire Community will be insufficient to keep you contained here." The communicator turned away, muttering, "As strength goes."

Marika had become accustomed to such chatter. Braydic had hinted and implied similar ideas a dozen times in a dozen different ways during their stolen moments. This time the meth was more direct, but her remarks made no more sense now than when Marika had first slipped in to visit her.

Marika was devouring books and learning some about her talent, but discovering almost nothing of the real internal workings of the Reugge sisterhood. She could not refrain from interpreting what she heard and saw in Degnan pack terms. So she often interpreted wrong.

Silth spoke the word "Community" with a reverence the Degnan reserved for the All. Yet daily life appeared to be every sister for herself, as strength goes, in a scramble that beggared those among frontier "savages." Never did the meth of the upper Ponath imperil their packs with their struggles for dominance. But Marika suspected she was getting a shaded view. Braydic did seem to dwell morbidly upon that facet of silth life.

It did not then occur to Marika to wonder why.

She left her seat, began pottering around. Braydic's talk made her restless and uneasy. "Distract them with other matters," Braydic said. "You are, almost literally, fighting for your life. Guard yourself well." Then she shifted subject again. "Though you cannot tell by looking, the thaw has begun. As you can see on the flow monitors."

Marika joined Braydic before one of the vision screens. She was more comfortable with things than with meth. She had a flair for manipulating the keyboards, though she did not comprehend a third of what Braydic told her about how they worked. In her mind electronics was more witchcraft than was her talent. Her talent was native and accepted fact, like her vision. She did not question or examine her vision. But a machine that did the work of a brain . . . Pure magic.

Columns of numeral squiggles slithered up the screen. "Is it warmer in the north than it is here, Braydic?" She had sensed no weakening of winter's grasp.

"No. Just warmer everywhere." The communicator made a minor adjustment command to what she called an outflow valve. "I am worried. We had so much snow this winter. A sudden rise in temperature might cause a meltoff the system cannot handle."

"Open the valves all the way. Now."

"That would drain the reservoirs. I cannot do that. I need to maintain a certain level to have a flow sufficient to turn the generators. Else we are without power. I cannot do my work without power."

Marika started to ask a question. A tendril of something brushed her. She jumped in a pup's sudden startle reaction. Braydic responded with bared teeth and a snarl, an instinctual reaction when a pup was threatened. "What is it, Marika?" She seemed embarrassed by her response.

"Someone is coming. Someone silth. I have to leave." She was not supposed to be in the communications center, exposed to its aura.

There were many things she was not supposed to do. She did them anyway. Like make sneak visits to Grauel and Barlog. The silth could not keep watch all the time. She slept so little. And the fortress's huntresses seemed disinclined to watch her at all, or to report observed behavior that was not approved.

She suspected Grauel and Barlog were responsible, for all they admonished her incessantly in their brief meetings. She caught occasional hints that her packmates had developed fierce reputations among Akard's untalented population.

Marika slipped away through a passage which led to the roof and the metal tree. Up there the aura still disoriented her, though not so she was unable to slide away in the moonlight and take a place upon the northern wall, staring out at the bitter snowscape.

To her, winter did not appear to be loosening its grip.

From the edges of her eyes she seemed to see things moving. She did not turn, knowing they would not be there if she looked. Not unless she forced her talent with hammer-blow intensity.

She did not look up at the great cold sky either, though she felt it beating down upon her, calling.

Someday, she thought. Someday. If Braydic was right. Someday she would go.

III

The moons tagged across the night in a playful band, in a rare conjunction that seemed impossible in the two-dimensional view available from the ground. They should be ricocheting off one another.

Sometimes smaller ones did collide with Biter or Chaser, according to Marika's instructresses. But the last showy impact had come two centuries ago, and the last before that a thousand years earlier still. For all the matter skipping across the nighttime skies, collisions remained rare.

"You are daydreaming again, Marika," a gentle voice said into her ear. She started, realized she had stopped marching. Barlog had overtaken her. Barlog, who was with the rear guard several hundred yards behind. There was a gentle humor in the huntress's voice when she asked, "Will

you make these packfast meth over in your own image,
rather than they you in theirs?"

Marika did not reply. She yanked the butt of her javelin
from the soggy earth and trotted forward, up the topless hill.
She understood. Barlog had made another of her sly obser-
vations about the stubborn resistance of a certain pup to
assimilation into silth life. A resistance that was quiet and
passive and almost impossible to challenge, yet immutable.
She studied and she learned with a ravenous appetite, but
she remained a savage in outlook, the despair of most silth.

Unconsciously, or perhaps instinctively, she had done the
right thing to avoid coming to the attention of more distant
members of the sisterhood. Pride would not permit the
Akard silth to report the unconquerable wild thing among
them.

Marika took her place near the rear of the main body,
falling into the rhythm of placing her feet into the tracks of
the sister before her. There were twelve silth and twelve
huntresses in the party. They were far north of Akard. The
moons appeared unnaturally low behind them. A few huntresses carried trophy ears, but it had not been the good hunt
expected. The nomads were avoiding contact expertly. Sisters capable of the far touch said the other parties had had
no better hunting. It was as if the nomads knew where their
stalkers were all the time. The few taken had been stragglers too weak to stay up with their packs, and mostly males.

A very frightening thing had happened. The nomad horde
had not broken into its bickering constituent packs with the
death of the wehrlen. The older silth in Akard were very
disturbed. But they were not explaining why. At least not to
Marika.

She had taken no part in the hunt so far, except to trudge
along with the pack and learn what was to be learned, to
marvel at endless alien vistas, at mountains and canyons and
waterfalls and trees like nothing she had imagined while
sealed up in her native packstead. To marvel at the world of
the night, with its strangely different creatures and perils
and aromas.

The hunting parties had departed Akard soon after winter's final feeble storm, while snow still masked the north. They had been instructed to harry the retreating nomads mercilessly, to press them back into the Zhotak, and beyond. Marika did not understand what the senior was doing, but had had no trouble comprehending why she had been sent along.

She was a disturbing influence in Akard. The old ones could not deal with her. They wanted her out of the way for a while, so they could regain their balance. And maybe so they could decide what to do about her.

She did not allow herself to dwell upon that. The possibilities were too grim. She was not as confident of her safety as Braydic said she should be. The senior and Khles and Gorry all had made the point repeatedly that she was at their mercy. And she had her responsibility to Grauel and Barlog. Why could she not conform more, at least outwardly? She tried, but invariably they would touch some unyielding chord of rebellion.

The party stopped moving. A huntress returned from the point to report, "We are there. Just beyond that loom of rock." She indicated a star-obscuring line ahead. Marika leaned on her javelin and listened, grateful for a chance to catch her breath. They had been climbing since sundown, and for three nights before that. And now they were just yards from the planned limit of their journey. Now they would turn and begin the long downhill return to Akard.

"You can see their campfires from the rim," the scout said. Marika became alert. The nomads? They were that close? And confident enough to show lights at night?

The pack responded with angry murmurs. Soon Marika found herself poised at the brink of an immense drop-off, staring at the patch of winking campfires, like a cloud of stars, many miles away.

"They feel safe beyond the Rift," muttered Rhaisihn, the silth who commanded the party. "They think we will not come on. Curse them. Far-toucher. Where is a far-toucher?

I need instructions from Akard. I need to touch the other parties, to let them know that we have found the savages."

Even in the darkness the view's immensity awed Marika. When the others withdrew to carry out orders or begin making camp, she remained, staring at moonlight glinting off mists, streams, lakes, patches of unmelted snow. And at that constellation of campfires.

Whenever her gaze crossed that far camp, she suffered a startling resurgence of emotion she had thought fully dulled. But the hatred and anger remained, buried. She wanted revenge for what had been done to the Degnan.

The first ghost light of approaching day obscured the feeble eastern stars. Marika went down to her own camp, where she found Rhaisihn with two far-touchers, muttering angrily. Her request for permission to carry the pursuit beyond the Rift had been denied.

There were ceremonies upcoming at Akard, and it would be hard enough now to get back in time to participate. If they pressed on north the ceremonies would have to be forgone.

Marika was indifferent to ritual obligations. She interrupted. "Mistress? May I have the watch on the nomad camp?"

The silth looked up, startled. "You? Volunteering? I am amazed. I wonder what ulterior motive you may have. But go ahead. You may as well be of *some* use."

Rhaisihn did not like Marika. Marika did her share and more, yet Rhaisihn persistently accused her of malingering, perhaps because she tended to daydream. Marika stilled her anger and returned to the rim of the Rift. She found a prominence and seated herself.

The light had grown strong enough to obscure all but the westernmost stars.

There were few stars in the skies of Marika's world. No more than a few hundred. Most were so feeble only the sharpest eye could discern them. The only truly bright heavenly bodies were the moons and nearest planets.

The light continued to grow, and Marika continued to sit,

as fixed as part of the landscape, her awe unabated. The lighter the dawn, the more grand the view. The lighter the dawn, the more she was astounded by the spectacle before her.

The Rift was a break in the earth's crust tilted like a monster paving stone ripped up by an earth giant's pry bar. The fall before Marika was at least two thousand feet. The Rift extended to either paw as far as she could see. The north spread out like a map. A map now partly obscured by mists over lakes and rivers and their verges. Most of the ground seemed flat and meadowy, maybe even marshy, but in the far distance there were darker greens that could only be forests. Beyond those the tundra began.

She looked to the east for some sign of the Great Gap, a wide break in the Rift wall through which both nomads and kropek migrated, and through which the nomads would have withdrawn. Those who had gone, for it was rumored that many had decided to remain in the upper Ponath. Parties from Akard were hunting them, too.

There was no sign of the Gap.

That vast sprawl of northland was hypnotic. There was no way a Marika could gaze upon it and not fall into a daydream.

A light, wandering something touched her mind as lightly as gossamer on the wind. Startled, she evaded automatically, then focused her attention. . . . And became very frightened.

That silth was not one of her party. That silth was out *there*.

For all her determination to learn, she had as yet mastered only the rudiments of silth mind exercise and self-control. She applied what she did know, calmed herself, let go of emotion, then went down inside herself seeking the gateway Gorry had been teaching her to find.

This was one of those rare moments when the gateway opened easily and she slipped through into the realm of ghosts, where the workaday world became as unreal as a chaphe dream. She captured a little fluttering wisp of a

ghost, commanded it to carry her toward the nomad camp.
To her astonishment, it complied.

She had tried that often before, and had had success only
on a few occasions when she had wanted to do harm, when
she had commanded by instinct, her will an iron engine
driven by black hatred.

Luck was not enough. She could not guide the ghost with
precision. She caught only random glimpses of the camp.

But those were enough.

She was aghast.

There were thousands of the nomads. Most were but fur
and bones, clad in tatters, a little better shape than the few
Marika's party had taken on the hunt. For all they had
plundered the upper Ponath, they had done themselves little
good. The sight of starving pups caused her the most discomfort, for it was hard to hate, and easy to have compas-
sion, for the very young.

The ghost passed something in black. Someone not rav-
aged by malnutrition. Someone arguing with several dominant nomad huntresses. Marika tried to turn back, to take
another look, but her control was inadequate. She caught
one more glimpse of someone in black from a distance. The
costuming appeared to be silth, yet it was different, subtly,
from that which she knew.

A dwindling shrieking sound hammered upon her, filter-
ing in from that other world where her flesh waited, petri-
fied, upon an outcrop overlooking the sprawl of the north.
There were harmonics of terror, of death, in that cry. She
fought to drive her ghost away from the nomad encampment, back to her body.

She had no skill. It was like trying to herd a butterfly. It
fluttered this way and that, only tending in the proper
direction.

Her flesh relayed hints of a disturbance back there. Of
excitement. Of danger. She felt tendrils of panic touch the
edge of her. Then came the light caress of an investigative
silth touch. A touch that became more firm, an anchor. A
lifeline along which she could pull herself back to her flesh.

She returned to a body gripped by an intense flight-fight reaction. There were meth all around her, all chattering but Rhaisihn, who was just coming back from helping Marika return. The commander stared at her when she opened her eyes, slightly puzzled, slightly angry, a whole lot disconcerted. The leader turned to her chief huntress. "Get these meth out of here."

The huntress tried to do as instructed. But one meth would not go. One who carried a heavy hunting spear and appeared willing to fight rather than be budged. Barlog.

"What happened?" Marika asked in a small voice, certain something dramatic had happened while she was away.

"That was a foolish thing to try at your level," Rhaisihn said, her concern surprising Marika. "You *must* learn with a guide."

"What happened?" Marika demanded. "I sensed something terrible."

"Obrhothkask fell off the ledge." Rhaisihn indicated a point just two feet from Marika. "The All only knows what she was doing." Rhaisihn glared at Barlog. The huntress had not yet set the butt of her spear to earth. Her teeth were bared in a snarl so fierce Marika knew she would take anything as a challenge, and would fight rather than be moved an inch.

"We will discuss this later," Rhaisihn said. "Under more favorable circumstances. Settle her down. Then rest. We start south tonight."

"There are silth in that camp," Marika told Rhaisihn's back.

"Yes. There would be." Rhaisihn skirted Barlog carefully. The huntress faced her as she passed, turning slowly, spear at the ready. Only after the commander disappeared among the rocks did she begin to relax.

Marika practiced her calming exercises. She waited on Barlog. Once the huntress was no longer in the grip of her fury, she asked, "What happened? How did Obrhothkask fall?"

Barlog's eyes were hard and narrow and calculating as

she settled beside Marika, stared at the nomad encampment. No awe of nature in her. "The butt of a spear struck her in the small of the back. She lost her balance."

"Oh?"

"Rumor says you were warned to remain alert. Perhaps you did not take the warning seriously." Barlog reached inside her jacket, produced a steel knife. It was the sort for which the tradermales demanded a dozen otec furs. "Let this talisman be a reminder. Save for a timely spear butt, it would be through your heart now. And you would lie where the witch lies."

Marika accepted the shining blade, barely able to comprehend. Barlog rose and strode toward the camp, spear upon her shoulder.

Marika remained where she was, thinking for half an hour, staring at that knife. Obrhothkask's knife. But Obrhothkask was only a few years her senior, and they had hardly known one another. Obrhothkask had no reason to attack her. Surely she would not have done so on her own. She was the most dull and traditional of silth trainees.

"Guard your tail," Braydic had said so often. And she had not taken the warning with sufficient seriousness. So a meth had died.

She snapped upright and peered over the edge. There was no sign of the fallen silth. The body was too far below, and in shadow. After a glance toward camp, Marika tossed the knife after its owner.

Twelve otec furs just thrown away. Barlog would have been appalled. But it might have been construed as evidence of some sort.

The homeward journey was a quiet one. Obrhothkask's death hung over the party, never forgotten. Silth and huntress alike avoided Marika and Barlog. The Degnan huntress seldom allowed Marika out of her sight.

Marika concluded that everyone knew exactly what had happened, and everyone meant to pretend that it had not.

For the sake of history Obrhothkask's passing would be recalled as accidental.

Marika wondered about the form and substance of a silth Mourning. Would she be allowed to witness it? Would it be a form she could memorize and secretly apply to the account of her unMourned packmates?

Thinking of old debts and a time of life that now seemed as remote as the tale of another meth's puphood, she realized that she had had no dreams since leaving Akard's environs. Would that haunt be waiting when she returned?

After that she was not incautious again, ever. And never again was there so crude and direct an attempt to displace her.

Marika got the sense of much hidden anger and activity generated by the attempt, the death, and perhaps even the attempt's failure. She suspected the meth responsible was never identified.

She did not get to witness a silth Mourning. There was no such rite, as she understood a Mourning.

Summer fled quickly and early, and winter stormed into the world again.

Chapter Ten

I

It was a winter like the one preceding, when the doom had come to the upper Ponath. Harsh. But it began with a lie, hinting that it would be milder. After it lulled everyone, it bared its claws and slashed at the upper Ponath with storm after storm, dumping snow till drifts threatened to overtop Akard's northern wall. Its chill breath howled without respite, and left everything encrusted with ice. For a time the Akard silth lost touch with their Reugge sisters in the south.

It was a winter like the one preceding. The nomads again came down out of the north in numbers greater than before. Many of the packs that survived the first invasion succumbed to this one—though much of the bad news did not reach Akard till after winter's departure. Still, scores of refugees appealed for protection, and the silth took them in, though grudgingly.

Twice small bands of nomads appeared on the snowfields beyond the north wall, fields where during summer meth raised the fortress's food crops. They examined the grim pile of stone, then moved on, not tempted. Marika chanced to be atop the wall, alone and contemplating, the second time a group appeared. She studied them as closely as she could from several hundred yards.

"They are not yet suicidal in their desperation," she told Braydic afterward.

"The key phrase is 'not yet,' " Braydic replied. "It will come." The communicator was a little distracted, less inclined to be entertaining and instructive than was her custom. The ice and cold kept her in a constant battle with her equipment, and in some cases she did not possses the expertise to make repairs. "This cannot go on. There is no reason to expect the winters to get better. They had best send me a technician. Of course, they do not care if they never hear from us. They would be pleased if the ice just swallowed us."

Marika did not believe that. Neither did Braydic, really. It was frustration talking.

"No. They will not try it yet, Marika. But they will one day. Perhaps next winter. The next at the latest. This summer will see a stronger effort to stay in the upper Ponath. We have given them little difficulty. They will be less inclined to run away. And they are becoming accustomed to being one gigantic pack. This battle for survival has eclipsed all their old bitternesses and feuds. Or so I hear when my truesister and the others gather to discuss the matter. They foresee no turns for the better. We will get no help from Maksche. And without help we will not stem the flood. There are too many tens of thousands of nomads. Even silth have limitations."

What little news filtered in with the fugitives was uniformly grim and invariably supported Braydic's pessimism. There was one report of nomads being spotted a hundred miles south of Akard, down the Hainlin. Braydic received some very bitter, accusing messages because of that. Akard was supposed to bestride and block the way to the south.

The communicator told Marika, "My truesister will not send anyone—not even you—hunting nomads in these storms. We are not strong. We do not have lives to waste. Come summer. Then. When there is only the enemy to beware."

Enemy. As a group. The concept had only the vaguest possibility of expression in the common speech of the upper Ponath. Marika had had to learn the silth tongue to find it. She was not pleased with it.

Indeed, the senior and silth of Akard did nothing whatsoever to arrest the predations of the nomads. Which left Marika with severely mixed feelings.

Packs were being exterminated. Her kind of meth were being murdered daily. And though she understood why, she was upset because their guardians were doing nothing to aid them. When some pawful of refugees came in, bleeding through the snow, frostbitten, having left their pups and Wise frozen in the icy forests, she wanted to go howling through the wilderness herself, riding the black, killing ghosts, cleansing the upper Ponath of this nomad scourge.

It was in such moods that she made her best progress toward mastery of the silth magic. She had a very strong dark side.

That winter was a lonely one for her, and a time of growing self-doubt. A time when she lost purpose. Her one dream involved the stars ever obscured by the clouded skies. It seemed ever more pointless and remote in that outland under siege. When she reflected upon it seriously, she had to admit she had no slightest idea what fulfilling that dream would cost or entail.

She did not see Grauel or Barlog for months, even on the sly—which was just as well, probably, for they would have recognized her dilemma and have taken the side which stood against dreams. They were not dreamers. For wilderness huntresses maturation meant the slaying of foolish dreams.

Braydic encouraged the dreamer side, for whatever reasons she might have, but the communicator's influence was less than she believed. Coming to terms with reality was something Marika had to accomplish almost entirely for herself.

The lessons went on. The teaching continued throughout long hours. Marika continued to learn, though her all-devouring enthusiasm began to grow blunted.

There were times when she feared she was a little mad. Like when she wondered if the absence of her nightmares of the previous year might not be the cause of her present mental disaffection.

The Degnan remained unMourned. And there were times now when she felt guilty about no longer feeling guilty about not having seen the appropriate rites performed.

It was not a good year for the wild silth pup from the upper Ponath.

II

The kagbeast leapt for Marika's throat. She did not move. She reached inside herself, through the loophole in reality through which she saw ghosts, and saw the animal as a moving mass of muscle and pumping blood, of entrails and rude nervous system. It seemed to hang there, barely moving toward her, as she decided that it was real, not an illusion conjured by Gorry.

A month earlier she would have been so alarmed she would have frozen. And been ripped apart. Now her reaction was entirely cerebral.

She touched a spot near the kagbeast's liver, thought fire, and watched a spark glow for a fragment of a second. The kagbeast began turning slowly while still in the air, clawing at the sudden agony in its vitals.

Marika slipped back through her loophole into real time and the real world. She stood there unmoving while the carnivore flailed through the air, missing her by scant inches. She did not bother to turn as it hit the white floor behind her, claws clacking savagely at the stone. She did not allow elation to touch her for an instant.

With Gorry directing the test, there might be more.

She was not surprised that Gorry had slipped a genuine killer into the drill. Gorry hated her and would be pleased to be rid of her in a fashion that would raise few questions among her sisters.

The old silth had warned her often enough publicly that her education could be deadly. She had made it clear that the price of failure might have to be paid at any time.

Gorry had had to explain the price of failure only once.

Marika could not sneak into Gorry's mind the way she had Pohsit's. But she did not need to do so. It was perfectly evident that Gorry had inherited Pohsit's mantle of madness. Gorry scarcely bothered concealing it.

The kagbeast howled and hurled itself at Marika once more. Once again she reached through her loophole. This time she touched a point at the base of its brain. It lost its motor coordination. When it hit the floor it had no more control than a male who had stolen and drunk a gallon of ormon beer.

She considered guiding the beast to the stair leading up to the balustrade. But no. She pushed that thought aside. There would come a better time and place.

The kagbeast kept trying. Tauntingly, Marika reached through and tweaked nerve ends so that it felt it was being stung.

While she toyed with her adversary, Marika allowed a tendril of touch to drift upward to where Gorry leaned upon the balustrade. She looked at the old silth much as she had done with the kagbeast. She did not touch the silth's mind, though. Did not alert Gorry to the true extent of her ability. That would come some time when the old silth was not alert.

Marika had waited almost two years. She could wait awhile longer to requite her torment.

Gorry's heart was beating terribly fast. Her muscles were tense. There were other signs indicating extreme excitement and fear. Her lips were pulled back in an unconscious baring of teeth, threatening.

Marika allowed herself one brief taste of triumph.

The old one was afraid of her. She knew she had taught

too well in her effort to make the teaching deadly. She knew her pupil. Knew a reckoning had to come. And feared she could not survive it even now.

The faintest quiver at the edge of Gorry's snarl betrayed her lack of confidence. Pushed, she might well respond with one of the several yielding reflexes genetically programmed into female meth. Triggering reflexive responses in Marika—and robbing her of the taste of blood she anticipated.

Marika withdrew carefully. She would avoid arousing old instincts.

She brought her attention back to the kagbeast and to the space around him. Another of Gorry's taunts, selecting a male. Another of the old fool's errors of pride. Another stitch in her shroud of doom, as far as Marika was concerned. Another petty insult.

Something small and shimmering and red drifted close by, drawn by the kagbeast's pain. Marika snapped a touch at it and caught it. It wriggled but could not escape. She impressed her will upon it.

The ghost drifted into the kagbeast's flesh, into its right hindquarter, into a hip joint. Marika compressed it to the size of a seed, them made it spin. At that concentration the ghost was dense enough to tear flesh and scar bone.

The kagbeast shrieked and dropped to its haunches. It tried to drag itself toward her, to the end single-minded in its purpose. When she searched for it, Marika could feel the thread of touch connecting the beast's mind with that of her instructress.

She would shatter Gorry's control.

Each time the kagbeast pulled itself forward, Marika made her compressed red ghost spin again. Each time the kagbeast howled. Driven or not, it learned quickly.

As Marika had learned quickly, under Gorry's torments.

The beast screamed and screamed again, the power in its mind trying to drive it forward while the pain in its flesh punished every attempt to obey that will. Gorry did have one advantage. She knew less of mercy than did her pupil.

Marika was sure one reason Gorry had volunteered to

become her instructress was that she had no champions. No ties. No backing. Certainly not because she had seen a chance to waken and ripen a new silth mind. No. She had seen Marika as a barbarian who would make a fine toy for her secret desire to do hurt. An object on which she could use her talent to hurt. With a slight twist of the mind she was able to justify it all by believing Marika was a terrible danger.

All the Reugge sisters at Akard seemed to have twists to their minds. Braydic was not telling the truth, or the whole truth, when she insisted that these silth were in exile because they had made enemies elsewhere in the sisterhood. They had been sent to the edge of beyond because their minds were not quite whole. And the lackings were dangerous.

That Marika had learned, too. Her education ran broader than she had expected, and deeper than her teachers suspected. She had a feeling that Braydic herself was not quite what she pretended, was not quite sane.

The communicator pretended she had accompanied her truesister into exile for fear of reprisals once her protection vanished elsewhere. About that Marika was certain Braydic was lying.

Caution was the strongest lesson Marika had learned. Absolute, total caution. Absolute, total distrust of all who pretended friendship. She was an island, alone, at war with the world because the world was at war with her. She barely trusted Barlog and Grauel, and doubted she might retain that trust much longer. For she had not seen either huntress in a long time, and they had been exposed to who knew what pressures.

She hated Akard, the Reugge, silthdom.

She hated well and deeply, but she waited for the time of balance to ripen.

The kagbeast moved closer. Marika pushed distractions out of mind. This was not the time to reflect. Gorry might have more deadly tests in reserve. Might think to overwhelm her. It was a time to be on guard continuously, for Gorry did suspect the truth: that she was stronger than she pretended. There would be no more attacks like that on the Rift, but there would be something beyond the customary limits.

If the kagbeast was not an indication that the limits had been exceeded already. Marika knew of no other silth trainee who had been tested this severely this early in her training.

Had Gorry hoped she would be taken unsuspecting, thinking the monster an illusion?

Of course.

Enough. Toying with the beast was overweening pride. She was betraying herself, revealing hidden strength. She was giving too much information to one who meant her harm.

She reached through her loophole and stilled the beast's heart. It expired, almost grateful for the inflow of darkness and peace.

Marika spent a minute relaxing, then looked upward, her face carefully composed in an expression of inquiry.

Gorry continued to stare vacantly for several seconds. Then she shuddered all over, like a wet meth getting the water out of her fur. She said, "You did very well, Marika. My confidence in you has been justified. That is enough for today. You are excused from all classes and chores. You need to rest." All spoken in a feeble voice quivering with uncertainty.

"Thank you, mistress." She was careful not to betray the fact that she felt no weariness as she departed, pushing past servants hurrying to remove the kagbeast to the kitchens. Several eyed her warily, which she noted without paying attention. There were servants everywhere these days, and one paid them no mind at all. The influx of refugees meant work had to be created.

She went directly to her cell, lay on her pallet contemplating the afternoon's events, unaware that she had adopted a silth mind-set. Every nuance of what had—and had not—transpired had to be examined for levels of meaning.

Somehow, she was sure, she had gone through a rite of

passage. A rite not planned by Gorry. But she was not sure what it was.

She willed her body to relax, muscle by muscle, as she had been taught, and pushed herself into a light sleep. A wary sleep, like that of a huntress in the field, overnighting in the forest far from her home packstead.

A part of her remained huntress. That would never change.

Never would she relax her guard.

III

Another year of exile passed. It was no happier than its predecessor.

Marika went to that part of the wall which overlooked the dam and powerhouse. There was a place there that she thought of as her own. A place only the newest refugees failed to respect as private and hers alone. A place surrounded by an invisible barrier that not even Gorry or her cronies among the old silth would cross when Marika was present. Marika went there when she wanted to be entirely free of care.

Each silth had such a place. For most it was their quarters. But the identity of such places developed in a tacit, unconscious fashion, within the shared awareness of the silth community. The silth of Akard gradually became aware that this place on the wall was the one where the wild pup was sovereign.

She liked the wind and the cold and the view. More, she liked the fact that she could not be physically approached without time to arrange her thoughts. There were those few who would and did dare intrude—the senior and Khlees Gibany, for example—though they would do so only with sound cause.

The Husgen was frozen. Again. The silth had scores of refugee workers out keeping the ice from choking the pipes to the powerhouse. It was a winter worse than the previous two, and each of those had set new records for inflicting misery. There were fewer storms this year, and less snow, but the wind was as fierce as ever, and its claws of cold were sharper than ever. The ice wind found its way even into the heart of the fortress, mocking the roaring fires burning in every fireplace. The edge of the forest, a third mile beyond the bounds of the tilled ground, had retreated two hundred yards last summer. Deadwood had been gathered from miles around. Firewood clogged every cranny of the fortress. And still Braydic shivered when she ran calculations of consumption against time left to withstand.

Foraging parties were not going out this winter. No one was allowed beyond reach of the massed power of the Akard silth. It was rumored that none of the Zhotak nomads had stayed behind this winter.

That first bleak winter only a relative few had come south. Though the Degnan had been consumed, most of the upper Ponath packs had survived. The few nomads who had not fled north had been destroyed by the silth. The second winter had seen fully half the upper Ponath packs destroyed, and the summer following had been a time of constant blood as the silth strove to overcome those masses of nomads trying to hang on in the captured packsteads. Many nomads had perished, but the silth had failed to force a complete withdrawal.

The nomads had no wehrlen to lead them now, but they no longer needed one. They had become melded into one vast superpack. This year the northern horde had come early, during the harvest season. The silth did all they could, but the savages were not intimidated by slaughter or silth witchcraft. Always there were more desperate packs to replace those consumed by the Reugge fury.

Most of the surviving packsteads had been destroyed or overcome and occupied. Braydic predicted that none of the nomads would retreat come spring.

Marika sensed that this third winter of her exile marked the end of the upper Ponath as the frontier of civilization.

This year the more mobile of the forerunner nomads were ranging far south of Akard. They gave the fortress a wide berth, then followed the course of the Hainlin, which had become a twisting road of ice carrying their threat down to the lands of the south. Only one other fastness of civilization remained unscathed, the tradermale packfast downriver, Critza.

Marika had seen Critza but once, briefly, from afar, during the nomad hunts of the previous summer. It was a great stone pile as forbidding as Akard itself. A great many refugees had fled there, too. More than to Akard, for the tradermales were not feared the way silth were.

They were not feared by the nomads either. The savages had attacked Critza once the second winter and twice already this year—without success. The tradermales were said to possess many strange and terrible weapons. The nomads had left many hundreds of dead outside Critza's walls.

Marika had been only vaguely aware of Critza's existence till she had seen it. Then she had been amazed that the silth would permit so much independent strength to exist within their demesne. Especially in the hands of males. For the silth had very strong convictions about males. Convictions which beggared the prejudices of the meth of the upper Ponath.

They would not permit an unneutered male inside Akard. That imposed a terrible burden upon those pawfuls of survivors who fled to the fortress, especially those packs with hopes of someday breeding back up.

There was a small village of unneutered males almost below the point where Marika stood, scratching for life in shelters pitched against the wall and appealing to the All for help that would not come from those who protected them. Even a few stiff-necked huntresses stayed out there rather than bow to silth demands.

Marika suspected most of those meth would move on to Critza when travel became less hazardous.

But Critza—why did such a place exist here? Not one of

the old silth had a kind word for the tradermales, nor trusted them in the least. They were the next thing to rogue, a definite threat to their absolute power, if only because they carried news between the packsteads.

Braydic said tradermales were necessary to the balance. They had a recognized niche in the broader law of the south, which was accepted by all the sisterhoods. The silth did not like the tradermale brotherhood, but had to accept it—as long as the tradermales remained within certain carefully defined professional strictures.

Marika shuddered but ignored the savage wind as she surveyed the view commanded by the packfast. Never in the entire history of the packfast—which reached back centuries before the coming of the Degnan to the upper Ponath—had there been a winter so terrible, let alone three in a row, each worse than the last.

Marika tried to recall winters before the coming of the nomads, and what the Wise had said about them. But she had only vague recollections of complaints that winters were becoming worse than they had been when the complainers were younger. The huntresses had scoffed at that, saying it was just old age catching up.

But the Wise had been right. These past three winters were no fluke. The sisters said the winters were getting harsher, and had been worsening for more than a generation. Further, they said this was only the beginning, that the weather would worsen much more before it began getting better. But what matter? It was beyond her control. It was a cycle she would not see end. Braydic said it would be centuries before the cycle reversed itself, and centuries more before normalcy asserted itself again.

She spied a familiar figure climbing the treacherously icy steps leading to the ramparts. She ignored it, knowing it was Grauel. Grauel, whom she had not seen in weeks, and whom she missed, and yet . . .

Grauel leaned into the teeth of the wind as she approached, determined to invade Marika's private space. Her teeth were chattering when she reached Marika.

"What're you doing up here in weather like this, pup? You'll catch your death."

"I like it here, Grauel. Especially at this time of year. I can come out here and think without being interrupted."

Grauel ignored the hint. "They're talking about you down there, pup." Marika noted the familiar form of speech—which even now Grauel turned to only when she was stressed—but maintained her aloofness. Grauel continued, "I just heard them. I had the duty. Gorry again. Talking to the senior. As viciously as ever, but this time I think she may have found a sympathetic ear. What have you done?"

"Nothing."

"Something, certainly. You've frightened Gorry so badly she is insisting you be sent to the Maksche cloister come spring."

That startled Marika. It was an about-face for Gorry, who till now had wanted her very existence concealed from the cloister at Maksche, of which Akard was a subservient satellite. Though she had done nothing specific to alarm Gorry, the old instructress had read her better than she had suspected. Yet another argument for exercising caution. The old silth counted experience and superior knowledge among her advantages in their subtle, bittersweet, unacknowledged duel.

"I still don't understand them, Grauel. Why are they afraid of me?" Gorry she understood on a personal level. Gorry feared because she had whelped a powerful hatred in her pupil. But Gorry's fear was far more than just a dread of Marika's vengeance. Without comprehending, Marika knew it was far more complex than that, and knew that part of Gorry's fear was, to some extent, shared by all the older silth of the packfast.

Grauel said what had been said before, by herself, Barlog, and especially by Braydic. But Marika did not relate to it any better now.

"It's not that they fear what you are now, Marika. They dread what you might become. Gorry insists you're the strongest pupil she's ever encountered, or even heard of.

Including those with whom she trained, and she claims those were some of the strongest talents of the modern age. What truth there? Who knows? They're all self-serving liars. But one fact remains undeniable. You have an air of doom that makes them uneasy."

Marika almost turned. This was something a little different from what she usually heard. "An air of doom? What does that mean?"

"I don't know for sure. I'm just telling you what I've heard. And what I've heard is, Gorry believes you are something more than you. Something mythic. A fang in the jaws of fate, if you will. Gorry came up with the idea a long time ago. The others used to scoff. They don't anymore. Even those who try to find ways to thwart Gorry. You have done something that makes even your champions uneasy."

Marika reviewed the past few months. There had been nothing at all that was different from what had gone before. Except that she had reached the brink of physical maturation and been ordered to take a daily draft of a potion which would prevent the onset of her first estrus.

"I don't see it, Grauel. I don't feel like I'm carrying any doom around."

"Would you know if you did, pup? Did Jiana?"

Gorry's word. Jiana. In a moment of anger the old silth had called her Jiana one day recently. "That's a myth, Grauel. Anyway, Jiana wasn't even meth."

The demigoddess Jiana had been the offspring of a rheum-greater and the all-father avatar of the All, Gyerlin, who had descended from the great dark and had impregnated Jiana's dam in her sleep. It was not accepted doctrine. It was a story, like many other tales from the dawn of time. A prescientific attempt to explain away mysteries.

When Jiana had become an adult, she had carried curses around the world, and in her wake all the animals had lost their powers of speech and reason. All but the meth, who had been forewarned by Gyerlin and had hidden themselves away where Jiana could not find them.

It was an ancient tale, distorted by a thousand generations of retellings. Any truth it might have held once had to have been leached away by the efforts of storytellers to improve upon the original. Marika accepted it only as what it was upon its face, an explanation of why the meth were the only intelligent, talking animals. She did not see that the myth had any connection with her present situation.

She said as much to Grauel.

"Myth or not, Gorry is calling you her little Jiana. And some of the others are taking her seriously. They are certain you have been touched by the All." Which expression could have two meanings. In this case Marika knew she could interpret it as a polite way of saying she was insane.

"Someone has been touched by the All, Grauel. And I don't think it is me. These silth are not very down to earth when you look at them closely."

Marika had been very much surprised to discover that the silth, for all their education and knowledge resources, were far more mystically and ritualistically inclined than the most primitive of nomads. They honored a score of days of obligation of which she had never before heard. They offered daily propitiation to both the All and the lesser forces with which they dealt. They made sacrifices on a scale astonishing to one for whom sacrifice had meant a weekly bowl of gruel set outside the packstead gate, with a pot of ormon beer, and a small animal delivered to Machen Cave before the quarterly conjunction of the two biggest moons. The silth were devil-ridden. They still feared specters supposedly cast down when the All had supplanted earlier powers. They feared shadows that had come with the All but which were supposed to be enchained irrevocably in other worlds. They especially feared those—always wehrlen—who might be able to summon those shadows against them.

Marika had observed several of the higher ceremonies by sneaking through her loophole. Those rituals had almost no impact upon those-who-dwell, as the silth called the things Marika thought of as ghosts. And those things were the only supernatural forces Marika recognized. At the moment she seriously questioned the existence of the All itself, let alone those never-seen shadows that haunted her teachers.

The ghosts needed no propitiation that Marika could see. Insofar as she could tell, they remained indifferent to the mortal plane most all the time. They responded to it, apparently only in curiosity, at times of high stress. And acted upon it only when controlled by one with the talent.

Doomstalker. That was Jiana's mystic title. The huntress in search of something she could never find, something that was always behind her. Insofar as Marika could see, the doomstalker was little more than a metaphor for change.

The doomstalker was a powerful silth myth, though, and Marika suspected that Gorry, fearful of what her own future held, was playing upon it cynically in an effort to gain backing from the other older sisters. None of the Akard silth liked Gorry, but they grudgingly respected her for what she had been before being sent into exile.

Even so, she would have to do some tall convincing before being permitted more blatant excesses toward her pupil. Of that Marika was confident.

Caution. Caution. That was all it would take.

"I am no doomstalker, Grauel. And I have no ambitions. I'm just doing what I have to do so we can survive. They need not fear me."

She had slipped into a role she played for Grauel and Barlog both, in their rare meetings, for she feared that Grauel, at least, in her own effort to survive reported her every remark. "I sincerely believe that I will become the sort of sister who never leaves the cloister and seldom uses her talent for anything but teaching silth pups."

Were her suspicions insane? It seemed mad to suspect everyone of malice. One meth, certainly. In any packstead there were enmities as well as friendships. Every packstead had its old-against-young conflicts, its Gorry-against-Marika. Pohsit had been proof of that. But to suspect the entire packfast of being against her, subtly and increasingly—even though the suspicion was encouraged by Braydic, Grauel, and Barlog—particularly for reasons she herself found mystical and inaccessible, stank of the rankest madness.

So it might be mad. She was convinced, and being convinced she dared do nothing but act as if it were true. Any concession to reason would be folly.

Why did the silth play their games of sisterhood? Or did every silth sister come to stand to all others as Marika was coming to stand to hers? Was sisterhood just a mask shown the outside world? An image with which the rulers awed the ruled? Was the reality continual chaos within the cloister wall? The squabble of starving pups battling over scraps?

Grauel intruded upon her thoughts. "I can't make you believe me, Marika. But I am bound to warn you. We are still Degnan."

Marika had definite, powerful feelings about that, but she did not air them. Grauel and Barlog both became sullen and hurt if she even hinted that the Degnan pack was a thing of the past. They had taken the Chronicle from her when they had discovered she was no longer keeping it up. Barlog had gone so far as to learn a better style of calligraphy so she could keep the Chronicle.

They were good huntresses, those two. They had given the packfast no reason to regret taking them in. They served it well. But they were fools, racked by sentimentality. And they were traitors to their ideals. Were they not working against her, their own packmate?

"Thank you, Grauel. I appreciate your concern. Please excuse my manners. I had a difficult morning. One of Gorry's more difficult tests."

Grauel's lips pulled back in a fierce snarl. For a moment Marika was tempted to press, to test the genuineness of the show. To employ Grauel as a blade in her contest with Gorry. But no. That was what someone had tried against her on the Rift. And the effort had earned nothing but contempt for the unknown one who had manipulated another into acting in her stead. The reckoning with Gorry was something she would have to handle herself.

So, when Grauel showed no sign of departing, she continued, "Thank you, Grauel. Please let me be. I need the song of the wind."

"It is not a song, pup. It is a death wail. But as you will."

Give Grauel that much. She did not subscribe to the clutch of honorifics which Marika was due, even as a silth in training. Had there been witnesses . . . But she knew Marika abhorred the whole artificial structure of honor in which the silth wrapped themselves.

As Grauel stalked away, cradling her spear-cum-badge of office, Marika reflected that she was becoming known for communing with the wind. No doubt Gorry and her cronies listed that as another fragment of evidence against her. Jiana had spoken with the wind, and the north wind had been her closest ally, sometimes carrying her around the world. More than one sister had asked—teasingly so far— what news she heard from the north.

She never answered, for they would not understand what she would say. She would say that she heard cold, she heard ice, she heard the whisper of the great dark. She would say that she heard the whisper of tomorrow.

Chapter Eleven

I

Gorry failed in her effort to rid Akard of its most bizarre tenant. Marika did not go to the Maksche cloister with the coming of spring. The senior was not yet sufficiently exercised with her most intractable student silth to accept the loss of face passing the problem would bring.

Hopeless as their hopes were, the exiles of Akard tried making themselves look good in the eyes of their distant seniors. Sometimes the winds of silth politics shifted at the senior cloisters and old exiles were derusticated. Not often, but often enough to serve as an incentive. A whip, Marika thought. A fraud.

Whatever, the senior did not wish to lose face by passing along such a recalcitrant student.

She was not shy, though, about getting her least favorite pupil out of Akard for the summer.

The orders had come not from Maksche but from beyond, from the most senior cloister of the Reugge sisterhood. The nomads were to be cleared from the upper Ponath. No

excuses would be accepted. Dread filled Akard. To Marika
that dread seemed unfocused, as much caused by the sisterhood's far, mysterious rulers as by the more concrete threat
of the hordes close by.

Marika went out with the first party to leave. It consisted
of forty meth, only three of whom were silth. One young far-
toucher. One older silth to command. Thirty-seven huntresses, all drawn from among the refugees. And one dark-
sider. Marika.

Maybe they hoped she would be inadequate to the task.
Maybe they hoped her will would fail when it came time to
reach down and grasp the deadly ghosts and fling them
against the killers of the upper Ponath. Or maybe they had
not had the webs drawn over their eyes the way she thought.
Maybe they knew her true strength.

She did not worry it long. The hunt demanded too much
concentration.

They went out by day, in immediate pursuit of nomads
seen watching the fortress. The nomads saw them coming
and fled. The huntresses slogged across the newly thawed
fields. Within minutes Marika's fine boots were caked with
mud to her knees. She muttered curses and tried to keep
track of the prey. The nomads could be caught up when
night fell.

Barlog marched to her left. Grauel marched to her right.
The two huntresses watched their own party more closely
than they watched the inimical forest.

"You look smug," Marika told Grauel.

"We are." Both huntresses were in a high good humor
Marika initially assessed as due to the fact that they were
outside Akard for the first time in six months. "We tricked
them. They thought they would be able to send you out
without us along to look out for you."

Maybe that explained the scowls from Arhdwehr, the
silth in charge. Marika peered at the older silth's back and
expressed her own amusement.

The hunt was supposed to follow the north bank of the

east fork of the Hainlin as far as the nether edge of country formerly occupied by settled meth. Then it was to swing through the hills to the south, loop again north almost to the Rift, drift down to the east fork again, then head home. That meant five hundred miles of travel minimum, in no real set pattern after leaving the Hainlin in the east. Basically, they were to wander the eastern half of the upper Ponath all summer, living off the land and slaughtering invaders. Marika's would be but one of a score of similar parties.

For a long time very little happened. Once again, as in the summer of the journey to the Rift, the nomads seemed capable of staying out of their path. When the hunt passed below the site of the Degnan packstead, Marika, Barlog, and Grauel gazed up at the decaying stockade and refused to take a closer look. The Laspe packstead they did visit, but nothing remained there save vaguely regular lines on the earth and cellar infalls where loghouses had stood.

Stirring a midden heap, Marika uncovered a scorched and broken chakota doll—and nearly lost her composure.

"What troubles you, pup?" Barlog asked.

Throat too tight for speech, she merely held out the broken doll. Barlog was puzzled.

Marika found her voice. "My earliest memory is of a squabble with Kublin. I broke his chakota. He got so mad he threw mine into the fire." She had not thought of, or dreamed of, her littermate for a long time. Recalling him now, with a chakota in her paw, brought back all the pain redoubled. "The Mourning. We still owe them their Mourning."

"Someday, pup. Someday. It will come." Barlog scratched her behind the ears, gently, and she did not shy away, though she was too old for that.

Approaching the Plenthzo Valley, they happened upon a packstead that had been occupied till only a few hours before. "Some of them have changed their ways," Grauel observed.

It was obvious the place had been abandoned hurriedly.

"They *do* know where we are and what we are doing," Marika said. She frowned at the sky for no reason she understood. And without consulting Arhdwehr—who was plundering deserted food stores—she ordered a half dozen huntresses into the surrounding woods to look for signs of watchers.

Arhdwehr was very angry when she learned what Marika had done. But she restrained her temper. Though just a week into the venture, she realized already that the savages with whom she traveled responded far better to the savage silth pup than they did to her. Too strong a confrontation might not be wise.

Marika had sent those huntresses that Grauel felt were the best. So she believed them when they returned and reported that the party was not being stalked by nomad scouts.

"They must have their own silth with them," she told Grauel and Barlog. "So they sense us coming in time to scatter."

"That many silth?" Barlog countered. "If there were that many, they would fight us. Anyway, sheer chance ought to put more of them into our path." The only encounters thus far had been two with lone huntresses out seeking game. Those the Akard huntresses had destroyed without difficulty or requiring help from the silth.

While searching for the best food stores, Arhdwehr made a discovery. She told the others, "I know how they are doing it. Staying out of our way." But she would not explain.

Marika poked around. She found nothing. But intuition and Arhdwehr's behavior made her suspect it came down to something like the devices Braydic used to communicate with Maksche.

Which might explain how the packstead had been warned. But how had the reporter known where the hunting party was?

Ever so gently, so it would seem to be Arhdwehr's idea, Marika suggested that the party might spend a day or two inside that packstead, resting. It had been a hard trail up from Akard. Arhdwehr adopted the idea. Her point won, Marika collected Grauel and Barlog. "Did you find any of the herbs and roots I told you to watch for?"

"Everything but the grubs," Grauel replied. She was baffled. Almost from her first contact with them after their arrival at Akard, Marika had had them gathering odds and ends from the woods whenever they left the fortress.

She replied, "I did not think we would find any of those. It is far too early yet. And too cold. Even the summers have become so cool that they have become rare. However . . ." With a gesture of triumph she produced a small sealed earthenware jar she had brought from the fortress. "I brought some along. I found them the summer we went to the Rift. Find me a pot. And something I can use as a cutting board."

They settled apart from the others—which drew no attention because it was their custom already—and Marika went to work. "I hope my memory is good. I only saw this done once, when Bhlase made the poison for our spears and arrows."

"Poison?" Barlog looked faintly distressed.

"I am not without a certain low, foul cunning," Marika said lightly. "I have been gathering the ingredients for years, waiting for this chance. Do you object?"

"Not with the thought," Grauel said. "They deserve no better. They are vermin. You exterminate vermin." Her hatred spoke strongly. "But poison? That is the recourse of a treacherous male."

Barlog objected, too. Eyes narrow, she said, "Why do I think you will make poison here where none will know what you do, and test it on those none will object to seeing perish, and someday I will find myself wondering at the unexplainable death of someone back at the packfast?"

Marika did not respond.

The huntresses exchanged looks. They understood, though they did not want to do so. Barlog could not conceal her disgust. Perhaps, Marika thought, she would now discover if they were the creatures of the senior.

They continued to object. Poison was not the way of a huntress. Nor even of the Wise. The way of a stinking silth, maybe. But only the worst of that witch breed. . . ."

They said nothing, though. And Marika ignored their silent censure.

She cooked the poison down with the utmost care. And just before the hunting party departed the packstead—where everything had been left much as found, at her insistence—she put three quarters of the poison into those nomad food stores she thought likely to see use soon.

The hunting party crossed the Plenthzo and continued on eastward for three nights. Then, after day's camp had been set, Marika told Grauel and Barlog, "It is time to return and examine our handiwork."

Grauel scowled. Barlog said, "Do not spread the blame upon us, pup. *You* played the male's poison game."

They were very irked, those two, but they did not refuse to accompany her.

They traveled more quickly as a threesome with a specific destination and no need to watch for prey. They returned to the packstead the second evening after leaving camp.

The nomads had not been forewarned of their approach. Marika filed that fact for future consideration. Then she crouched outside the stockade and ducked through her loophole, went inside the packstead.

As she had guessed from evidence seen on site, the packstead was home to a very large number of nomads. More than two hundred adults. But now half those were dead or in the throes of a terrible stomach disorder. And there were no silth there to contest with her.

She did what she believed had to be done, without remorse or second thoughts. But dealing with so many was more difficult than she had anticipated. The invaders realized the nature of the attack within seconds and responded by counterattacking. They very nearly got to her before she succeeded in terrorizing them into scattering.

Then it was over. And she was chagrined. She had managed to destroy no more than fifteen.

Grauel and Barlog, ever taciturn, were quieter than usual on the return trail as they pursued the main party. Marika pretended to be unaware of their continued displeasure. She said, "We were able to get close without difficulty. I wonder why. Two possibilities suggest themselves. The fact that we were a small party and the fact that we came by day. Which do you suppose it might have been? Or might it have been a combination of the two?"

Neither Grauel nor Barlog cared to sustain her speculations. She let them drop. And once they reached the site of the camp they had deserted, she bothered them no more, for from then on they were too busy tracking.

II

Arhdwehr flew into a rage. "You will not do that again, ever, pup! Do you understand? You will not go off on your own. If you had found more trouble than you could handle, there would have been no hope for you. No help. I had no idea where to look for you."

"If I had gotten into more trouble than I could handle, all your problems would have been solved for you," Marika countered. Her tone was such that Arhdwehr understood immediately exactly what she was implying. For a moment the older silth looked abashed, which was a happening so rare Marika savored it and decided she would treasure it.

Arhdwehr controlled herself. After a time, in a reasonable tone, she asked, "Have you decided how it was that you were able to approach them undetected?"

Marika shared her speculations.

"We will experiment. There must be other such packsteads. We will seek them out. We will pass them by if they are abandoned, then we will turn back and strike swiftly a few days later. We will try it with small parties, approaching both by day and by night."

Arhdwehr assumed that a large circle around the hunting party was alert to the presence of the hunting party. Given the nomad propensity for evasion, she felt safe scattering scouts widely in search of packsteads occupied by nomads.

Marika was pleased. "She has a temper," she told Grauel. "But she is flexible."

Still sullen, the huntress replied, "I admit it is seldom one sees that in a silth sister."

Marika was irked at the way her two packmates had distanced themselves, but she said nothing. They would have to learn flexibility themselves. Without coaching, which they would resist, if only because they were older and believed that gave them certain rights.

The huntresses discovered that a packstead could not be approached in large numbers by day, or even in small numbers by night. But by day twos and threes could close in and remain undiscovered till it was too late for the nomads.

The far-toucher reported the news to Akard. The sisters at the fortress passed the word to the other parties in the field, none of which had had much luck.

"They have their means of communication," Marika mused one evening. "They will figure it out and respond. Probably by abandoning their packsteads altogether. Which means we must begin considering ways to hunt them down once they revert to old ways."

Arhdwehr said, "That will be easier, if more work. Being on the move will rob them of much of their communications capacity." She would not expand upon that when Marika asked questions.

"They are weird, that is why," Grauel said when Marika later wondered why most silth refused to discuss some subjects with her. "Everything is a secret with them. Ask them what color the sky is and they will not tell you."

The daytime sneaking worked well for several weeks. The hills south of the Hainlin were spotted heavily by packsteads taken over by the nomads. The party fell far behind its planned schedule. Then a turn back found a packstead still empty. And the next packstead located had been abandoned a week.

Arhdwehr tightened the party up, not wanting to be too scattered if hostiles appeared. She expected the nomads to become less passive. She, though, seemed to be increasingly disaffected, muttering imprecations upon the silth of Maksche. Marika did not understand. And, of course, Arhdwehr would not explain.

III

The hunting party had given up hope of catching any more nomads unaware. They were headed toward the Hainlin, hoping for better hunting on the northward leg. Arhdwehr was pleased with what had been accomplished, though she would have liked even longer strings of trophy ears. Marika had begun to believe the entire hunt was an exercise in futility. She suspected that a score of nomads were escaping for each one even located, let alone destroyed. And Akard's strength was being sapped.

Out west of the fortress the nomads were fighting back. There had to be a better way.

The far-toucher wakened suddenly in the middle of the day, when the party was just a day's travel south of the east fork. She squeaked, "A touch! Pain. A sister . . . just west of us. They are being attacked. She is the only silth left alive."

Marika stared at the far-toucher, who seemed panicky and confused. Then she felt the touch, too. It was a strong one, driven by the agony of a wound. She felt the direction. "Up!" she snarled. "Everybody up. Weapons only. Leave your packs." She snatched her bow and javelin. Grauel and Barlog did likewise, questioning nothing, though they had many questions. Marika trotted toward the source of pain.

Two thirds of the huntresses did not so much as glance at

Arhdwehr for approval. The others scarcely delayed long enough to see the older silth begin to fall into a rage.

It had been coming from the beginning. Marika had not seen it, but Grauel and Barlog had and had spoken with most of the huntresses. Marika realized there was, and would be, a problem only after she had done the thing.

Grauel admonished her softly as they ran through the forest. "You must learn to reflect on the consequences of your actions, pup," the huntress said. "You could have done that politely and let Arhdwehr claim it as her own idea."

Marika did not argue. Grauel was right. She had not thought. And because she had not taken a few seconds there might be trouble. Certainly, what sympathy she had won from Arhdwehr was now dead.

Silth were extremely jealous of their prerogatives.

The party under attack was just five miles away. An easy run for huntresses. Half an hour. But half an hour was too long.

Forty-seven multilated bodies in Akard dress lay scattered through the woods. Twice that many nomads lay with them, many twisted in that way they did after silth magic touched their hearts. Marika stared at the massacred, filled with a hard anger.

"They know we are close," Grauel said. "They fled without their dead." She knelt. "Mercy-slew their most badly wounded."

"Which way did they go?"

Grauel pointed. Marika looked to Arhdwehr, deferring this time. The older silth's lips pulled back in a snarl of promise. "How long ago did they run?"

Grauel replied, "Ten minutes at most."

The far-toucher said, "We left our things. We could lose them."

Marika gave her a fierce look. And, to her surprise, Arhdwehr did the same. The older silth said, "Marika, you and your friends take the point." To Grauel, she added, "Point out individual trails if they start scattering."

Everyone fell silent, froze. A far *tak-tak-takk*ing echoed

up the valley along which the nomads had fled. Then came several sounds like far, muted thunder.

"What in the All?" Arhdwehr exploded angrily. "Go! But slow down after the first mile."

Marika leapt down the trail a step behind Grauel. Barlog panted at her heels. The others came behind, making no effort to keep quiet. The rustle of brush would be heard by no one above that ferocious uproar ahead.

The sound swelled quickly. After a mile Grauel slowed as instructed. Marika guessed the noise's source to be a half mile farther along. Grauel trotted another five hundred yards, then suddenly stabbed sideways with her spear and cut into the brush, headed uphill. Marika followed. Three minutes later Grauel halted. The hunting party piled up behind Marika.

The hillside gave a good view of a fire burn where tree trunks lay strewn like a pup's pick-up sticks. It was an old burn, with most of the black weathered away. Several hundred nomads crouched or lay behind the fallen trees. The *tak-tak-takk*ing noise came from a slope beyond the nomads.

Something went *whump!* over there. Moments later earth geysered near a clutch of nomads. Thunder echoed off the hills. Meth screamed. Several nomads tried to flee. The *tak-tak* redoubled. All who were erect jerked around and fell, lay still.

They were dead. Marika sensed that instantly. "What is going on over there?" she asked Arhdwehr.

It was something secret. The older silth ignored her question. "You stay put," Arhdwehr told her. "Use your talent. The rest of you follow me." She let out an ululation that would have done any huntress proud.

The huntresses hesitated only a moment, saw Marika do as she was told, followed. A howl of despair went up from the nomads.

The chatter from the far woods lasted only moments longer.

Marika wasted only a moment more speculating. The

odds were heavy against her party. The nomads would obliterate them unless she did what she was supposed to do.

It was not a long fight, and scarcely a pawful of nomads escaped. When Marika walked through the burn afterward, she stepped over scores of bodies contorted but unmarked by wounds. A bloody Arhdwehr watched her with an odd look. "You did exceptionally well today, pup." A trace of fear edged her voice.

"The rage came," Marika said. She kicked a weapon away from fingers still twitching. "Would it not have been wiser to have stayed on the hillside and used our bows?"

"The rage came upon me also. I wanted to feel hot blood upon my paws."

Marika stared up that slope whence the strange sounds had come. "What was that, Arhdwehr?"

The elder silth shrugged.

"Males," Marika said. "I sensed that much. And you must know. Why is it hidden?"

Arhdwehr's gaze followed hers. "There are rules, pup. There are laws." To the huntresses, most of whom had survived, she said, "Forget the ears. This day's work is not done." She started toward the source of the mysterious sounds, traveling in a squat, darting from one log to another.

The huntresses all looked to Marika. Even the far-toucher hesitated. Marika could not help being both flattered and dismayed. She waved them forward.

"You made the move," Grauel whispered.

"What move?" Instead of hurrying after Arhdwehr, she took time to examine her surroundings.

"As strength goes."

Marika slipped a finger into a hole something had drilled through four inches of hard word. She stared at the torn bodies lying near the site of the explosion she had witnessed. "No, Grauel. It was not that. I just did what needed doing without thinking about the politics." That was a word that existed only in the silth secret languages. "What could have done this?"

"Maybe you will find out if you are there when she catches whoever it is she is chasing."

Marika scowled.

Grauel was amused, but only briefly. She surveyed the carnage. "Who would have thought this could occur in this world? And for what, Marika?"

Barlog was studying the corpses nearby, trying to read pack fetishes and having no luck. Few of the dead even wore them. She rolled a corpse, knelt, pulled something from its chest. She presented it to Marika a moment later.

It was a blood-encrusted, curved fragment of metal. Marika examined it briefly, tossed it aside. "I don't know. We'd better catch up."

The run was long and hard. Marika sensed the males in front in a tight group of twenty, loping along at a steady, ground-devouring pace. They seemed to know exactly where they were going and what they were doing. And that a band of huntresses was on their trail. They increased their pace whenever Arhdwehr increased hers.

"Who would have thought it?" Grauel gasped. "That males could run us into the ground."

"We ran six miles before they started," Barlog countered.

"Save your breath," Marika snapped.

They moved up through the party till Marika was running at Arhdwehr's heels. She was young and strong, but the pace told. Why were they doing this?

Someone farther back said, "We will catch them after dark."

Arhdwehr tossed back one black look and increased her pace. Marika had to admire the silth. She was showing exceptional endurance for one who led a sedentary life. Marika started a warning. "Mistress. . . ."

Arhdwehr held up. "I sense it," she gasped.

They had crested a ridge. The valley beyond reeked of many meth. All male meth.

Silth senses were not needed to detect the presence of meth, though. Smoke tainted the air, a smoke filled with the aromas of cooking and trash burning. There was another smell, too, an unfamiliar, penetrating, acrid scent that brought water into Marika's nose.

A flurry of activity broke out below, out of sight. There was a series of soft, rising whines that, one after another, in less than a minute began fading into the distance.

Arhdwehr cursed and sprang downhill at a dead run. She trailed an anger as great as any Marika had managed to inspire.

More whines faded away.

Marika charged after the older silth. Moments later Arhdwehr broke into a clearing, a dozen steps ahead. With a howl she launched her javelin. Marika broke cover just as the missile flashed into the darkness between two trees a hundred feet away. The gray curve of something big disappeared in that same instant, behind a swirl of dust and flying needles. The javelin did it no harm.

Marika gagged and gasped. She needed air desperately. But that male camp was choked with the foul smell that had stung her nose on the ridge. She fought for breath while she surveyed the clearing.

"Khronen!"

At least twenty males—tradermales—sat around a campfire to one side, all gazing at the huntresses. They appeared to be cooking and pursuing other mundane chores. Among them was the tradermale Khronen.

Grauel and Barlog recognized him, too. They followed as Marika stalked toward the males—none of whom bothered to rise or even to cease performing whatever tasks they had at paw. Marika noted the presence of a lot of metal, all of it pointed or edged.

Khronen rose. His eyes narrowed. "Do I know you, young sister?"

Marika glanced at Arhdwehr, who had gone to reclaim her javelin. Marika sensed the swift movement of males pulling away far beyond the elder silth. "Yes," she replied. "Or, say, you knew me when I was something else. What is this? What are you doing here?"

"Preparing our evening meal. We would invite you to join us, but I do not think we have enough to guest so many."

"So? Grauel. How many tradermale-made weapons have you seen these past two months?"

"I have not kept count. Too many."

"Look around. Perhaps we have found the source."

Grauel's teeth appeared in a snarl of anger and surprise. The thought had not occurred to her.

Barlog said, "Let me, Marika." Her tone suggested a strong emotional need.

"All right. You stay, Grauel."

Something flashed across Khronen's features when Barlog spoke. He had recognized her voice, perhaps. He said, "You have not answered my question directly."

"I will ask, male. You will answer."

Twenty-some pairs of eyes turned toward Marika. And she very nearly backed away, startled by the smoldering emotion she saw there.

"You think, perhaps, that we are some of your tame packstead chattels?" Khronen asked. "Ah. The costume distracted me. I know you now. Yes. Very much the image of your dam. Even in your arrogance." He looked over her shoulder. Marika sensed that Arhdwehr had come up behind her. But she did not look back.

A hard-eyed male near Khronen said, "And at such a young age, too. Pity." His gaze never left her face.

All those eyes continued to bore into her.

It was a moment of crisis, she knew. A moment when the wrong word could cause a lot of trouble. Khronen was right. These were not the sort of males to which she was accustomed. She sensed that they would as soon battle her as be polite. That there was no awe of her in them, either because she was female or because she was silth.

What sort of male did not fear silth?

Barlog returned. "This is the only blade I found." Other than those close to male paws, of course.

Marika took it. "Grauel, give me one of those we captured." One was in her paw in a moment. She examined both blades, shrugged, presented both to Arhdwehr. Arhdwehr scarcely glanced at them.

"Not the same maker. Pup, suppose you take this opportunity to restrain your natural exuberance and allow one with a more diplomatic nature to handle communication?" She stepped past Marika, passed both weapons to Khronen, who was the oldest of the males. Some were little older than Marika. In fact, many had the look of upper Ponath refugees.

Grauel whispered, "That was well-done."

"What?" Marika asked.

"She saved you from trouble, salvaged your pride, and put you in your place with a single sentence. Well-done, indeed."

Marika had not seen that in it. But when she glanced around she saw that the other huntresses had read it that way. Instead of being irked, though, she was relieved to be out of the confrontation with Khronen.

She stepped up behind Arhdwehr, who had settled to the earth facing Khronen. The tradermale had seated himself, too. He barely glanced at the blades before passing them to the tradermale on his right. That one had not shifted his eyes to Arhdwehr. His gaze, frankly curious, bored into Marika as though trying to unmask her secret heart. There was an air of strength about him that made Marika suspect he was as important here as was Khronen.

He passed the blades back to Arhdwehr.

Khronen continued, "I know, sister. That is why we are here. Seeking the source. And doing much what you are."

"Which is?"

"Exterminating vermin."

"The last I heard, the upper Ponath was classified a Tech Two Zone."

"Your communications are more reliable than mine, sister. I have no far-toucher. I presume it still is. Is the pup your commer? I would not have guessed it of one of the Degnan."

Marika's ears twitched. Something about the way he said that. . . . He was lying.

"Dark-walker," Arhdwehr replied. She slipped a paw into a belt pouch, removed something shiny, passed it over. "Those who shatter the law should take care to clean up their back trail."

Khronen fingered the object, grunted, passed it to his right. Both males stared at Marika. Khronen's face became blank. "Dark-sider, eh? So young, and with her dam's temperament. A dangerous combination."

"Impetuous and undisciplined, yes. But let us discuss matters more appropriate to the moment. You will be in communication with Critza after we depart. Remind your seniors that Critza's walls mark the limit of brethren extra-territoriality in the upper Ponath. Only within those limits is overteching permissible. Most Senior Gradwohl is immutably determined on such points."

"We will relay your admonition, if we should discover a male far-toucher hidden in the crowd here. Though I doubt anyone there needs the reminder. How was the hunting, sister?" He did not look at Arhdwehr at all, but continued to stare at Marika. So did the male on his right.

She wondered what was on their minds.

"You would know better than I, I suspect," Arhdwehr replied. "You have eyes that see even where silth cannot."

"Here? In a Tech Two Zone? I fear not, sister. We have had a bit of luck, I admit. We have helped a few hundred savages rejoin the All. But I fear it is like bailing a river with a leaky teacup. They will breed faster than we can manufacture javelins."

Marika had noticed few pups anywhere. The numbers of old and young both were disproportionately small among the nomads she had encountered.

Some sort of fencing was going on between Arhdwehr and the tradermale. But whatever it was about, it was not dangerous. The other males went back to what they had been doing, occasionally glancing her way as though she were some strange beast that talked and behaved with inexcusable manners. She began to feel very young and very ignorant and very self-conscious.

She backed several steps away. "Grauel, there is more going on in this world than we know."

"You are catching on only now?"

"I mean—"

"I know what you mean, pup. And I had thought your innocence was feigned. Perhaps you do not hear as much in silth quarters as we do in ours."

"Silth do not gossip, Grauel."

Barlog said, "Perhaps she does not hear because she does not listen. She sees no one but that communicator creature." Barlog continued to watch Khronen with as much intensity as he watched Marika. "They say you may be in line for a great future, pup. *I* say you will never see it until you begin to see. And to hear. To look and to listen. Each dust mote has a message and lesson, if you will but heed it."

"Indeed?" Barlog sounded like one of her teachers. "Perhaps you are right. Do you know Khronen, Barlog? Is there something between you two?"

"No."

"He was Laspe. Dam knew him when he was a pup."

Barlog had no comment.

Arhdwehr rose, walked back to where she had left her javelin stuck into the earth. She yanked it free, trotted up the trail along which the hunting party had approached the male camp. The others followed in a ragged file. Baffled, Marika joined them. Grauel trotted ahead of her, Barlog behind. She glanced back before she left the clearing. Khronen was watching her still. As was his companion. They were talking.

Marika wondered if the party ought not to double back after a while. . . .

Arhdwehr kept a steady pace all the way to the place where they had left their packs. Marika fell into the rhythm of the run and spent the time trying to unravel the significance of what had happened during that long and bloody day.

* * *

Two nights later the hunting party crossed the east fork of the Hainlin, headed north. The remainder of the season was uneventful. Marika spent most of her time trying to learn the lesson Barlog claimed she needed to learn. And she practiced pretending to be what she was supposed to be. She succeeded well enough. She managed to get back on Arhdwehr's good side. As much as ever anyone could be.

Early snows chased them back to Akard ten days earlier than planned. Marika suspected the upper Ponath was in for a winter more fierce than the past three.

She also felt she had wasted a summer. All that blood and anger had done nothing to weaken the nomads. The great hunt had been but a gesture made to mollify those shrill and mysterious silth who ruled the Reugge from afar. Only one result was certain. Many familiar faces had vanished from among Akard's population.

Marika visited Braydic even before she made her initial courtesy call upon Gorry. She told Braydic all about her summer, hoping the communicator's reactions would illuminate some of what she had seen. But she learned very little.

Braydic understood what she was doing. She was amused. "In time, Marika. In time. When you go to Maksche."

"Maksche?"

"Next summer. A certainty, I think, from hints my truesister has dropped. If we get through this winter."

If.

Chapter Twelve

I

Marika was four years too young to be considered a true silth sister, yet she had exhausted the knowledge of those who taught her. In less than four years she had devoured knowledge others sometimes did not master in a lifetime. The sisters were more frightened of her than ever. They very much wanted to pass her on to the Maksche cloister immediately, but they could not.

It was yet the heart of the fourth winter. Nothing would move for months. The snows lay fifteen to twenty feet deep. In the north, in places, the wind sweeping across the fields had drifted it to the top of the packfast wall. The workers had dug tunnels underneath in order to connect the fortress with the powerhouse. It was essential that the plume water be kept running. If the powerhouse froze up, there would be no communication with the rest of the Reugge sisterhood.

The times were strange in more than the personal way Marika knew. By staying near Braydic whenever she was free, she had begun to catch snatches of messages drifting in from Maksche. Messages that disturbed the older silth more then ever.

For a long time the Reugge Community had been involved in a sort of low-grade, ongoing conflict with the more powerful Serke sisterhood. Lately there had been some strong provocations from the stronger order. There were some who suspected a connection with strange events in the upper Ponath, though no hard accusations were made even in secret. The Akard sisters were afraid there was truth in that, and that the provocation here would escalate.

As near as Marika could tell, it seemed to be packwar on a grand scale. She had never seen packwar, but she had heard. In the upper Ponath that meant a few isolated skirmishes, harassment of another pack's huntresses, a rather quick peak into a confrontation which settled everything. Often the fighting was ritualized and consisted entirely of counting coup, with the big battle ending the moment of the first death.

Unless there was blood in it. Bloodfeud was different. Bloodfeud might be fought till one side fled or boasted no more survivors. But bloodfeud was exceedingly rare. Only a few of the Wise of the Degnan had been able to recall the last time bloodfeud plagued the upper Ponath.

The louder the north wind howled and the more bitter its bite, the more Marika met it in her place upon the wall, and whispered back of the coldness and darkness that had found their homes within her mind. There were moments when she suspected she was at least half what Gorry accused, so savage were some of her hatreds.

So it was that she was in her place when the messengers came from Critza, with nomad huntresses upon their tails. She saw the males floundering, recognized their outer wear, saw they were on the edge of collapse from exhaustion. She sensed the triumph in the savages closing in behind them, climbing the slope from the river. She went down inside herself, through her loophole, and reached out over a greater distance than ever before. She ripped the hearts out of the chests of the savages, setting the Hainlin canyons echoing with their screams. Then she touched the messengers and guided them to a point where they could clamber up the snowdrifts to the top of the wall.

She went to meet them, gliding along the icy rampart, not entirely certain how she knew what they were or why their visit would be important, but knowing it all the same. She would bring them inside.

Males inside the packfast proper was unprecedented. The older silth would be enraged by the desecration. Yet Marika was absolutely certain she would be doing right by bringing them across the wall.

Their breaths fogged about them and whipped away on the wind. They panted violently, lung-searingly. Marika sensed that they had been forced to travel long and hard, with death ever snapping at their tails. One collapsed into the powder snow before she reached them.

"Welcome to Akard, tradermales. I trust you bear a message of the utmost importance."

They looked at her with awe and fear, as most outsiders did, but the more so because she was young, and because she still radiated the darkness of death. "Yes," said the tallest of the three. "News from Critza. . . . It is you. The one called Marika. . . ."

She recognized him then. The male who had sat beside Khronen during last summer's confrontation with males. That unshakable self-certainty and confidence were with him no more. That anger, that defiance, had fled him. He shivered not only from the wind.

"It is I," Marika replied, her voice as chill as the wind. "I hope I have not wasted myself guarding you from the savages."

"No. We believe the sisterhood will be very interested in the tidings we bring." He was resilient. Already he had begun to recover himself.

"Come with me. Stay close. Do not stray. You know that an exception is being made. I alone can shield you once we go inside." She led them down, inside, into the great chamber where so often she had faced Gorry's worst, and where all the convocations of the cloister took place. "You will wait here, within the confines of this symbol." She indicated the floor. "If you stray, you will die." She went in search of Gorry.

Logic told her Gorry was not the one to inform. Gorry ran a bit short on basic sense. But tradition and custom, with virtually the force of law, demanded that she deal with her instructress first. It was up to Gorry to decide whether or not the situation required the attention of Senior Koenic.

Perhaps fate took a hand. For Gorry was not alone when Marika found her. Three sisters were with her, including Khles Gibany, who was her superior. "Mistress," Marika said, after impatiently working her way through all the appropriate ceremonials, "I have just come from the wall, where I watched a band of savages pursue three tradermales across the river. Deeming it unlikely that tradermales would be abroad in this weather and near Akard unless they had some critical communication to impart, I helped them to escape their pursuers and allowed them to scale the snow-drifts to the top of the wall. Upon inquiry, I learned that they did indeed bear a message from their senior addressed to the Akard cloister."

"And what was this message, pup?" Gorry asked. Her tone was only as civil as she deemed needful before witnesses. These days Gorry was civil only when appearances required. The passing of time made her ever more like Pohsit.

"I did not enquire, mistress. The nature of the situation suggested that it was not for me to do so. It suggested that I should turn to sisters wiser than I. So I led them down to the main hall, where they might shed the chill in their bones. I told them to wait there. They did suggest that their senior wished them to relate their message before the assembled cloister. It would seem the news they bring is bad."

Gorry became righteous in the extreme. Outsiders allowed into the packfast! *Male* outsiders. Her sisters, following the lead of Khles Gibany, proved to be more flexible. They shushed Gorry and began questioning Marika closely.

"I can tell you no more, sisters," she said, "unless you wish to review my feelings while I stood upon the wall, and the consequent reasoning which lent credence to them."

Gibany rose and manipulated herself onto her crutches. "I will be back soon. I agree with your feelings, Marika. There is something afoot. I will speak with the senior." She departed.

While Gorry glared daggers at Marika for further unsettling her life, the other two silth continued questioning her. They were only killing time, though. Already it was in the paws of Senior Koenic.

They saw the implications Marika had seen. The implications Gorry wished to ignore.

Once upon a time, years earlier, Khles Gibany had told Marika, in response to a question about Gorry: "There are those among us, pup, who prefer to live in myth instead of fact." Marika saw that clearly now.

Tradermales liked silth even less than the run of meth. The silth stand on male role assumption was harder than any packstead female's. The message brought by these males would have to be earthshaking, else they would not have come. And these days earthshaking news meant news about the nomads.

The myth-liver was the first to articulate what everyone was thinking. "The damned Critza fester has been overrun. They are trying to get us to take them in. No, say I. No. No. No. Let them stay out there in the wilderness. Let them fill the cookpots of savages. It is their ilk who have armed the grauken."

Grauken. Marika was startled to hear the word roll off a silth tongue.

"I do not believe they bear tidings of the fall of Critza, mistress. They did not look dispossessed. They just look exhausted and distressed." She did not put much force into her statement. She was being extremely careful with Gorry these days. And striving to build goodwill among the other sisters.

Gibany returned. "We are to report to the hall. We will

hear what the males have to say. Nothing will be decided till
they have spoken."

II

The leader of the tradermales, who made Marika so uneasy,
called himself Bagnel. He was known to some of the sisters.
He had spoken for his packfast before, though Marika did
not recall having ever seen him anywhere but in that far
clearing.

Another lesson: pay attention to everything happening.
There was no telling what might become important in later
days.

Bagnel's history of dealing with silth had led to his selec-
tion as leader of his mission.

"There were seven of us who left Critza," he said, after
explaining his circumstances. "Myself and our six strongest,
best fighters. Nomads caught our wind immediately, though
we followed your own example and traveled by night. Four
of us fell along the way, exhausted, and were taken by
savages. We could not stop to help."

Gorry made nasty remarks about males and was ignored
by all but a small minority of the assembled sisters. Clever
Bagnel had placed a debt upon Akard with his opening
remarks. He implied that the news he carried was worth
four of his brethren's lives.

"Go on," the senior told him. "Gorry. Restrain yourself."

Marika stood behind her instructress, as was proper, and
was embarrassed for her when she heard someone remark,
"Old Gorry is getting senile." It was an intimation that
Gorry would not be taken seriously much longer. Though
Marika nursed her own black hatred, she felt for the old
female.

"The journey took two days—"

"This is not relevant," the senior said. "If the tidings you bear are worthy, we will be in your debt. We are not here to trade. Be direct."

"Very well. Four days ago the nomads attacked Critza again. We drove them off, as we have before, but this time it was a close thing. They have acquired a quantity of modern weapons. They caused us a number of casualties. Their tactics, too, were more refined. Had they been more numerous the fortress would have fallen."

The senior stirred impatiently, but allowed Bagnel to establish the background. Silth exchanged troubled glances and subdued whispers. Marika felt the fur on her spine stir, though she did not quite understand what was being said.

Bagnel's gaze strayed her way several times while he spoke. That did nothing to make her more comfortable.

"We took prisoners," Bagnel continued. "Among them were several huntresses of standing. Upon questioning them we made several interesting discoveries. The most important, from the viewpoint of the sisterhood here, was the unmasking of a plan for an attack upon Akard."

That caused a stir, and considerable amusement. Attack Akard? Savages? That was a joke. The nomads would be slaughtered in droves.

"One of those prisoners had been in on the planning. We obtained all the details she knew." Bagnel drew a fat roll of hide from within his coat. He stripped the skin away to reveal a sheaf of papers. "The master directed that a copy of her testimony be given you." He offered the papers to the senior.

"You appear to take this more seriously than seems warranted," Senior Koenic said. "Here we are in no danger from savages, come they singly or in all the hordes of the north."

"That is not true, Senior. And that is why we risked seven fighters sorely needed at Critza. Not only have the nomads acquired modern weapons; they are convinced that they can neutralize most of your power. They have both silth and wehrlen with them and those will participate in the attack.

So our informant told us. And she was incapable of invention at the time."

Bagnel's gaze strayed to Marika. To her consternation, she found she was unable to meet his eye.

From the reaction of the silth around her, Marika judged that what Bagnel had described was possible. The sisters were very disturbed. She heard the name "Serke" whispered repeatedly, often with a pejorative attached.

Senior Koenic struck the floor three times with the butt of her staff of office. Absolute silence filled the hall. "I will have order here," the senior said. "Order. Are we rowdy packsteaders?" She began to read the papers the tradermales had given her. Her teeth showed ever more as she proceeded. Black anger smoldered behind her eyes.

She lifted her gaze. "You are correct, tradermale. The thing they propose is hideous, but it is possible—assuming they surprised us. You have blessed us. We owe you a great deal. And the Reugge do not forget their debts."

Bagnel made gestures of gratitude and obeisance Marika suspected to be more diplomatic than genuine. He said, "If this is the true feeling of the Akard senior, the Critza master would present a small request."

"Speak."

"There is equally a master plan for the capture of Critza. And it will work even though we know about it. Unless . . ."

"Ah. You did not bring us this dark news out of love." The senior's voice was edged with a brittle sarcasm.

It did not touch the messenger. "The master suggests that you might find it in the Reugge interest to help sustain at least one other civilized stronghold here in the Ponath."

"That may be true. It may not be. To the point, trader."

"As you will, Senior." Bagnel's gaze strayed to Marika once again. "The master has asked that two or three sisters, preferably dark-siders, be sent to help Critza repel the expected attack. They would not be at great risk, as the nomads would not expect their presence. The master feels that, should the nomads suffer massive defeats at both fortresses in rapid succession, they will harass us no further.

At least for this winter. Their own dead will sustain them through the season."

Marika shuddered.

The evidence had been undeniable in the packsteads she had seen last summer. The nomads had let the grauken come in and become a working member of their society. Whatever had shattered the old pack structure and driven them into hording up had changed much more than that.

"Your master thinks well. For a male. He may be correct. Presuming these papers carry the whole story." A hint of a question lurked around the edges of the senior's remark.

"I participated in the questioning, Senior. I am willing to face a silth truthsaying to attest to their authenticity and completeness."

Marika was impressed. A truthsaying was a terrible thing to endure.

"Send Marika," Gorry blurted. "She is perfect for this. And no one will miss her if she were lost."

"Ought to send you," someone muttered. "No one would miss you."

Gorry heard. She scanned the assembly, her expression stricken.

The senior glared at Gorry, angered by the unsolicited suggestion. But then she turned thoughtful.

Marika's heart fell.

"There is truth in what you say, Gorry," Senior Koenic said. "Even though you say it from base motives. Thus does the All mock the littleness in our hearts, making us speak the truth in the guise of lies. Very well, tradermale. You shall have your sisters. We will send three of our youngest and strongest—though not necessarily our most skillful— for they face a journey that will be hard. You will not want to lose any along the way."

Bagnel's face remained stone.

"So? What say you?"

"Thank you, Senior."

Senior Koenic clapped paws. "Strohglay." A sister opened a door and beckoned. A pair of senior workers stepped inside. The senior told them, "Show these males to cells where they may spend the night. Give them of the best food we possess. Tradermale, you will not leave your quarters under any circumstances. Do you understand?"

"Yes, Senior."

Koenic gestured to the workers. They led the males away.

The senior asked, "Are there any volunteers? No? No one wants to see the inside of the mysterious Critza fortress? Marika? Not even you?"

No. Not Marika. She did not volunteer.

Neither did anyone else.

III

Marika did not volunteer. Nevertheless, she went. There was no arguing with Senior Koenic.

Much of the time they traveled in Biter's light, upon snow under which, yards below, the waters of the Hainlin ran colder than a wehrlen's heart. In places that snow was well packed, for the nomads used the rivercourse as their highway through the wilderness, though they traveled only by day.

Braydic said most of the nomads were south of Akard now, harrying the meth who lived down there. She said the stream of invective and impossible instructions from Maksche never ceased. And never did any good. The only way they could enforce their orders was to come north themselves. Which was what Senior Koenic wished to compel.

Marika was miserable and frightened. The stillness of the night was the stillness of death. Its chill was the cold of the grave. Though Biter lingered overhead, she felt the Hainlin canyon was a vast cave, and that cave called up all her old terrors of Machen Cave.

There was something wicked in the night.

"They only sent me because they hope to be rid of me," she told Grauel and Barlog. Both her packmates had volunteered to come when they heard the call for huntress volunteers and learned that Marika had been assigned to go. Marika wondered if the silth could have kept them back had they wanted.

"Perhaps," Barlog said. "And perhaps, if one might speak freely before a sister, you attribute the motives of the guilty few to the innocent many."

Grauel agreed. "You are the youngest, and one of the least popular silth. None can dispute that. But your unpopularity is of your own making, Marika. Though you have been trying. You have been trying. Ah. Wait! Listen and reflect. If you apply reason to your present circumstance, you will have to admit there is no one in Akard more suited to this, the rest of the situation aside. You have become skilled in the silth's darkest ways. The deadly ways. You are young and strong. And you endure the cold better than anyone else."

"If one might dare speak freely before a sister," Barlog said again, "you are whining like a disappointed pup. You are shifting blame to others and refusing responsibility yourself. I recall you in your dam's loghouse. You were not that way then. You were a quiet one, and a dreamer, and a pest to all, but mistress of your own actions. You have developed a regressive streak. And it is not at all attractive in one with so much promise."

Marika was so startled by such bold chiding that she held her tongue. And as she marched, pressed by the pace the tradermales set, she reflected upon what the huntresses had said. And in moments when she was honest with herself, she could not deny the truth underlying their accusations.

She had come to pity herself, in a silth sort of way. She had come to think certain things her due without her having to earn them, as the silth seemed to think the world owed them. She had fallen into one of Gorry's snares.

There had been a time when she had vowed that she would not slip into the set of mind she so despised in her instructress. A time when she had believed her packstead background would immunize her. Yet she was beginning to mirror Gorry.

Many miles later, after much introspection, she asked, "What did you mean when you said 'so much promise,' Barlog?"

Barlog gave her a look. "You never tire of being told that you are special, do you?"

When Marika threatened to explode, Grauel laid one hard paw upon her shoulder. Her grip tightened painfully. "Easy, pup."

Barlog said, "One hears things around the packfast, Marika. They often talk about you showing promise of rising high. As you have been told so many times. Now they are saying you may rise higher than anyone originally suspected, if they teach you well at Maksche cloister."

"If?"

"They're definitely going to send you come summer. This is fact. The senior has asked Grauel and I if we wish to accompany you when you go."

There was a chance that had not occurred to Marika. Always she had viewed Maksche with great dread, certain she would have to face a totally alien environment alone.

A hundred yards along, Grauel said, "She is not all ice water and stone heart, this Koenic. She knew we would follow, even if that meant walking all the miles down the Hainlin. Perhaps she recalls her own pack. They say she came as you did, half grown, from an upper Ponath pack, and Braydic with her as punishment for their dam having concealed them from the silth. Their packstead was one of those the nomads destroyed during the second winter. There was much talk of it at the time."

"Oh." Marika marched on, for a long time alone with her thoughts and the moonlight. Three moons were in the sky now. Every riverside tree wore a three-fingered paw of shadow.

She began to feel a subtle wrongness in the night. At first it was just something on the very edge of perception, like an irritating but distant sound mostly ignored. But it would not be ignored. It grew stronger as she trudged along. Finally, she said, "Grauel, go tell that Bagnel to stop. We are headed into something. I need time to look ahead without being distracted by having to watch my feet."

By the time Grauel returned with Bagnel, she knew what it was. The tradermale asked, "You sense trouble, sister?" In the field, working together, he seemed to have an easy way about him. Marika felt almost comfortable in his presence.

"There is a nomad watchpost ahead. Around that bend, up on the slope. I can feel the heat of them."

"You are certain?"

"I have not gone out for a direct look, if that is what you mean. But I am sure here." She smote her heart.

"That is good enough for me. Beckhette." He waved. The tradermale he called Beckhette was what he called his "tactician," a term apparently from the tradermale cult tongue. The male arrived. "Nomad sentries around the next bend. Take them out or sneak past?"

"Depends. They have any silth or wehrlen with them?" The question was addressed to Marika. "Our choice of tactics must hinge on which course allows us the maximum time undiscovered by the horde."

Marika shrugged. "To tell you that I will have to walk the dark."

Both Bagnel and Beckhette nodded as if to say, go ahead.

She slipped down through her loophole, found a ghost, rode it over the slopes, slipping up on the nomads from the far side. She was cautious. The possibility that she might face a wild silth or wehrlen disturbed her.

They were sleepy, those nomad watchers. But there were a dozen of them huddled in a snow shelter, and with them was a male who had the distinctive touch-scent of a wehrlen. And he was alert. Something in the night had wakened him to the possibility of danger.

Marika did not withdraw to confer. She struck, fearing the wehrlen might discover her party before she could go back, talk, and return.

He was strong, but not trained. The struggle lasted only seconds. Pulling away, craft touched her. She squeezed her ghost down to where it could affect the physical world, undermined the shelter, brought tons of snow down upon the nomads before they fully realized they were under attack.

She returned to flesh and reported what she had done.

"Good thinking," Bagnel said. "When they are found it will look like a regrettable accident."

From that point onward Marika did not daydream. She lent all her attention to helping her sisters locate nomad watchers.

The tradermales insisted on taking the last few miles over a mountain. They were convinced they would encounter a strong nomad force if they continued to follow the watercourse. They did not want to waste their silth surprise by springing it in a struggle for the survival of a pawful.

They made that last climb in sunlight, among giant, concealing trees far larger than any Marika had yet seen in any of her wanderings. She was amazed that life could take so many different forms so close to her ancestral home—though she did reflect that she and Grauel and Barlog had wandered more of the world than any of the Degnan since the pack had come north in times almost immemorial.

They smelled smoke before they reached the ridgeline. Some of the huntresses thought it from the hearth fires of Critza, but the tradermales showed a frightened excitement which had nothing to do with an anticipation of arriving home. They hurried as if to an appointment with terrible news.

Terrible news it was.

From the heights they looked down on the hold which had been the traders' headquarters. Somehow, one wall had been broken. Smoke still rose, though no fire could be seen. The snowfields surrounding the packfast were littered with bodies. Marika did not immediately recognize what they were, for they appeared small from her viewpoint.

Bagnel squatted on his hams and studied the disaster. For

a long time he said nothing. When he did speak, it was in an emotionless monotone. "At least they did not take it cheaply. And some of ours escaped."

Not knowing why she did so exactly, Marika scratched his ears the way one did when comforting a pup. He had removed his hat to better listen for sounds from below.

He looked at her oddly, which caused her to feel a need to explain. "I saw all this happen at my packstead four years ago. Help came too late then, too."

"But it came."

"Yes. As it did here. Seen from an odd angle, you might think me repaying a debt."

"A small victory here, then. At horrible cost we have gotten the silth to be concerned." He donned his hat, stood. His iron gaze never left the smoking ruins. "You females stay here. My brothers and I will see what is to be seen." He and the other two started down the slope. Ten paces along, he stopped, turned to Marika. "If something happens to us, run for Akard. Do not waste a second on us. Save yourselves. It will be your turn soon enough."

Return to Akard? Marika thought. And how do that? They had come south carrying rations for three days, no one having given thought to the chance that they might find Critza destroyed. They had thought there would be food and shelter at the end of the trail, not the necessity to turn about and march right back to Akard.

No matter. She would survive. She had survived the trek to Akard when she was much younger. She would survive again.

She closed her eyes and went into that other place she had come to know so well, that place where she had begun to feel more at home than in the real world. She ducked through her loophole into a horde of ghosts in scarlet and indigo and aquamarine. The scene of the Critza massacre was a riot of color, like a mad drug dream. Why did they gather so? Were they in fact the souls of meth who had died here? She thought not. But she did not know what to think them otherwise.

It did not matter. Silth did not speculate much on the provenance of their power. They sensed ghosts and used them. Marika captured a strong one.

She rode the ghost downhill, floating a few yards behind Bagnel.

He did not much heed the fallen nomads. Marika ignored them, too, but could not help noticing many were ripped and torn like those she had seen at the site of the tradermale ambush last summer. Only a few—and all those inside the shattered wall—bore cut or stab wounds. And she never saw a one with an arrow in his or her corpse.

Odd.

Odder still the fortress, much of which recalled Braydic's communications center. Though Marika was sure much of what she saw had nothing to do with sending or receiving messages. Strange things. She would have liked to have gone down and laid on paws.

The agony of the tradermales was too painful to watch. Marika withdrew to her flesh. With the others she waited, crouched in the snow, leaning upon her javelin, so motionless winter's breath might have frozen her at last.

Bagnel spent hours prowling the ruins of Critza while the silth and huntresses shivered on the hillside. When he returned, he and his companions climbed slowly, bearing heavy burdens.

They arrived. Bagnel caught his breath, said, "There is nothing here for any of us now. Let us return and do what we may for Akard." His voice was as cold as the hillside, edged with hatred. "There is a small cave a few miles along the ridge. Assuming it is not occupied, we can rest there before we start back." He led off, and said nothing more till Marika asked what he had learned in the ruins.

"It was as bad as you can imagine. But a few did break out on the carriers. The pups, I suppose. Unless the nomads carried them off to their pots. There was very little left, though they did not manage to break the door to the armory. We recovered what weapons and ammunition we could carry. The rest . . . you will know soon enough."

Marika looked at him oddly. Distracted, he was using many words she did not know.

"They stripped the place like scavengers strip a corpse. To the bone. Stone still sits upon stone there, but Critza is dead. After these thousand years. It has become but a memory."

Marika festered with questions. She asked none of them. It was a time for the tradermales to be alone with their grief.

A mile along his trail Bagnel halted. He and his brethren faced the direction they had come. Marika watched them curiously. They seemed to be waiting for something. . . .

A great gout of fire-stained smoke erupted over the ridge recently quit. It rolled high into the sky. A great rumbling thunder followed. Bagnel shuddered all over. His shoulders slumped. Without a word he turned and resumed the march.

Chapter Thirteen

I

"Thank the All," Grauel said with feeling as they rounded the last bend of the Hainlin and dimly saw Akard on its headland, brooding gray and silver a mile away. "Thank the All. They have not destroyed Akard."

There had been a growing, seldom voiced fear that their trek north would be rewarded with the sight of another gutted packfast, that they would round that final bend and find themselves doomed to the mocking grasp of the hunger already gnawing their bellies. Even the silth had feared, though logically they knew they would have received some sort of touch had the fortress been attacked.

But there the fortress stood, inviolate. The chill of the north wind was no longer so bitter. Marika bared her teeth and dared that wind to do its damnedest.

"This is where they ambushed us," Bagnel said. "One group pushed us while the other waited in that stand of trees there."

"Not this time," Marika replied. She looked through the blue-gray haze of lightly falling snow, seeing evidence of a nomad presence. The other silth did the same. The hunt-resses stood motionless, teeth chattering, arms ready.

Marika sensed nothing untoward anywhere. The only meth life lay within the packfast, brooding there upon its bluff.

"Come." She resumed walking.

There was no trail. Enough snow had fallen, and had been blown, to bury their southbound trail.

When they were closer and the packfast was more dis-tinct, Marika saw that there had been changes. A long feather of rumpled snow trailed down the face of the bluff below the fortress, like the aftermath of an avalanche. Even as she walked and watched, meth appeared above and dumped a wheelbarrow load of snow, which tumbled down the feather.

The workers had been doing that all winter, keeping the roofs and inner courts clear, but the mound had never been so prominent. It had grown dramatically in five days. Marika was curious.

The workers saw them, too. Moments later something touched Marika. The other silth received touches too. The sisters would be waiting when they arrived, anticipating bad news.

Why else would they have returned so soon?

Marika sensed a distant alien presence as they began the climb from the river. The other silth sensed it, too. "On our trail," one said.

"No worry," the other observed. "We are far ahead, and within the protection of our sisters."

Even so, Marika was nervous. She watched the rivercourse as she climbed, and before long spotted the nomads. There were a score of them. They were traveling fast. Trail had been broken for them. But they never presented any real threat. They turned back after reaching the point were the travelers had begun their climb to the packfast.

The sisters—and many of their dependents—were wait-ing in the main hall. Many were males. Marika was astonished. She asked Braydic, "What happened? What is this? Males inside the fortress."

"My truesister decided to bring everyone inside the wall. Nomads were prowling around out there every day while you were gone. In ever greater numbers. Only the workers have been going out. Armed."

Marika had noted the workers clearing the snow away from the north wall, hoisting it to the wall's top and barrowing it around to the spill visible from the river.

"They have gotten very bold," Braydic reported. "My truesister feared they might have good reason. We might even need the males."

Senior Koenic called for a report from Marika's party.

Bagnel did the talking. He kept it simple. "They were all slain," he said. "Everyone in Critza, both brethren and those we gave shelter. Except a pawful who got out on the carriers. The wall was breached with explosives. The nomads took some arms and everything else. They were unable to penetrate the armory. We blew that before we left the ruin. Though I am sufficiently realistic to know you would not, if you were to ask my advice, I would tell you you should ask your seniors to evacuate Akard. The stakes have been raised. The game has sharpened. This is the last stronghold. They will come soon and come strong, and they will make an end of you."

Marika was both mystified and startled. The former because she did not understand all Bagnel was saying, the latter because Senior Koenic was considering the advice seriously. After reflection, Senior Koenic replied, "All this will be reported. We are in continuous contact with Maksche. I have my hopes, but I do not believe they will take us out. It seems likely the Serke Community is helping the nomads in an effort to push the Reugge out of the Ponath. I expect policy will be to stand fast even in the face of assured disaster. To maintain the Reugge face and claim."

The tradermale shrugged. He seemed indifferent to the world now that his mission was complete. His home had

been destroyed. His folk were all dead. For what did he have
to live? Marika understood his feelings all too well.

She worried his remarks about the Serke and evacuation.
That baffled her completely. It had something to do with
those parts of her education that had been left vague deliberately. She did know that competition between sisterhoods
could become quite vigorous, and that there were centuries
of bad blood between the Serke and Reugge. But she never
imagined that it could become so intense, so deadly, that, as
the senior implied, one sisterhood would help creatures like
the nomads to attack another.

That meeting did nothing but frighten everyone. Only a
few of the older silth, like Gorry, refused to believe that the
danger was real. Gorry remained convinced that any nomad
assault would see the surrounding countryside littered with
savage corpses while leaving Akard entirely unscathed.

Marika was convinced that Gorry was overconfident. But
Gorry had not seen Critza. . . .

Even that might not have convinced the old one. She had
reached that stage of life where she would believe only what
she wished to be true.

II

Marika visited Braydic in the communications center the
morning after her return. Even now she became mildly
disoriented if she passed too near the tree and dish on top,
but her discomfiture was nothing like that experienced by
most of the Akard silth. Braydic believed she would conquer
it entirely, given time.

Braydic had several communications screens locked into
continuous operation. Each showed different far meth at
work in very similar chambers. "Is that Maksche we are
seeing, Braydic?" Marika asked.

"That one and that one. They are not going to evacuate

us. You know that? But they want to keep close watch on what happens here. I believe they hope the nomads do attack."

"Why would they want that?"

"Maybe so they can find out for sure if the Serke are behind everything. The nomads will not be able to break in against silth without silth help. Though that would not be proof enough in itself. If we take prisoners and questioning reveals a connection, then Reugge policies toward the Serke would harden. So far it has been one of those cases where you know what is happening and who is doing it, but there has been no court-sound proof. No absolute evidence of malice." Braydic shuddered.

"What?" Marika asked.

"I was thinking of Most Senior Gradwohl. She is a hard, bitter, tough old bitch. Cautious on the outside but secretly a gambler. As we all do, she knows the Reugge are weaker than the Serke. That we stand no chance in any direct confrontation. She might try something bold or bizarre."

Marika did not understand all this talk of the Serke and whatnot. She did know there was no friendship between the Reugge and Serke communities, and that there seemed to be blood in it. But the rest was out of that knowledge that had been concealed from her for so long. Now the meth spoke as if she were as informed as they.

She was not as naive as she pretended either.

"What might be an example?"

Braydic was more open than the silth, but there were things she never discussed either. Now, in her distraction, she might be vulnerable to the sly question.

Braydic had learned her trade at the cloister in TelleRai, which was one of the great southern cities. In her time she had encountered most of the most senior sisters of the Reugge and other orders. She had been a technician of very high station till her truesister's error had gotten the pair of them banished to the land of their birth. Marika often wondered what had caused their fall from grace, but never had asked. About that time and that event Braydic was very closed.

"A sudden direct attack upon the Ruhaack cloister springs to mind. An attempt to eliminate the seniors of the Serke Community. Or even something more dire. Darkwar, perhaps. Who knows? Bestrei cannot remain invincible forever."

"Bestrei? Who is Bestrei? Or what?"

"Who. Bestrei is a Mistress of the Ship. The best there is. And she is the Serke champion, thrice victorious in darkwar."

"And darkwar? What is that?"

"Nothing about which you need concern yourself, pup. Of faraway meth and faraway doings. We are here in Akard. We would do well to keep our minds upon our own situation." Braydic eyed a screen spattered with numbers. Marika could now read displays as well as her mentor. This was a reference to a problem with a generator in the power-house. "You will have to leave now, pup. I have work to do. We are getting some icing out there, despite the fires." Braydic called the powerhouse technicians. While she awaited their response she muttered something about the All-be-damned primitive equipment given frontier outposts.

Braydic was not in a communicative mood. Marika decided there was no need pressing for something she could not get. She abandoned the communications center for her place upon the wall.

The wind was in its usual bitter temper. A steady but light snow was falling, confining the world to a circle perhaps a mile across. It was a world without color. White. Gray shadows. The black of a few trees, most of which appeared only as blobbish shapes floating on white. Marika wished for a glimpse of the sun. The sun unseen for months. The peculiar sun that had changed color during the few years she had been in this world, fading slowly through deeper shades of orange.

At long last Braydic had let fall what the winters were about. She said the sun and its gaggle of planetary pups had

entered a part of the night that was extremely thick with
dust. This dust absorbed some of the sun's energy. It had
hastened a planetary cooling cycle already centuries old.
The system would be inside the dust cloud for a long time to
come. The world would get very much colder before it
passed out. That would not happen in Marika's time.

She shivered. Much worse before it got better.

Below, workers continued the endless task of carrying
snow away from the wall. The restless north wind brought
drifts down almost as fast as they could carry it away.

Farther up the headland, other workers were building a
plow-shaped snowbreak intended to divert blowing, drifting
snow into the valley of the eastern fork of the Hainlin, away
from both the wall and the powerhouse on the Husgen side.

Marika spotted Grauel among the huntresses watching
over the workers on that project. She raised a paw. Grauel
did not see her. She was wasting no attention on the
packfast.

Nomad parties had come within touch of the silth twice
during the past night. One party had been large. Their
movements suggested they were maneuvering according to
the plan Bagnel had wrung from a prisoner down at Critza.

Several silth were out with the workers, adding their
might to that of the guardian huntresses. Marika was surprised to see Khles Gibany among them. But Gibany never
had permitted her handicap to control her life.

She looked very strange bobbing around on crutches
specially fitted so she could travel on snow.

Marika went inside herself and found her loophole. She
slipped through into the realm of specter. And was startled
to find it almost untenanted.

Strange. Disturbingly strange.

There were moments when the population of ghosts numbered more or less than normal, times when finding one
appropriate to one's purpose was difficult, but never had she
seen the realm so sparsely occupied. Marika came back out
and looked for a sister on watch.

The first she found answered her question without her

having to ask. The truth was graven on the silth's face. She was frightened.

This, if ever there was one, was a time for a nomad attack. The power of the Akard silth would never be weaker.

Marika hurried back to her place, waved at the workers and Grauel.

The news had reached Senior Koenic, Marika saw. The silth of Akard had begun to come to the rampart. Outside, the working parties had begun gathering their tools. Everything seemed quite orderly, indicating preparation beforehand.

Indicating planning not communicated to Marika.

She was irked. They never bothered telling her anything, though *she* considered herself an important factor in Akard's life and defense. What was wrong with these silth? Would they never consider her as more than a troublesome pup? Did she not have a great deal to contribute?

Workers already within the walls were being armed. Another facet of planning of which she had been left ignorant. She was surprised to see males mount the walls bearing javelins.

Marika sensed the nomads approaching before the last workers started for the packfast gate. She did not bother reporting. She reached out and touched Khles Gibany. *They come. They are close. Hurry up.*

Hobbling about, Gibany hurried the workers and formed a screen of huntresses bearing spears and shields. But she allowed no one to become precipitate. Even for silth tools were too precious to abandon.

Marika sensed the enemy in the snow. They were approaching Akard all across the ridge. There were thousands of them. Even now, after so many years of it, Marika could not imagine what force could have drawn so many together, nor what power kept them together. The horde the wehrlen had brought south had been implausible. This was impossible.

The forerunners of the host appeared out of the snow only a few hundred yards beyond Khles Gibany and the workers.

They halted awhile, waiting for those behind to come up. Gibany remained cool, releasing no one to return to the fortress unburdened with tools.

Perhaps she was unconcerned because she believed she was safely under the umbrella of protection extended by her silth sisters.

Marika sensed a far presence not unlike that of her sisters. She tried to go down through her loophole to take a look, but when she got down there she could not find a single usable ghost. Without ghosts she could but touch, and there was little chance of touching without her reaching for someone she knew. It was certain she could effect nothing.

She returned to the world to find the forerunner nomads howling toward Gibany's group. Fear seized her heart. Grauel was out there! Javelins arced through the air. A couple of nomads fell. Then the attackers smashed against huntress's shields. Spears and swords hacked and slashed. The nomads screeched war cries. The line of huntresses staggered backward under the impact of superior numbers. A few nomads slipped through.

Marika realized that these attackers were the best the nomads had. Their most skilled huntresses. They were trying to effect something sudden. One nomad suddenly shrieked and clasped her chest, fell thrashing in the snow. Then another and another followed. The silth had found something to use against them, though their range seemed limited and the killing was nothing so impressive as other slaughters Marika had witnessed.

The swirl of combat began to separate out. Still forms scattered the snowfield. Not a few were Akard huntresses, though most were nomads. The nomads retreated a hundred yards. The silth seemed unable to reach them there. Marika went down through her loophole and found that it was indeed difficult to reach that far. There were a few ghosts now, but so puny as to be jokes. She retired and watched the nomad huntresses stand watch while the Akard workers and huntresses continued their withdrawal.

Khles Gibany. Where was Gibany? The crippled silth was

no longer there to direct the retreat. Marika ducked through her loophole again and went searching.

She could not find a body. . . . There. Somehow, the nomad huntresses had managed to take Gibany captive. What had they done? The Khles was unable to call upon her talent to help herself. And Marika, though she strained till it ached, could not apply enough force to set her free.

Nomad males with farming tools came forward. Two hundred yards from the snow break they began excavating trenches in the old hard-packed snow. They threw the dug-out snow to the Akard side of the trench, used their shovel to beat it into a solid wall.

Marika became aware that someone had joined her. She glanced to her right, saw the tradermale Bagnel. "They learned at Critza," he said. "Curse them." He settled down on the icy stone and began assembling a metal contraption he had been carrying since his initial appearance at Akard. Marika saw his two brothers doing likewise elsewhere.

Out on the snow, beyond the trench, nomad workers had driven a tall post deep into the snow. Now they were laying a layer of rock and gravel around it. Others stood by with arms loaded with wood. Marika was puzzled till she saw several huntresses drag Gibany to the post.

They tied the one-legged silth so her foot dangled inches from the surface. They they piled wood around her. Even from where she watched Marika could sense Gibany's fear and rage. Rage founded in the fact that she could do nothing to halt them, for all she was one of the most powerful silth of Akard.

"They are taunting us," Marika snarled. "Showing us we are powerless against them."

Bagnel grunted. He mounted his metal instrument upon a tripod, peered through a tube on top. He began twisting small knobs.

A runner carrying a torch came out of the snowfall, trotted up to where Gibany was bound. Marika slipped through her loophole once more, hearing Bagnel mutter "All right," as she went.

There was not a ghost to be found. Not a thing she could do for Gibany, unless—as several silth seemed to be doing already—she extended her touch and tried to take away some of the fear and agony soon to come.

Thunder cracked in her right ear.

Marika came back to flesh snarling, in the full grip of a fight-flight reflex. Bagnel looked at her with wide, startled eyes. "Sorry," he said. "I should have warned you."

She shook with reaction while watching him fiddle with his knobs. "Right," he said. And the end of his contraption spat fire and thunder. Far out on the snowscape, the nomad huntress bearing the torch leapt, spun, shrieked, collapsed, did not move again.

Marika gaped.

Facts began to add together. That time in the forest last summer, when she had heard those strange *tak-takk*ing noises. The time coming down the east fork with Khles Gibany and Gorry when the nomads attacked . . .

The instrument roared again. Another nomad flung away from Gibany.

Marika looked at the weapon in awe. "What is it?"

For a moment Bagnel looked at her oddly. Along the wall, his brethren were making similar instruments talk. "Oh," he murmured. "That is right. You are Tech Two pup." He swung the instrument slightly, seeking another target. "It is called a rifle. It spits a pellet of metal. The pellet is no bigger than the last joint of your littlest finger, but travels so fast it will punch right through a body." His weapon spat thunder. So did those of his brethren. "Not much point to this, except to harass them." *Bam!* "There are too many of them."

Below, the last of the workers and huntresses were coming in the gate. Only one of Akard's meth remained unsafe: Khles Gibany, tied to that post.

The nomad huntresses and workers had thrown themselves into the trench the workers had begun. Now Marika saw another wave hurrying forward from the forest beyond the fields. She could just make that out now. The snowfall was weakening.

Pinpoints of light flickered along the advancing nomad line, accompanied by a crackle like that of fat in a frying pan.

"Down, pup!" Bagnel snapped. "They are shooting back."

Something snarled past Marika. It took a bite out of the earflap on her hat. Another something smacked into the wall and whined away. She got down.

Bagnel said, "They have the weapons they captured at Critza, plus whatever else someone gave them." He sighted his weapon again, fired, looked at her with teeth exposed in a snarl of black humor. "Hang on. It is going to get exciting."

Marika rose, looked out. Someone had managed to get the torch into the wood piled round Gibany's foot. Gibany's fear had drawn her. . . . Once more through the loophole. Once more no ghosts of consequence. She reached with the touch to help Gibany endure. But half the silth on the wall were doing that, almost in a passive acceptance of fate. "No!" Marika said. "They will not do that. You. Bagnel. Show me how to use that thing." She indicated his weapon.

He eyed her a moment, shook his head. "I am not sure what you want to do, pup. But you will not do it with this." He patted the weapon. Snowflakes touching its tube were turning to steam. "It takes years to learn to use it properly."

"Then you will do it. Put one of your deadly pellets into Khles, to free her from agony. We cannot save her. The talent is denied us today. But we can rob the savages of their mockery by sending her to rejoin the All."

Bagnel gaped. "Mistress. . . ."

Her expression was fierce, demanding.

"I could not, mistress. To raise paw against the silth. No matter the cause. . . ."

Marika stared across the snow, ignoring the insect sounds swarming past her. Gibany had begun writhing in her bonds. The pain of the fire had torn all reason from her mind. She knew nothing but the agony now.

"Do it," Marika said in a low and intense voice so filled with power the tradermale began looking around as if seeking a place to run. "Do it now. Free her. I will take all responsibility. Do you understand?"

Teeth grinding, Bagnel nodded. Paws shaking, he adjusted knobs. He paused to get a grip on himself.

His weapon barked.

Marika stared at Gibany, defying the nomad snipers.

The Khles bucked against her bonds, sagged. Marika ducked through her loophole, grabbed the best ghost available, went looking.

Gibany was free. She would know no more pain.

Back. "It is done. I am in your debt, tradermale."

Bagnel showed her angry teeth. "You are a strange one, young mistress. And soon to be one joining your elder sister if you do not get yourself down." A steady rain of metal pounded against the wall. Swarms whined past. Marika realized most must be meant for her. She was the only target visible to the nomads.

She sped them a hand gesture of defiance, lowered herself behind a merlon.

One of Bagnel's brethren shouted at him, pointed. Out on the snowfield meth were running forward in tight bunches. Each bunch carried something. Bagnel and his comrades began shooting rapidly, concentrating on those groups. Some of the silth, too, managed to reach them. Marika saw nomads go down in the characteristic throes of silth death-sending. But three groups managed to carry their burdens into the snow trenches, where workers were still digging. Marika now understood why they were heaping the snow the way they were. It would block the paths of the pellets from the tradermales' weapons.

More nomads came from the woods. Some carried heavy packs, some nothing at all. The latter rushed to the burdens their predecessors had dropped, grabbed them up, hustled them forward.

The crackle of nomad rifles continued unabated. Twice Marika heard someone on the wall shriek.

"Get down as flat as you can," Bagnel told her. "And

snuggle up tight against the merlon. They are going to start throwing the big stuff."

Puffs of smoke sprouted and blossomed above the nomad trenches, vanished on the wind. Muted crumpings came a moment later, a sort of soft threatening thumping. Where had she heard that before? That time when tradermales ambushed the nomads she and Arhdwehr were chasing . . .

"Down," Bagnel said, and yanked at her when she did not move fast enough to suit. He pressed her against the icy stone.

Something moaned softly in a rising pitch. There was a tremendous bang outside the wall, followed by a series of bangs, only one of which occurred behind the wall. That one precipitated a shriek which turned into the steady moan of a badly injured meth.

"They are getting the range," Bagnel explained. "Once they find it the bombs will come steady."

Where were the ghosts? How could silth battle this without their talents?

Why were the ghosts absent just when the savages elected to attack?

A second salvo came. Most fell short, though closer. Several did carry past the wall. They made a lot of noise but did little damage. The packfast was constructed of thick stone. Its builders had meant it to stand forever.

The entire third salvo fell inside the fortress. Marika sensed that that presaged a steady hammering.

A river of meth poured from the woods, burdened with ammunition for the engines throwing the bombs. Workers left their trenches and darted forward, hastily dug shallow holes in which to shelter. They worked their ways toward the snow break. Nomads carrying rifles followed them, only sporadically harassed by Bagnel and his brethren. The crackle of nomad rifle fire never slowed.

Several more packfast meth were hit.

"This is hopeless," Marika whispered. "We cannot fight back." She went down through her loophole again, and

again found the ghost world all but barren. But this time she
stayed, hoping for the stray chance to strike back. She
sensed that many sisters were doing the same, with occasional success. Those who did find a tool spent their fury
upon the crews of the bomb-throwing instruments.

Why was the ghost world so naked?

Marika waited with the patience of a hunting herdek, till
the ghost she needed happened by. She pounced, seized it,
commanded it, rode it out over the snowfields, past the
nomads and their strange engines, through woods where
thousands more nomads waited to move forward, and on to
the very limit of her ability to control that feeble a ghost.
And there she found the thing that she had sensed must
exist, if only on the dimmest level.

A whole company of silth and wehrlen, gathered in one
place, were pulling to them all the strong ghosts of the
region. The air surrounding them boiled with color, denser
than ever Marika had imagined. She thought the ghosts
must be so numerous they would be visible to the eyes of
untalented meth.

They were weak, these wild silth and wehrlen. Poorly
trained. But in the aggregate they were able to summon the
ghosts to them and so deny the Akard sisters access to their
most potent defense.

Marika sought a focus, one strong silth controlling the
group. Sometimes her Akard sisters linked under the control
of the senior to meld into a more powerful whole.

A greater whole there was here, but not under any immediately evident central direction.

Straining her ghost, Marika picked a female and plucked
at her heart.

The distance was too extreme. She was able to injure the
wild silth but not to kill her.

Might that not be enough?

She moved among the nomads rapidly, stinging, and for a
moment they lost control. A moment was enough. The
ghosts scattered, driven by some mad pressure.

Marika felt her hold on her self growing tenuous. She had strained it too much. She hurried back to Akard. She was a moment slow getting though her loophole, and nearly panicked. There were stories about silth who did not get back. Terrible stories. Some might be true.

It took a moment to get oriented in her flesh.

She opened her eyes to discover the nomad rifle fire grown ragged, to the sight of nomads fleeing toward the woods, and many not making it.

This was the slaughter Gorry had prophesied and insisted would be visited upon the savage.

Feebly, Marika attained her feet and made her way toward Senior Koenic. The senior was out of body when she arrived. She waited till her elder came back from the place of ghosts. When the senior's eyes focused Marika reported all that she had seen and done.

"You are a strong one, pup," Koenic said while a nearby Gorry scowled at such praise. "I sensed them out there myself, but I did not have the strength to reach them. Will you be able to do it again?"

"I am not certain, mistress. Not right away. It is an exhausting thing to do." She was shaking with fatigue.

Senior Koenic stared out across the snowfields. "Already they begin to gather those-who-dwell to them again. Soon they will resume their attack. In an hour, perhaps. Marika, go down into the deepest cells, where their weapons cannot reach you. Rest. Do not come back up, for you are our final weapon and you must not be risked. When you are ready, scourge them again."

"Yes, mistress."

Gorry glowered, angered because her pupil should receive so much direct and positive attention. A glance told Marika that her instructress was scheming to take advantage of the day. She would have to watch her back. The moment the danger receded. . . .

Senior Koenic mused, "Those of us who can will seize what you give us and punish the savages. They may take

Akard from the Reugge, but they will pay dearly for the theft."

Marika was surprised at such negativity in the senior. It frightened her.

Grauel appeared from somewhere unseen. Marika felt pleased, restored, knowing her packmate was watching over her. The huntress followed her down into the courtyard, where bombs had destroyed everything not constructed of the most massive stone. In a strained, flat tone, Grauel said, "We had four years, Marika. Four more than seemed likely when last the nomad threatened us."

"Yes? You, too? Even you have surrendered to despair?" She could think of nothing else to say. "Express my regards to Barlog."

"I will. She will not be far away."

Marika passed through the great hall. It was a shambles. The overhead windows had been shattered by bombs. Its interior had been damaged badly. Though there had never been much in that chamber not made of stone, a few small fires burned there, being fought by worker pups too young to make a stand upon the wall. Marika paused to watch.

The word seemed to have run ahead. The pups looked at her in awe and fear and hope. She shook her head, afraid that too many meth, for whatever reason, had suddenly invested all their hopes in her.

It did not follow logically in her mind that because she had aborted the savage strategy once she should become the heartpiece of the packfast's defense.

While she stood there she thought of going to the communications center to see what news Braydic had, in hopes there would be a hope from Maksche, but she decided she would be drained too much by the electromagnetic fog. If she was to be the great champion of Akard—foolish as that seemed to her—then she must conserve herself.

She went down to her own cell, not as deep inside the fortress as Senior Koenic might have liked, but deep enough to be safe from bombs, and psychologically more comfortable than anyplace but her retreat upon the wall.

Chapter Fourteen

I

Jiana! You have brought this upon Akard and the Reugge.

Marika started out of her resting trance, shaken by the touch. What? . . .

Someone scratched at her cell door. She sat up. "Enter."

Barlog came in. She carried a tray laden with hot, high-energy food. "You'd better eat, Marika. I hear the silth need much energy to work their witchery."

The smell of food made Marika realize how hungry she was, how depleted her energies were. "Yes. You are wise, Barlog. I had not thought of it."

"What is the trouble, pup? You seem distracted."

She was. It was that touch. She took the tray without answering, dug in. Barlog stationed herself beside the door, beaming approval like a fussy old male.

Another scratch. Barlog met Marika's eye. Marika nodded. Barlog opened the door.

Grauel stepped inside, apparently relieved to see Barlog there. She carried a whole arsenal of weapons: shield, sword, knives, heavy spear, javelins, even a bow and arrows, which

would be useless inside the fortress's tight corridors.
Amused, Marika asked, "What are you supposed to be?"

"Your guardian."

"Yes?"

Grauel understood. "The old one. Gorry. She is saying
wicked things about you."

"Such as?"

"She is walking the walls calling you doomstalker. She is
telling everyone that the nomads have come down upon
Akard because of you. She is telling everyone that you are
accursed. She is saying that to end the threat the packfast
must rid itself of the Jiana."

"Indeed?" That was a change from moments ago. "I
thought that the senior had designated me Akard's great
hope."

"There is that school of thought, too. Among the younger
silth and huntresses. Especially those who have shared the
hunt with you. Arhdwehr follows her around, giving the lie
to all she says. But there are those among the oldest silth
who live in myth and mystery and hear only the magic in
Gorry's claims. One savage packstead pup is a cheap price
to pay for salvation."

"It is sad," Marika said. "We have ten thousand enemies
howling outside the walls, so we divide against ourselves."

Grauel said, "I know huntresses who have served the
Reugge elsewhere. They say it is ever thus among silth.
Always at one another's throats—from safely behind the
back. This time could be dangerous. There is much anxiety
and much fear and a great desire for a cheap, magical
solution. I will stand guard."

"I, too," Barlog said.

"As you will. Though I think you two would be of more
value upon the wall."

Neither huntress said a word. Each had a stubborn look
that said no command would return them to the wall while
they fancied Marika threatened. Barlog took weapons from
Grauel. After a last look at their charge, the two stepped
outside.

Marika wondered if a bomb would blast them away from her door.

She did feel more secure, knowing they were there.

She ate, and returned to her resting trance.

Jiana. Your time is coming.

Angrily, Marika flung back, *Someone's time is near. The grauken is about to snap at someone's tail.* She felt Gorry reel under the impact of the unexpected response. She felt Gorry's terror.

She was pleased.

Yes. Someone's time was near, be it hers or that of the mad old instructress.

For a time Marika had difficulty resting. Memories of kagbeasts and other surprise horrors kept creeping into her mind.

II

She felt the bombs falling in the far distance, sending muted vibrations running through Akard's roots. The nomads were back. Their silth had recovered control of the ghost realm. She ignored the sounds, remained calm, waited till she had regained her full strength. Then she probed out through the cold stone, searching for a suitable ghost.

The hunt took much longer this time. In time she captured a weaker one and rode it farther afield in her search. And it was while she hunted that she witnessed the disaster on the Husgen.

The third dam, the far dam, up the Husgen several miles, erupted suddenly. A wild volcano of ice and snow went charging down the river, driven by the reservoir water. So mighty was its charge that it smashed through the ice upon the middle lake, poured over the face of the middle dam, gnawed at its foundations where it abutted the canyon walls, and broke it, too. The combined volume of two lakes rushed toward the final dam.

The disaster seemed to occur in slowed motion because of its scale. Marika had ample time to grow angry.

Her anger, perhaps, allowed her to scale another barrier, as she had done during the attack upon the Degnan packstead. She found she was able to detect the presence of a far, strong ghost. She called it to her, mounted it, took it under control as the fury in the canyon reached the third dam, broke it, swamped the powerhouse, and bit deep into the face of the bluff on which Akard stood, so that great pillars of stone collapsed into the flood, taking a section of fortress wall with them. Several score huntresses, silth, and dependents tumbled down with the wall.

Whipped by rage, Marika drove her ghost steed out to the gathering of nomad silth. She hit them the way a kagbeast hit a herd of banger, slaughtering everything in reach. There would be time to savor and linger over the kill later.

Once again the nomad silth lost their concentration. And once again Marika's strength expired and she had to race back to her self, past the second rout of the besiegers, who were scourged much more terribly this time.

This time, as she parted from the wild silth gathering, Marika did sense the presence of a central control, a trained silth. But this control was stationed far from the main gathering, directing them from both safety and anonymity in the eyes of the sisters of Akard.

A trained silth, yes, certainly. And a powerful one. Perhaps the Serke guiding influence the senior suspected, and so wanted to capture.

Perhaps she was the key, Marika thought.

Marika slipped into her own flesh and lay there gasping.

"Are you ill, pup?"

Grauel was bending over her, face taut with concern.

"No. It is hard work, making the silth magic. Bring me some sweetened tea. A lot of sweetened tea." Her head was pounding. "Make it one cup of goyin to begin." She tried to sit up. Grauel had to help her. "I stopped them, Grauel. For a while. But they destroyed the dams."

She wondered what Braydic was doing now she could get

o more power from the powerhouse. What would they be thinking down in Maksche? Would loss of contact force them to move finally? When it was too late?

Grauel went for the teas while Barlog stood in the doorway, heavy spear in one paw, sword in the other. When Marika gave her a querying look, she said only, "Gorry has found a new slander to spread. She is accusing you of murdering Khles Gibany, and of trafficking with males."

An accusation that would be hard to deny, Marika realized. Anyone who had been trying to help Gibany weather the agony of burning would have realized a trademale projectile had ended her trial.

Senior Koenic came down soon after Grauel returned with the teas. It seemed an age since she had come back to flesh, but it could not have been more than fifteen minutes. "You did very well this time, pup." There was a light in the senior's eyes that baffled Marika. Mixed fear and respect, she supposed.

"Senior . . . Senior, I think I touched a true silth that time. She was beyond the nomads, hiding, but I am sure she was fully trained and exceptionally strong. And there was an alien flavor about her."

"Ah! Good news and dark. We may not die in vain. I must relay this to Maksche immediately, before Braydic's reserve power fails. It is not proof, but it is one more hint that the Serke are moving against us." She vanished in a swish of dark clothing.

Marika allowed the goyin free run and lay back to sleep. Many hours passed while her body recovered from the drain she had placed upon it. When she finally awakened, she was instantly aware that there was fighting inside the packfast proper. Panicky, she dove through her loophole and explored.

Nomad huntresses had gotten inside, coming around the end of the wall where it had collapsed. More were coming all the time, despite the arrows of Akard's huntresses and the rifles of the trademales. Two thousand nomads lay dead

upon the snowfields, but still they came, and still they died
They were a force as unstoppable as winter itself.

It was insanity. It was nothing any meth of the upper
Ponath could have imagined in her worst nightmare. It was
blood-soaked reality.

Most of the day had passed. It was late. If she could turn
the attack once more, Akard would have the night to
recuperate, to counterattack, to something. Night was the
world of the silth. . . .

Grauel and Barlog heard her stirring. They looked in.
"Finally coming around?" Barlog asked.

"Yes. You look awful. You need some rest."

"No. We have to guard this door." And there was that in
Barlog's stance which said that the guardianship had been
tested, though the huntress appeared unwilling to say how.

Grauel said, "There are those now willing to appease the
All with the sacrifice of a doomstalker."

"Oh."

Just the slightest hint of fear edged Barlog's voice as she
asked, "Is there anything you can do to stop the nomad
Marika? They are inside the packfast now."

"I was about to do what I can. Try to have me some tea
and food here when I come back."

"It will be here," Grauel promised.

Marika slipped through her loophole. Desperately, she
hunted for an appropriate ghost. And the thing she finally
found was a monster, discovered hovering high above the
packfast. It never had occurred to her to seek upward
before. A set of mind she realized was shared by all the silth
she knew. All were surface oriented.

Once she bestrode the monster, she immediately became
aware of others, higher still, even more monstrous, but the
sensing of them was dim, and they were too strong to
control. She stayed with the ghost she had, and rushed it
toward the nomad silth.

This time she sensed the control of the silth clearly as she
approached. Marika was stronger than she had ever been

She located the strange sister and stole toward her, and took her entirely by surprise.

She pounced. There was an instant of startled "Who are you?" before she ripped the female's flesh, scattering her heart and blood across an acre of snow.

Marika was appalled. The silth had, almost literally, exploded.

It was a strong ghost.

She savaged the nomad silth as well, slaying several score before she became so body-loose she had to withdraw. She fled to Akard, where her sisters were again slaughtering nomads by the hundreds.

But there were hundreds inside the fortress, unable to flee, and they continued fighting, as cornered huntresses would.

Too many silth sisters had been slain during the attack. Those who survived were hard pressed, even with their powers restored. And, one by one, they were succumbing to exhaustion.

Marika grabbed her flesh before she lost her grip entirely.

Grauel recognized her arrival in flesh, had her sitting up with a cup of sweet tea to her muzzle almost before she recognized her surroundings. "Drink. Did you do well? Is there hope?"

Marika drank. Almost immediately she felt the sugar spreading through her body, giving her a near high. "I did very well. But maybe not enough. Maybe too late. More of that. And chaphe. I will have to go back right away. The others haven't the strength to hold."

"Marika. . . ."

"You want a hope? The only hope I saw was for me to strike again. Soon. Closer to the fortress. The way it stands now, silth or no silth, we are destroyed."

Grauel nodded reluctantly.

"What of Gorry?"

"As vicious as ever. But lately she has been too busy to stir trouble. I think most of those who supported her have been killed in the fighting. So she may be no problem after all."

Marika downed another long draft. Her limbs were trembling. She knew risking the ghost realm in her state was not wise. But it was necessary. It seemed to be the choice between grave risk and certain death. Also, there was something she had to do. . . .

"Stay with me this time, Grauel. I don't know you could, but if something seems bad wrong, try to bring me back."

"All right."

Marika lay back and closed her eyes. She slipped through her loophole. A glance upward showed her the giant ghost she had used before still hovering over the packfast. She snatched at it, seized it, brought it down amid the ruins of the broken wall.

She spied Gorry almost immediately, surrounded by scores of nomad bodies, exulting in her killing. Gorry, whom she hated above all else in her world. Gorry, who was totally engrossed in her work. Gorry, who was wounded and likely to be struck down by some nomad missile at any moment.

That could not be. No nomad would steal the pleasure of that death.

It was time.

Marika reached, found the point at the base of Gorry's brain, struck quickly but lightly, paralyzing not only the old silth's body but her talent. She held Gorry there for a long moment, letting the terror build.

It is time, Gorry. And, *Good-bye, Gorry.*

She left the paralyzed silth for the nomads. Their imaginations were far more gruesome than hers. She hoped Gorry suffered a long wait in impotent terror.

She hacked, slashed, battered, left a hundred nomads twisted and torn. Then she could stay out no longer. Blackness hovered at the edges of her perception. If she did not get out of the ghost realm soon, she never would.

She slipped into her own present and fell into a sleep of total exhaustion. Her final thought was that she needed food if she were to recover. She had pressed too hard, taken herself too far.

Self-mockery echoed through her fading consciousness. This was the last sleep from which she would never return.

She tried to beg the All to spare her awhile longer. She had one mission yet to perform before she departed the world. The Degnan dead remained unMourned.

III

To Marika's amazement, she wakened. The hammer of tradermale weapons wakened her. She opened her eyes. She was lying on a pallet in Braydic's comm room. Grauel sat beside her, a bowl of soup in her paw. Relief flooded her features.

Marika turned her head slowly. It ached terribly. She needed more goyin tea. She saw Bagnel and one of his comrades firing through narrow windows. Huntresses with bows waited behind them, occasionally stepped forward to loose an arrow while the males reloaded. Bombs were falling outside. They did little damage. Occasionally a metal pellet whined through one of the windows. Most of Braydic's beautiful equipment had been wrecked. All of it was dead. Marika could not feel a spectre of the electromagnetic fog.

Barlog knelt beside Grauel. "Are you all right, Marika?"

"My head aches. I need a double draft of goyin tea." She then realized it was daylight out. She had slept a long time. "How bad is it? How did I get here?"

"It is very bad, pup." She presented the tea, which had been prepared. "We are the last." She gestured. The two tradermales. A dozen huntresses, counting herself and Grauel. Braydic. A dozen worker pups cowering in the nether reaches of the room. "We carried you up when it became clear the nomads would take the underparts of the packstead. Take as little of that tea as you can. You have been drinking too much."

"The sisters. Where are the sisters?"

"All fallen. All but you. A valiant struggle, I am sure. One the savages will recall for a thousand generations. We will be sung into their legends."

Grauel exchanged glances with Barlog. "Are you too weak, Marika? You are the last silth. And we need to hold them off awhile longer. Just awhile."

"Why? What is the point? Akard is fallen."

Braydic replied, "Because help is coming, pup. From the Maksche cloister. Because of what you discovered about the Serke sister. They want to see the body for themselves. You see? Never abandon hope. You may then be too late to profit from what the All has in store."

"I killed her," Marika said. "Gruesomely. They will not find enough left of her to identify."

"They did not need to know that down there," Braydic countered. "Shall we turn them away?"

A burst of explosions sounded outside. Marika turned to Grauel and Barlog. "Help is too late once again, eh?"

Barlog looked at her oddly, with a hint of awe. "Perhaps. And perhaps the All is moving through the world."

Puzzled, Marika glanced at Grauel and surprised the same look there. What were they thinking?

She said, "More food. I am starving. Famished." When no one moved, she pouted. "Find me something to eat. I can do nothing till I have eaten." Her body did feel as though she had fasted for days. "Those pups are beginning to look tasty."

They brought her food. It was dried trail rations of the sort prepared for the summer nomad hunts. Tough as hide. And right then very tasty.

Outside, the racket of the siege continued to rise. Bagnel and his comrade looked ready to collapse. But those two were, for the moment, the only line of defense.

Marika went among the ghosts again, for the last time at Akard. They were few, but not so few as when the nomad silth had been more numerous. And the big dark killer still hovered on high, as though waiting to be used and fed. She called it down.

She ravened among the besiegers, fueling herself with fear and anger and an unquenchable lust for requiting what had been done to the Degnan. She allowed all the hidden shadows, so long repressed, to the fore, and gave them free rein. But she was one silth alone, and the nomads were growing skilled at evading silth attack, at hiding under a mantle of protection extended by their own wild silth, who were in the packfast themselves. Blood ran deep, but Marika feared not deep enough. The savages continued to hammer at the last bastion.

The day proceeded, and despite Marika's efforts the siege turned worse. One after another, her companions were hit by fire coming through the two windows. There was no place to hide from ricochets. The nomads tried to throw explosives inside, and that she forestalled each time, but each time it distracted her from her effort to destroy the wild silth.

Collapse was moments away She knew she could hold no longer, that her will *did* have its limits. And as she faced the absolute, resolute, and unyielding herself, she found that she had only the old regret. There would be no Mourning for the Degnan. And a new. There would be no journey to Makesche, which might have been the next step on her road leading toward the stars.

The hammer of weaponry rose toward the insane. Bagnel dared not return fire, for a swarming buzz of metal now came through the windows. The pellets were chewing Braydic's machines into chopped metal and glass.

The firing ceased. Bagnel bounced up for a look. Braydic whimpered. "Now they will come."

Marika nodded. And did something she never did before. She hugged Grauel and Barlog in turn.

Pups of the upper Ponath packs hugged no one but their dams, and that seldom after their first few years.

The two huntresses were touched.

Stray nomad weapons resumed a sporadic fire apparently meant to keep Bagnel away from his window.

Grauel rejoined the tradermale. She was trying to learn to use a rifle. Bagnel's companion could no longer lift his.

A slumping Marika suddenly went rigid. Her jaw dropped. "Wait! Something. . . ."

Something mighty, something terrible in its power, was roaring toward her up the valley of the Hainlin. For a moment she was paralyzed by her terror of that raging shadow. Then she hurled herself to the one window facing down the river.

She saw three great daggerlike crosses hurtling up the river's course, above the devastation left by the flood released with the collapse of the dams. They charged into the teeth of the wind, flying like great raptors fifty feet above the surface in an absolutely rigid V formation.

"What are they?" Grauel whispered from Marika's side.

"I do not know."

"Looks like meth on them," Barlog murmured from Marika's other side.

"I do not know," Marika said again. She had begun shaking all over. A fierce and dreadful shadow-of-touch rolled ahead of the crosses, boiling with a mindless terror.

A tremendous explosion thundered out behind them. Its force threw the three of them together, against the stone of the wall. Marika gasped for breath. Grauel turned, pointed her rifle. It began to bark counterpoint to Bagnel's, which was speaking already.

Nomad shapes appeared in the dust boiling around the gap in the wall blown by the charge.

Marika clung to the window and stared out.

The three rushing crosses rose, screaming into the sky, parting.

QUESTAR®

... MEANS THE BEST SCIENCE FICTION AND THE MOST ENTHRALLING FANTASY.

Like all readers, science fiction and fantasy readers are looking for a good story. Questar® has them—entertaining, enlightening stories that will take readers beyond the farthest reaches of the galaxy, and into the deepest heart of fantasy. Whether it's awesome tales of intergalactic adventure and alien contact, or wondrous and beguiling stories of magic and epic quests, Questar® will delight readers of all ages and tastes.

___**PASSAGE AT ARMS**　　　　　(E20-006, $2.95, U.S.A.)
　　 by Glen Cook　　　　　　　　(E20-007, $3.75, Canada)
A continuation of the universe Glen Cook develops in *The Starfishers Trilogy*, this is a wholly new story of an ex-officer-turned-reporter taking the almost suicidal assignment of covering an interstellar war from a tiny, front-line attack ship.

___**PANDORA'S GENES**　　　　　　(E20-004, $2.95, U.S.A.)
　　 by Kathryn Lance　　　　　　 (E20-005, $3.75, Canada)
A first novel by a fresh new talent, this book combines a love triangle with a race to save humanity. In a post-holocaustal world, where technology is of the most primitive sort, a handful of scientists race against time to find a solution to the medical problem that may mean humanity's ultimate extinction.

___**THE DUSHAU TRILOGY #1: DUSHAU** (E20-015, $2.95, U.S.A.)
　　 by Jacqueline Lichtenberg　　　(E20-016, $3.75, Canada)
The Dushau see the end of a galactic civilization coming—but that's not surprising for a race of near-immortals whose living memory spans several thousand years. The newly crowned emperor of the Allegiancy wants to pin his troubles on Prince Jindigar and the Dushau, but Krinata, a plucky young woman who works with the Dushau, determines to aid their cause when she discovers the charges are false.

WARNER BOOKS
P.O. Box 690
New York, N.Y. 10019

Please send me the books I have checked. I enclose a check or money order (not cash), plus 50¢ per order and 50¢ per copy to cover postage and handling.*
(Allow 4 weeks for delivery.)

_____ Please send me your free mail order catalog. (If ordering only the catalog, include a large self-addressed, stamped envelope.)

Name _____

Address _____

City _____

State _____ Zip _____

*N.Y. State and California residents add applicable sales tax.　　135

MORE FROM QUESTAR®...
THE BEST IN SCIENCE FICTION AND FANTASY

___**FORBIDDEN WORLD**   (E20-017, $2.95, U.S.A.)
by David R. Bischoff and Ted White   (E20-018, $3.75, Canada)

This is a novel about a distant world designed as a social experiment. Forbidden World recreates regency London, Rome in the time of the Caesars, and a matriarchal agrarian community in a distant part of space—with devastating results!

___**THE HELMSMAN**   (E20-027, $2.95, U.S.A.)
by Merl Baldwin   (E20-026, $3.75, Canada)

A first novel that traces the rise of Wilf Brim, a brash young starship cadet and son of poor miners, as he tries to break the ranks of the aristocratic officers who make up the Imperial Fleet—and avenge the Cloud League's slaughter of his family.

___**THE HAMMER AND THE HORN**   (E20-028, $2.95, U.S.A.)
by Michael Jan Friedman   (E20-029, $3.75, Canada)

Taking its inspiration from Norse mythology, this first novel tells the story of Vidar, who fled Asgard for Earth after Ragnarok, but who now must return to battle in order to save both worlds from destruction.

WARNER BOOKS
P.O. Box 690
New York, N.Y. 10019

Please send me the books I have checked. I enclose a check or money order (not cash), plus 50¢ per order and 50¢ per copy to cover postage and handling.* (Allow 4 weeks for delivery.)

_____ Please send me your free mail order catalog. (If ordering only the catalog, include a large self-addressed, stamped envelope.)

Name _____

Address _____

City _____

State _____ Zip _____

*N.Y. State and California residents add applicable sales tax.   136